After the Fear

BY ROSANNE RIVERS

IMMORTAL INK
PUBLISHING

AFTER THE FEAR

AFTER THE FEAR
by Rosanne Rivers

AFTER THE FEAR

dedication

For my amazing Mum.

AFTER THE FEAR

one

Sola Herrington has not attended a September Demonstration

Sola Herrington is attending <u>Coral's 17th!!!!!</u> tonight (touch to follow link)

I SHOVE MY DIGIPAD back into my jeans. The last place I want to be is at Coral's birthday party, but Dad needs to get cosy with the Shepherds' Liaisons if he's ever going to get promoted. Unfortunately, Coral is the daughter of such a Liaison. 'You received an invitation and it would look strange if you weren't there,' so Dad thinks.

Really, it wouldn't be strange at all, seeing as Coral hates my guts and was probably forced to invite me, but there's no way I can tell Dad that. So now I'm standing on the rail, obsessively checking Debtbook for updates of a cancellation.

I recognise a couple of girls from school farther down; they hold onto the handles like clothes dangling in a wardrobe as we trundle through the city. I stay back, rearranging the silver pin which holds my frizzy hair in place. It's shaped like a four-leaf clover and is supposed to bring me luck. I figure I'll need it tonight.

One of the girls, Moni, carries a Book of Red Ink under her arm. *Suck up.*

'Uh oh . . .' Moni studies her digipad. 'Coral's written on Debtbook that she's wearing red and if anyone turns up in the same colour they'll be sent home immediately.' She looks down at her crimson halter-neck.

Now why didn't I think of that?

The other girl examines the screen. 'Hmm, she's put LOL, but maybe you should go back and change just in case. You don't want to miss you-know-who!'

She leans forwards and whispers something to cause Moni's eyes to widen.

'The Demonstrator?' Moni asks as the rail begins to slow.

I wait until the girls have hopped off the metal platform before scanning out myself. I have another rail ride and two short walks before I reach Coral's. The rail is the only way to get anywhere around here and the electric tracks run in perfect circles, situated a mile apart from each other until they reach city Juliet's border. Sometimes I imagine if I looked down from the sky all the circular tracks would look like target practice, with the Stadium sitting right in the bull's eye.

The girls must have decided to change, because when I arrive at Coral's street there's no one around. Not even Herd officers. I do a little run and jump up her path, just because I can.

'Sola.' Coral's tall, thin father opens the door before I've even knocked. His fixed smile makes me want to shrivel up and disappear. When he turns away to look back down the long hall behind him, it's as if I can hear the creak of his bones moving.

'Evening, Mr Winters. I'm here for the party,' I say, batting a drifting balloon away from my face. The whole house is covered in them, like colourful bubble-wrap.

He turns back.

'Coral is in the guest-living-room. The Demonstrator is giving a speech so please slip in quietly.'

I repress a shudder. Why does he speak so slowly? It's as though everyone to do with the Shepherds are forced to pronounce each and every syllable: heaven forbid we miss one precious word of theirs. Still, I'm quite impressed he managed to remind me I'm late while implying no one will be happy to see me all in one greeting. Hey, like father, like daughter.

I run the scan chip in my palm over the discreet scanner fitted into the front door and step in. The stench of new leather hits me straight away. If Mr Winters wasn't walking right behind me, I would cover my nose. He follows me through the hall until he finally turns into his study. It's silly, but I always associate Coral's father with needles. I think it's because when I was eight, I walked out of school with a cut knee. Mum was waiting with Mr Winters and when I showed her my leg he produced a needle from his Liaison uniform pocket. I remember crying, but he acted like he had misinterpreted my tears, voicing something about cleaning the wound. The last thing I saw before I blacked out was the tip of the metal disappearing into my skin.

Urgh. The perks of having a Liaison as a family friend.

I push the guest-living-room door open a fraction and peek through the gap. Standing opposite me, at the front of the room, is the Demonstrator. I recognise his face from Debtbook. Half the girls at school are in love with him, spending hours trawling over his profile. Yet I wasn't expecting that voice. It's low, his speech a song of unusual inflections and intonations.

His qualities aren't lost on anyone else, either. Every girl at the party practically salivates at the sight of him, and even the boys are paying attention to his speech. Coral lies to his side in a blood-red dress, taking up a whole chaise lounge to herself. Her sweet perfume mingles in with the leathery smell of the furniture.

I watch the Demonstrator as he talks, his voice creaking gently when he goes too low and his eyes never catching Coral's despite her legs writhing together like two snakes.

9

Something about the way he occasionally gestures with his hand—a seemingly unconscious flick here or there, as if he's trying to conjure his thoughts into words—makes me smile. I'm still gawping when his gaze darts to the back of the room. He's staring right at me.

Crap. He pauses mid-sentence. I need to do something—anything . . . Yet all I can concentrate on is the heat flushing my face. I've never gone along with the Demonstrator crushes, so what's wrong with me? Coral gives a little cough.

'Sorry, Miss Winters, but another one of your guests has arrived.' The Demonstrator speaks with a slight smile, not taking his eyes from me as he gestures to the door.

'Really? Oh, it's only Sola. Anyway—' She leans over and gives him a playful tap on the arm. 'I told you to call me Coral; everyone else does.'

Not everyone, I think. Not when you can't hear me, you spiteful, spoilt—

Her glare interrupts my thoughts and for a panicky moment, I worry I've been talking out loud. But I realise I'm still hovering in the doorway, and the Demonstrator is obviously waiting for me to come in. Ignoring everyone's eyes on me, I tiptoe across the room. A few of the boys shuffle away when I pass, but I just stare straight ahead, hoping the Demonstrator doesn't notice.

'Any other questions?' he asks once I've sat. His resigned tone tells me he knows there will be, and sure enough, most of the girls dart their hands up. A few wrestle and chuckle with each other, trying to stick the other's hand in the air. I can guess what kind of question they want to ask.

Eventually, a boy sitting near the front shouts out, 'What was it like being chosen to be a Demonstrator?'

'Not good,' the Demonstrator replies. When it's obvious the whole room is expecting more, he sighs.

'I found out from the status update on my Debtbook. I had been chosen to help pay back the Nation's Debt.' He stresses the last bit. I get the impression they're not really his words. 'My parents explained that I would help the Debt by either becoming a Demonstrator or working at the Demonstrator camp. What they didn't tell me was that only the elderly work at the camp, and, as you all know, I wound up in the tryouts.' His musical tone flattens during this speech.

'How did you survive?' a girl asks.

'By doing what I've done nearly every day since. By killing.'

I cringe at the gasps from the party-goers. They don't seem to register that this man isn't play-fighting, isn't spinning off propaganda for effect. He's telling the cold, hard truth. The excited questions go on and on. 'How many criminals have you killed?' 'Can you teach us some moves?' 'How much Debt do the other cities owe?'

'Where are you from?'

I look up at this one. The Demonstrator, whose name I now know is Dylan, smiles for a flicker of a second.

'City Victor. But it used to be called Belfast, Northern Ireland.'

An excited whisper spreads through the guests. We're not supposed to know the old names, and definitely not allowed to talk about them. If this was anyone else's home, the trigger camera would have sprung to life with that comment, but it hangs placidly in the corner. I doubt it's even wired into the system.

City Victor. I've heard what they're like over there. People say they believe in so many superstitions that they'd kill someone on sight who wasn't from their city. I'm pretty sure we've paid more of our Debt back than them; otherwise, Dylan probably wouldn't be so welcome.

'I thought so,' Coral says, nodding her head. 'Now, will you answer my one and only question?' She leans up so she's resting on one elbow. 'Do you like coming to these kinds of parties?'

I hate how perfect her smile is.

'Aye, it's my favourite part of being a Demonstrator,' he replies. His tone is still hard around the edges. If Coral had half a brain, she would notice that he was being sarcastic. But she doesn't, so she bites her lip and giggles.

'I lied. One more question! Will you stay for some drinks?'

'I'm contracted to stay for another 96 minutes, so yes, I'd be delighted.'

I don't stifle my snort quickly enough. Coral shoots me a glare but overall seems thrilled with his comment. She even moves up to let two of her friends share the lounger with her.

Within seconds, conversations have sprung up between groups, making the gap between me and everyone else devastatingly obvious.

The moment I stand, headed for the bathroom to kill some time playing on my digipad, Coral's silky voice calls out to me.

'Oh, Sola? Get us some more drinks if you're going that way?'

It isn't a request. I breathe in slowly, as if the extra air could quash my rising frustration. At least fetching drinks will take up more time of this awful party. Coral has already turned back to the Demonstrator and evidently does not intend to shout her order across the room, so I walk through the groups and over to the lounger.

'What would you like?' I ask, putting on my sickly sweet voice. It's not only for Dad's promotion that I have to suck up to Coral, but for our whole well-being. One wrong move and we could be monitored for a week; I know Coral has her influential parents wrapped around each ruby-painted fingernail.

'We'll have three virgin mojitos, and Dylan will have . . . ?' She looks up at him through curled lashes. Instead of answering her, he does the unthinkable. He turns to me.

'Are you a server here?' he asks. That heavy lilt makes it hard for me to think. I shake my head.

'Getting drinks is just my favourite part of being at a party,' I say, *nearly* quoting him back.

He raises his eyebrows, then laughs. A low chuckle which sounds like hollow bamboo sticks knocking against each other.

'In that case, I'll have whatever you're having.'

I have no idea what I'm having and doubt Coral planned on wasting a drink on me, but I turn away before I can say or do anything stupid.

There's a refreshments table set up in the hallway with a cocktail recipe stuck to the board. They're all non-alcoholic, seeing as most of us are seventeen, and I giggle at the ridiculousness of a virgin mojito. Without the rum it's just mint leaves and ice. Oh well, what the lady wants, the lady gets!

I pour two cokes for Dylan and me and load them onto a tray. As I go to pick it up, a manicured hand slaps down beside the glasses.

'I'll take those.'

Coral. Her red hair bounces around her back as she ushers me out of the way.

'Dylan's nice, isn't he?' she asks over her shoulder. 'My father paid the Shepherds a lot to get him here for me.'

She smiles at me, obviously expecting something. I twist my hands together and give her a half-smile that I hope says *good for you*. When she holds out a coke I go to take it, but Coral doesn't let go.

'Look, I'm saying this as a friend, Sola. Don't come back into the party. I know it's not your scene, and it's kind of embarrassing. To be honest, I only invited you because Father made me. I didn't expect you to come.'

'Oh. Right,' is all I manage. Coral's unfaltering smile slips into a genuine one and the full weight of the drink falls into my hand. With a flick of her hair, she retrieves the tray and floats back into the living room. All it takes is a delicate kick of the door, and I'm alone in the hallway.

I stare after her, unable to breathe. To stop my hand from shaking I take a controlled sip of my drink but the coke tastes bitter and lonely in my mouth. For a stupid, brilliant moment, I really thought I would be drinking and chatting with the others.

Humiliation burns behind my eyelids.

I can't run home. Dad will know something went wrong. I can't hang out on the streets, the Herd officers will have me escorted back in minutes. Most of all, I can't stay in this hall, waiting for my tears to break through.

I slam my drink onto the table and run through the kitchen, bursting out into the back garden. I used to play here all the time when I was a kid so I know the house inside-out. Sometimes I think it's the reason Coral hates me, because I know so much about her childhood. Or maybe it's because we were forced to be friends through our parents, but she became cool, I didn't, and now it's the most embarrassing thing in the world to have known me.

The worse thing about it all is that, if I'm honest, I miss her.

I breathe in that fresh, dewy smell of the garden, but as I reach the far end the scent goes bitter, like decaying plants. They keep a massive trampoline tucked away down here. It's covered in autumn leaves, and in the twilight, they kind of look like scales. I close my eyes, kick off my boots, and pretend I'm a kid again. Clambering onto the trampoline, I imagine it's a giant tortoise which will take me out of the city. It will keep me safe, and I'll see the sky without pollution, and the stars will shine so brightly that the light will burn into my eyelids forever.

I stretch my arms up and jump as high as I can. The leaves spin around me as if I were caught up in a tornado. They rustle together, crunching underneath my feet as the springs launch me into the sky again and again. When the wind rushes past my face, I pretend it's travelled all over England and Ireland and touched the faces of millions of people just like me.

Then I remember that anyone outside of Juliet would want me dead, and I stop pretending altogether.

Slowing down, I stretch my legs out so that I land on my bum. Trickles of sweat fall down my face and I gasp to catch my breath. With my hands tucked behind my head, I lean back, panting amid the bouncing array of cold leaves. As usual, the misty film of hanging, polluted sky blurs the image ahead. I wonder if the stars really are those dull shiny smudges or something more.

Dad told me that my great-grandfather used to live in the countryside—before England got into Debt and the cities had borders. I used to imagine him looking out a window with the sun on his face and no blanket of dead air in between. In school, they say the heat used to burn people, making their skin peel off and causing deathly diseases to spread within their bodies. I don't believe that. Thinking of the sun's undiluted rays makes me warm from the inside out. I bet it's like delving into a hot bath, only less like sinking and more like flying.

'You're enjoying this party about as much as I am.'

The low voice sends sharp impulses through me. I jolt up, trying to find purchase with my hands on the trampoline. They skid on the leaves, making my whole body bounce. After what seems like an age of making a fool of myself, the springs steady and I look out towards the voice. The outline of the Demonstrator's jagged hair is silhouetted from the lights of the house. He stands at the edge of the trampoline, facing me.

'You startled me,' I tell him. Witty, I know, but it's all I can think of.

His eyes are on me once again, and I get that same gasping excitement he stirred in me earlier. I try, unsuccessfully, to lean back onto the trampoline with grace.

'Aye, but you scared me too,' he replies.

'How on earth did *I* scare *you*?' I hope he doesn't notice the wobble in my voice or that my breathing hasn't calmed yet. He moves around the trampoline, getting closer.

'Well.' The leaves rustle once more. The trampoline dips slightly. Risking a glimpse over, I see he's leaning both elbows on the surface, palms cupping his face. 'I saw you jumping around with all those leaves and I thought you were being attacked by some sort of bush monster.'

I laugh a little too hard.

'So you came out here to rescue me then?'

'Hmm. Unfortunately, I came out here to rescue myself.'

Ah, Coral and her gaggle. No doubt they're scouring the house to try and find him right now.

'She's not that bad really,' I say. I don't know why I'm defending her, but I know how horrible it is to like someone only for them to dismiss me.

'I think you're being kind, Sola.'

He remembers my name. The sound of it in his voice makes my skin tingle, like every hair on my body is jumping up. For some reason, I'm not even surprised that he's nothing like the other people from Victor. I wonder what they say about our city where he's from.

Dylan pats the surface beside me.

'Can I?'

I swallow and shuffle over. Suddenly I don't know what to do with my body. How was I lying before? Everything seems unnatural; nothing fits into place like I want it to. Thankfully, he doesn't lie down, just sits up near my head, his legs dangling over the edge. He brings with him the faint smell of dirt and metal. I sense his eyes are on mine so I look directly ahead, acting as though I don't notice.

'Grand night, isn't it?' he asks. I keep my gaze upwards. I can't believe a killer is making small talk with me. Then again, he doesn't *act* like a killer. Ignoring him would be rude.

'It would be nicer if we could see the stars.'

'Aye. You're not wrong there.' He tilts his head back so I take the opportunity to glance over. His wild brown hair sprouts in layered tufts, sticking out in an adorable way. His cheekbones are high, his jaw set, and those deep blue eyes look through such long, thin eyelashes. His only imperfection is what looks like a twice-broken nose. Unfairly, it makes him more beautiful.

Without warning, he brings his gaze back to me. I let my lips part in surprise, unable to take my eyes from his. Maybe it's the leaves which surround us, the night which hides us away, but when he whispers that maybe one day he could show me the stars, I close my eyes.

His lips are on mine.

I don't have time to think, I just move my mouth gently. He tastes sweet and bitter all at once.

With a jolt in my stomach, my senses kick in. What on earth am I doing? One sweet line and I'm kissing a stranger? I push him off me in a violent movement and sit up straight, my breathing quick and shallow.

His eyes dart around wildly. 'I'm sorry. I don't know what I was—you just looked so—ah. I'm sorry.' He grabs the edge of the trampoline and pushes himself off in a fluid motion, before turning to me once more. His mouth opens. Nothing comes out. Eventually, he runs his hand through his hair and hurries back inside.

For the second time tonight, I've been left alone. But for the first time in my life, I've been kissed. I touch my bottom lip. When I look up, I swear I see two stars twinkling in the distance.

The stars move. An outline solidifies and Coral steps out from the shadows. She stares at me with eyes so narrow all of the light I saw before disappears.

A moment later she stalks back inside the house and it's as if I had never seen her at all. Yet I know I'm going to pay for my kiss with the Demonstrator.

A million different words jam into my mind, vying for my attention. *Demonstrator, killer, murderer, sweet-talker, party-goer, rule breaker?*

Or maybe, a strange part of my brain murmurs, *just Dylan.*

two

SOLA HERRINGTON is in bedroom 2 of Flat 436 Rotunda Building (home)

I spend the next week obsessively checking Coral's Debtbook profile. I'm not sure what I'm looking for—a mention of her party, perhaps—but there are only the usual updates: comments, whereabouts, events, friends' birthdays . . .

Nothing about Dylan.

I suppress a grin. The Demonstrator strides into my mind more than I care to admit, followed each time by a soft, hot flourish which causes me to draw breath. I *could* check his profile, but I'm scared. I can only access the profiles of those from Juliet, but public figures like Demonstrators are open to everyone as long as we sign up as a follower. So if I found him, he would know that I'd signed up.

Almost subconsciously, I tap Coral's name on my digipad. Her profile zooms up from the corner of the page.

Coral Winters is attending Demonstrator Tryouts—Two Teams, Only Winners Survive! tonight (touch to follow link)

Why am I not surprised Coral is attending the most horrific Demonstration around? The price of a ticket is probably more than the cost of this flat.

With a sigh, I grab the four-leaf clover hair pin from my desk. I've been wearing it all week, and each time I catch a glimpse of myself, I remember Dylan. I twist all of my hair into a messy bun and secure it with the pin, reliving the kiss in my mind one more time before school. That sensation swells again in my stomach, like when you're going backward on a swing and for a second, you trick yourself into thinking you're free falling.

Chasing the delicious smell of microwaved bacon, I scan into the kitchen. The beep makes Dad jump.

'Oh! Morning. How do you fancy a cooked breaky?' He sounds surprisingly cheery for before eight o'clock. There's not enough room in the kitchen for both of us to stand, so I manoeuvre around Dad and hop onto the stool in the corner.

A crazily loud advert makes me jump in my seat. I wait until it's over to look at the left wall where the large digiscreen incessantly flickers between mine and Dad's profiles, occasionally interrupted by some Shepherd propaganda. Sometimes I like looking at it 'cause when the pictures change from Dad's to mine, I see the resemblance between us: the button nose; eyes which are too far apart; the sloping grin we both share. I used to see my resemblance to Mum on the screen, too. If I had had my way, her profile would still be up there, living right between mine and Dad's, reminding us we're still related. I guess the Shepherds don't like to think of those who've passed.

I still remember hugging that screen, my tears smudging on the cold surface as the status changed.

Luna Herrington's profile will be deleted in 26 minutes. 25, 24, 23 . . .

I shake my head; profiles don't matter. If I *really* had my way, she wouldn't have been killed at all, wouldn't have left me and Dad alone for the last seven years.

'You sleep okay, Sola?' Dad stands right in front of me. I blink, take the plate he's offering, and balance it on my knees.

'Yeah. Thanks.' There's a whir above me. 'Why's that on again?' I whisper, watching the unblinking red dot in the corner of the trigger camera. Dad follows my stare.

'Oh, I didn't realise it was. You haven't been sleep-talking, have you?' He smiles and leans back easily against the fridge.

'Has something happened?' I ask. In my head I add, *with Coral.*

'Okay, okay. I wasn't going to say anything because nothing is certain, but—' He drops to a whisper. '—I've been asked to work crowd surveillance at the Demonstrator tryouts tonight.'

I let out a long breath. He expects me to be pleased. Looking at his hopeful face, I put on my best fake smile. It evidently doesn't convince him.

'Still a judger, are we?' He gives a little shake of his head. 'Do you have any idea how much crime has dropped since the Demonstrations were put in place?'

Oh man, here we go.

'Would you prefer having a bigger Debt, Sola? The Demonstrations tax those who can afford tickets. The more you attend, the less chance you have of being picked for the Debt, which offers people an incentive to work hard, save for the tickets and not spend money on frivolous things. We *all* have issues with the violence, but *"bad things only happen to people who deserve them".'* He repeats the Shepherds' motto.

I don't need to reply. I just stare. At least Dad has the courtesy to realise his mistake and look sheepish.

'Well done. It's a big step up from profile monitoring,' I say sarcastically, because I can't say what I'm really thinking with the trigger camera activated.

'Yes it is. *A big responsibility,* in fact. This is simply the start, Sola. If I get this right, there's no reason for Mr Winters not to give me the prom—' He looks towards the camera. 'Well, you know.'

21

My dad's smile is catching, so I set aside my disgust over the tryouts. As soon as I pop the last bit of sandwich into my mouth, he whips the plate from my lap.

'Right, you better get to school.'

I groan, sliding off the stool. 'Yeah, I couldn't possibly miss double cookery. We're making vegetable cake. Again.' I can almost hear Mr Laver's monotonous voice in my head. *It's the most efficiently balanced meal for both taste and vitamins. You receive your five fruit and vegetables a day, as well as fibre, calcium, and protein all in one meal.*

'Well, don't worry too much about saving any for me this time, okay?' Dad says.

I open my mouth in pretend outrage. 'Hey! I'll have you know I'm a great cook. I just don't work well with that recipe,' I lie.

Dad gives me a sarcastic 'yeah, yeah,' before I scan out and head to the lift.

As I walk down the hall, Dad's chuckles turn into a cheerful humming. I recognise the melody. It's the first time I've heard the tune in our flat since the morning before Mum died.

℣

I'M STILL HUMMING when I scan out of school. Cookery was a disaster, as usual, and my uniform is covered in dough, but I can't help but wonder if Dad's right, if things *are* looking up.

My smile is stopped by a flicker of glossy red hair. It catches my eye through the gaggle of school children running for the rail. Although my station is the other way, I run to catch up with Coral.

I need to make things right with her. We're taught at school that if you overlook problems, they get worse. Like with the Debt, it started as just a small deficit; England kept thinking it would get better. We kept borrowing and borrowing from other countries, increasing taxes until the whole country rioted. Finally, our grandparents voted in the Shepherds to take control, and since then, each city has been trying to pay back its Debt. Coral isn't exactly my best friend, but I can't ignore the fact that I kissed someone she liked.

'Coral!' I reach out and touch her arm. She spins around, a moment of panic flitting across her face before she pulls her earphones out and smiles at me. It catches me so off-guard that instead of talking, I just stare like an idiot. Eventually she sighs and looks over her shoulder at the rail. It's easier to speak when she isn't beaming at me.

'Um, I wanted to say I'm sorry. I would've done it earlier but I couldn't catch you after school. What happened at your party—'

'It's fine,' she says with a flick of her hand, turning back to me. 'It's sorted.'

Okay, I wasn't ready for this. All of a sudden, it's obvious why I haven't been punished for the kiss. Coral's actually too hurt to be petty.

'I really didn't know how much you liked him,' I say. 'I only went out to jump on the trampoline. You know, like how we used to?'

'Like how we were forced to, you mean?' She's still smiling, but it seems dead on her lips. Before I can speak, she touches her forehead as if she suffers from a headache. When she brings her hand down, her eyes are narrowed; the rim where she usually wears her eyeliner is a painful red.

I've never seen her cry before. Not even when we were kids. Tantrums, yes. Not real tears. My heart hammers and without thinking I bring my arm around her shoulders, pulling her towards me. She heaves a great sigh into my neck and the smell of marzipan drifts from her hair.

This second, right now, I forget about the bullying I've endured from her through secondary school. All the snide remarks and the shrug-offs from her friends. I think about the person she used to be—before she started wearing heels and makeup and going on diets. I think of the games we used to play, how we would pretend we were lost children and our parents were out looking for us. How we used to hide in her playhouse when Mum called for me to go home.

'You're so much like your mother, you know,' Coral says into my shoulder. Despite her cold tone, my chest swells with the compliment. Just as I think we might break apart and laugh about all those childhood memories, she pulls back, her plastered-on smile making a mockery of how I feel.

'Bye, Sola,' she says brightly before walking towards the rail.

A strange vibe creeps over me. I try to understand our embrace, to recapture that sense of friendship, but all I can hear are her sharp heels against the pavement.

Coral takes up nearly all of my thoughts on the walk home. One moment I'm annoyed with myself for hurting her, the next I'm annoyed with her for tainting the memory of my first kiss. By the time I scan into the flat, I've decided I'm actually annoyed with Dylan for turning me into the kind of girl who over thinks everything.

That's weird. Dad's briefcase is in the living room. He's meant to be at work.

'Dad?'

I peek into his room, then mine. Nothing. A faraway digger makes me jump, and I let out a half breath/half laugh to myself. I always creep myself out so easily. I'm actually relieved to hear a noise from the kitchen, because a noise that's *definitely* someone is better than a creak which *could be* someone.

'Why didn't you answer me?' I ask, rushing into the last room of the flat.

Three people crowd my kitchen. I bounce back from the threshold, as if I've hit an invisible wall. Mr Winters stands by the door, tall and gangly with his hands held behind his back. His grey face almost matches his white coat. The other two are surly-looking men I don't recognise, but their Liaison uniforms unite all of them against me. One eyes me greedily, his arm resting on my kitchen counter.

A sticky bubble forms at the back of my throat. Mr Winters holds a finger up to silence me, although I hadn't even opened my mouth to speak. He motions the digiscreen with a flick of his bony hand.

It's fixed on my Debtbook profile. My picture grins into the room. There's a new status underneath my name, but I can't read it. I glance at Mr Winters and something catches the light in his hand. From in between his curled fingers protrudes the long stem of a needle.

Everything slows, although I know it happens quickly.

I back away and hit the screen. The black dots of text shuffle and sharpen. Mr Winters moves behind me. I read the words.

Sola Herrington has been chosen to help pay the Nation's Debt.

three

ONE BLINK AWAKE. Then two. All around is thick nothingness, so black it seems blue. With every second that passes, my panic spreads. Why am I lying down? Why does my body hurt? I feel as though I've been dragged over rocks to get here.

Sweat. Blood. Medicine. Earth. Urine. I choke on the vile smells stealing their way down my throat and up my nose. Yet the stench is better than the memories which jam into my mind. The needle, my Debtbook status, Coral's father. I pretend for a second I'm still in the kitchen, that Dad will be here any minute to save me. Even as I grab the soil beneath me I wish for it to be true.

There's a gasping sound now, like a saw chewing through wood, again and again. It's coming from me. Hot tears sting my eyes, burning and desperate to escape, but I blink them away. *Won't cry, won't cry, won't cry.*

Slowly, I push myself up so that I'm sitting. My arm throbs in protest, telling me that's where Mr Winters stabbed me with the needle. Through the dark, I make out three walls. Bars cover the last side, as if I'm in an over-sized crate.

There's movement next to me. I jerk away, but my elbow collides with something warm and soft. No, not something. *Someone.*

I'm not alone.

I pause, struggling to breathe. I feel like I've been caught at lying. My stomach is hollow, and I'm just waiting, *waiting* for my brain to find a solution that I know isn't coming. Although I wish they wouldn't, my eyes adjust to the shade. More bodies. Every speck of soil is covered in mangled shapes. Hugging my arms around my knees, I make myself as small as possible. Maybe if I'm tiny enough, I can disappear and no one will notice me ever again. Not Coral, not Dylan, not the Shepherds.

Coral. There aren't enough horrible words to describe her right now. Did she send me here? To this prison which smells worse than a corpse? I need to find out what will happen to us, but my head is still foggy, and I have too many pains and aches to think straight.

The girl next to me shudders once again, and like that, she's awake and freaking out. I want to grab her and tell her to be quiet—instinct tells me we should keep the fact that we've woken a secret—but other groans stop me. Really, *really* slowly, I run my eyes over the room.

The mass of bodies begin to writhe and pulse. Everyone is waking, like some sort of mass resurrection. I cling to myself tighter. I know I'm watching something horrid unfold, like when I see something balanced on an edge, but I'm too far away to stop it from toppling over.

And after the fall, there's always a smash.

Groans become cries. Someone immediately starts sobbing, while one woman starts shouting to be let out. The panic is catching, seizing everyone. My breath quickens, but I won't beg to be freed. I sit perfectly still, clenching my fists into balls so that my fingernails make arcs of pain in my palm.

I make a list in my head of everything I know about being chosen.

-You either fight to become a Demonstrator, or if you're too old, you go to work in a camp of some sort.

-You don't come home until you've paid your Debt, but I don't know how that happens.

27

-You can avoid it by going to as many Demonstrations as possible.

Well, too late for number 3. Someone retches in the shadows, and the bitter smell of vomit filters through the dank air. My legs ache as I pull myself up, desperate not to be stamped to death. Aside from the grogginess of being drugged, there are no other aches or cuts down my body as far as I can tell, and I'm still wearing the dough-stained black trousers, white shirt and checked tie which signal my school uniform. That's some relief—I don't want to contemplate the thought of Mr Winters and his cronies undressing me.

My gaze latches onto something huddled in the corner. I step closer and squint through the moving people. But it's just a child, their knees pulled up to their chest. I clench my eyes shut against the image of them being chosen. Did they see the needle before they felt the jab? Were they alone, too?

A loud noise buzzes above us. Long, yellow lights attached to the ceiling flicker on, filling the room with stark brightness that burns my eyes. Even with my eyelids gritted shut, red fuzz stains the dark. Blinking away the smudges, I glance around.

Unlike me, everyone's dressed in brown. I was right, we *are* standing on soil and earth. I try to peer through the brown-clad swarm of people, but all I can see is the top of the bars and a thick brown gate a few paces behind it.

'Listen!' A sharp shout snaps everyone to attention. The voice is full of authority and kind of familiar. A Herd officer I've crossed before, perhaps?

'If you look down, you'll see a red cross painted across your chests. This means you're in the red team. You'll fight the blue crosses. Whoever is still standing when the other team is completely wiped out becomes a Demonstrator.'

What? No . . . My body shakes. I look down. The cross painted over my school shirt bleeds lines of crimson. That old saying from school jumps to mind, '*X marks the spot*'.

The man speaks again, and with his words it's as though he's reached into my chest and stolen any hope I had left.

'Welcome to city Juliet's Demonstrator tryouts.'

His voice is flat and trimmed with sad sarcasm . . . it's the same tone Dylan used to tell Coral he would be pleased to stay.

Dylan's here.

If I had the strength, I would be excited to see him again. Or scared. Or whatever I should be experiencing right now. Yet all I can do is hold back my tears. Others, however, aren't following suit. I hear someone's shouts to try and rally us all together, but mostly grief-stricken sobs filter through the room. The group shift in their terror, and I glimpse a look at Dylan.

He's standing in the space between the bars and the gate, dressed in the tooth-white uniform of a Demonstrator, his sword hidden in its scabbard. I dart behind a well-built man who's stretching his neck muscles. I don't want Dylan to see me. Not yet.

'There's a weapon for each of you on the bench. As you exit into the Stadium, be sure to pick one up.' Dylan's unusual accent carries over the bawling.

Another voice echoes from the distance, and I assume it belongs to Ebiere Okiro, commentator for most Demonstrations. I imagine her standing on the sands, spinning a tale of why the Demonstrations are necessary to raise money and pay back our Debt, dramatising the event in her smooth, low tone.

With a clang, the metal bars slide out of place. Nobody moves. After a second, one man breaks from the group and ducks underneath the ascending bars, towards the bench. Like a rush of water through open floodgates, the group surges forwards. I stumble with the force, crying out in frustration.

Then I'm really yelling because someone's gripping my arm.

'Let's look after each other, yeah? Look out for me, all right?' A girl nods frantically in my face. I muster an 'okay' and pull my arm from her. She latches onto the man in front. I bite my lip. If she dies early because she's panicking, she'll reduce our chances of winning as a team. I wonder if she's from Foxtrot; they're supposed to be cowards down there.

As soon as I think it, I curse myself. How can I be contemplating people's deaths as though they're nothing to me? I memorise her blonde hair and vow to look out for her.

Now that the bars have disappeared, the gate begins to rise. It cranks upwards with clicks, counting down to the big reveal. Cold air rushes in from the outside, and I clench my teeth to stop them chattering violently.

The open gate reveals a stone archway, and beyond that, a sight I've seen a hundred times before, only from a very different view.

The sands of the Stadium floor. They spew out before me, endless yet enclosed. The deafening screams of the crowd outside invades our little room. My fingernails scrape against the metal wall beside me; I didn't even know I was trying to grab hold of it.

From here, tucked out of the sight of the audience, I peer upwards. The inside of the Stadium is like an inverted dome, the wide circle of the edge facing the open sky. I'm standing before the apex, the furthest point from the escape, and it's as if the eager spectators are climbing up the curve, jeering as they make their way towards freedom.

I realise I'm shaking. Those around me have fallen quiet, too. We stand, letting the clamour of the Stadium wash over us. The panic has been replaced with a weird kind of calm as we look out onto the place where we fight, or we die.

'This is it!' Dylan shouts. 'Don't be put off by the cameras around the Stadium. They're projecting your image onto the screen so the people far away can see it. And don't dawdle in here, whatever you do. The blues will corner you.

Remember that the whole blue team must be killed before you can survive. Look out for each other.'

I'm not ready. I can't do this. My mind is telling me one thing, yet my feet move forwards. Until I hear the whimper behind me.

The child I spotted before is still folded up like a foetus in the corner. Light weaves around the other moving bodies and flutters onto his pale, unmoving face. I dawdle, needing to get to the bench but unable to look away from the boy.

Each clang of metal tells me another weapon has been taken. I have to go. I can't help him. I turn away just as Dylan's words about being cornered by the blues force their way into my conscience.

Already regretting this, I run over to the boy. A horrible roar emits from the Stadium, and I know the other reds must be stepping through the archway.

'We have to get out of here, come on,' I urge. He doesn't respond. His body bobs up and down with his sharp, shallow breathing. When I look down, I notice he's sitting on a patch of darkened, wet earth.

'Come on,' I say again, softer this time.

I lower my hand, palm upwards, and he looks up. Even his eyes are shaking.

More screams from the spectators. The blues must have been released. I bite my tongue so I don't scream at the boy. Every moment I stay, with my back to the arena and bent down to his level, goes against my instincts. Still, I unwind his hand from around his knees and hold it tight.

Finally, he allows me to guide him up. I resist running to the weapons bench. Dylan faces away from us, herding the last of my team into the arena.

'No.' I let out an involuntary whisper. Only two weapons remain on the bench: a ragged, wooden staff which looks as though it would snap before doing any damage and a short spear. Despite my urge to hang onto it, I hand the spear to the boy. He takes it with a violently quivering hand. I

31

wonder if he's more likely to stab himself before he has a chance to use the knife for defence.

'Sola?'

Dylan. He stands frozen, mouth wide, with a strange expression across his familiar face. It's something like surprise and realisation all at once. Despite everything, I glance at his lips before looking away. They were once on mine.

'Don't say this is because of me.' His voice is halfway between a growl and a breath, his face so full of pain that I can't possibly tell him he's right. I shake my head.

'Are, are you fighting?' I manage to ask, hoping that he isn't despite knowing he could more than protect himself. A flick of his head tells me no.

'Then, could you do something for me?' I don't give him time to respond. 'If I . . . if the blues win, could you tell my dad that I'm sorry. And that I'm—I'm—' the words won't come. Why won't they? This is my chance to tell my dad that I love him and that I'm proud and that he's done everything so well since Mum was killed even though he thinks he hasn't. But I can't, and my window of opportunity disappears along with my resolve. A loaded sigh escapes my lips.

'The blues won't win. Here, take this.' He drags his sword from its hilt and passes it to me. It pulls my arm down as soon as he lets go.

'It's too heavy. I can't fight with this,' I tell him, even more desperate now. He glances out to the Stadium, the fear in his eyes making my heart panic.

'Just take it! It might intimidate the blues.'

I don't know what to say and evidently, nor does he. So I take the sword with my bad, needle-injected arm as the boy grips my right hand, and hold Dylan's gaze. I need to see those sharp blue eyes for a moment more.

At the back of my mind, a stupid, not concentrating, girlish part of me thinks that at least I had a first kiss before I was chosen.

I turn towards the archway. Walk underneath the threshold.

The sands are already ruined with blood. Contestants scramble past us. I can't see whether they're reds or blues.

The child's grip tightens. I squeeze once.

Here goes.

I step out into the Stadium's thick air.

There's only a second to register the sickening sight of death, the smell of rust and iron, and the crunch of the sand before a dagger hurtles towards me.

No time to scream.

No time to react.

I just stare. Stare as the blade whizzes past me, missing my arm by inches, and plunges deep into the boy's stomach.

We're losing.

four

THE BOY shudders next to me. He looks down at the silver handle poking out from his small body. His desperate eyes plead for me to help.

Never in my life have I been so completely lost.

I go to pull him back into the metal room and away from the violence but I remember Dylan's words. We can't get cornered in there. I hook my arm underneath the boy's shoulders, tucking my hand into his armpit, and glance around the Stadium. Darting figures ruin my frantic search for a Shepherd or Liaison. I know when the authorities see him they'll understand how bad this is, how much of a mistake.

Bad things only happen to people who deserve them.

How can anyone think this boy deserves to die?

But no one will help us. We're alone with dancing bodies and manic shouts. In the stretched second it takes to scrutinise the Stadium, everything seems to lock into place. Leaning over rails, the spectators curse and yell. The cold air stinks like an overflowing rubbish bin left out too long; it circles the sands in a slow breath, making me shudder. Painful strokes of white light reflect in the blades of metal which clash together. The floodlights buzz above me; beyond that, the sky looks dark and purple, deeper than I've ever seen it.

Colour and light flicker. I squeeze the boy's hand with panic, but the colour is just the screen high above broadcasting the fight. That screen I've watched so many times before as a spectator. Now, it looks bigger, more threatening, as if it's mocking everything happening to us. It's saying *this doesn't matter, this isn't true.*

I almost trick myself into believing that. I'm safe and nothing is real. Not the sand which whips up between people's feet or the rips of flesh tearing. Not the blood which congeals in clots on the ground or the climactic music blaring from the speakers.

Then I see my own face staring back at me from the screen, gazing slightly off centre.

I snap into reality. This, down here, is the truth. And I'm in the middle of it.

The boy is heavy, his weight practically dead as I try to put more space between us and the main fracas. Dylan's sword drags my arm down and the tip makes a little line in the sand as I haul the child away.

That's when I see him.

On the screen, a bulky figure presses towards us. I whip my head around and the huge man is even closer than he appeared. A wide blue cross sprawls over his shirt. It creases as he stealthily avoids a would-be punch from an attacker and backs away from a neighbouring duel. My stomach flips, letting me feel each painful clench. I should be running away but I'm frozen still. A girl near him falls, and his gaze wavers as he blinks the specks of sand from his eyes. Before long, his glare settles back onto the tummy of the boy who holds my hand.

He wants his weapon back.

It's not this man's fault. I know he's trying to survive like everyone else. I just don't care. I listened enough in biology class to know that if he pulls that dagger out, this child is dead.

I lurch forwards. The boy falls back behind me. In the corner of my vision, I see my image on the screen run too. She bends as I bend to slice through the air faster. I focus on the bouncing cross on the man's chest as he hurtles

35

towards me. I don't know what I'm planning to do but my body works for me, pulling the heavy sword up to chest height.

My first mistake is thinking the man has overlooked me. In a neat blow, his fist jabs into the hilt of my sword. There's a sharp snap, like conkers colliding together in a game, and my fingers bend back unnaturally. I think that unearthly scream comes from me.

I'm still cursing, searching the floor for my weapon when pain fractures the side of my face, shooting up to my eye. I imagine a vein bursting, sending agony through all the rivulets like a tree growing in fast motion. My body twists as I reel backwards; sight blurred and with my eyes, head and nose all throbbing.

The man's already off, sprinting towards the boy now curled on the ground.

I don't even know the child's name. Why didn't I ask his name?

I'm running. The stinging pain from my hand goes numb and I force on through hazy vision. My eye's swelling too, the lid closing over it, yet I keep pushing my legs over the sand.

The man skids. Leans over the boy. His hand reaches out, and I do the only thing I can.

I jump.

My leap closes the distance between us and I land on his back, locking my hands around his neck. He jerks backward, his body twisting as we tumble to the ground. My knees and arms smack onto the sand, the force wrenching my hands from his neck. For a terrifying second, his arm swings for my face, but I roll away just in time, and his fist meets air. Almost as soon as we're down, we're both clambering to get up.

We scramble together in a frenzy. Somehow his kicks don't hurt, they're just stopping me from getting to my feet. My breath screams with exertion, like a siren in my ears with everything else dulled into a muffled roar. Let. Me. Go! The maniac's trying to grab my neck. I'm a trapped animal, scratching and scraping, using my fingernails, my teeth, every speck of strength and determination I have left to break free.

He's stronger, but I'm faster. I escape his grasp and right away I'm on my feet. I dive towards the discarded spear I gave to the boy moments ago.

With horrible agility for his size, the man rolls onto his front and pushes up with his hands.

That's when I see it.

The soft, exposed side of his neck.

I can't think. I just thrust the spear in a savage arc through the air and don't stop until the man's flesh hits the side of my fist.

Hot, sticky blood pulses over my hand and in between my fingers. It seeps into my balled palm. Blood which smells of iron and rot.

I didn't cause this. This is nothing to do with me.

I stare down at my hand and his neck. There's a droplet of sweat below his hairline. A constellation of freckles across his nape. He shudders and it runs from him to me through the spear which connects us. And just like that, he falls. Where there was a running, breathing man, there is now a dead mass of bones and flesh.

I snatch my aching fingers away from the spear as if it were aflame.

Screams. Cheers. Hoots. As though I've just popped my ears, my hearing bursts back.

There's drums. First a few, then the sound multiplies like the beginnings of an avalanche. I realise the spectators are stamping their feet—a Mexican wave of appreciation washing through the stands.

Is Coral one of those twisted-mouthed people? Does she want me to live or die?

Another thought paralyses me. Dad was asked to work at this event. He'll be watching me right now. Waiting to see whether his only child will survive. So that answers my question. Coral wants me to die, and she wants my dad to watch.

I swallow, unable to take my eyes from the adoring crowd. Why are they cheering a death? Did I do that when I was in the stands? I can't remember. All I see is the dead man in front of me. The spear sticks out from his neck, the wooden end bobbing up and down as if nodding its approval.

The unsteady sand rubs at my knees as I crawl away and towards the boy. I drag my guilt behind me; although I can't believe what I've just done, I'm sickeningly glad the spear isn't in *my* neck. What kind of person does that make me?

I don't want to touch the boy with my bloodied hand even though his own wound pumps blood nonstop. I place my clean palm on his forehead in what I hope is a soothing way.

'You're going to be fine.' I have to shout to make sure he hears me. 'What's your name?'

His mouth moves into an 'o' before he manages to croak out what I think is 'William.'

With no idea why, I smile. His hand shudders into life and in sudden, quaking movements he raises it towards me. I want to take it, but there's a note of fear in his eyes. They've lost focus, rolling backwards as though he is looking over my shoulder. It's obvious it takes all his effort to move and as his finger extends, I catch on to what he's trying to say.

There's someone behind me.

A woman slick with grime towers over us. In an instant her mace crashes down, missing my calf by an inch. Before I can react, an arrow from nowhere pierces her middle, spilling blood onto her brown shirt. Her back arcs with the impact; her face contorts with surprise. I crawl out of the way just in time for her twitching body to slump to the ground. On her chest, just above her wound, there's a thick red cross.

I want to cry, to scream out that she lost her life trying to kill members of her own team, but nothing will come from my mouth but heavy, laboured breaths. I wonder how many others she's killed in her hysteria.

My clothes are sticky with sweat although the air's still cool. I push the woman's body away from William's legs, ignoring the stained sand which creeps towards us.

The ground is plagued with bodies now, but I can't tell which team they belong to. Through the disturbed sand which shrouds the dead, I make out six people still left. Two of them are women, locked in a weaponless duel, grappling and pushing with their hands. My tummy flips as I recognise the blonde girl who panicked earlier. That's one more red.

On the other side of the arena, another two red men have ganged up on a huge-looking blue, and the only other figure stands farther away, fumbling with a bow and arrow. He must be the one who protected William and me. That makes him a red too, surely?

For the first time since I stepped onto the sands, I let myself wish. The man finally strings the bow and as he aims at the duel hope surges through me, flooding my body and mind.

We're going to win.

We're going to win! If only I could tell William. His coiled body shivers beside me. Despite his pale face, he's full of life compared to the murdered woman by his feet.

I look again at her red cross, nearly lost in her crimson blood. Then comes the realisation I should have made long ago.

If she was red, the man who shot her must be blue . . . he's going to shoot the blonde girl and the red men and there will be two blues against us—a half-blind school girl and a near-dead boy.

I jump to my feet. My mind is buzzing with a hundred thoughts. I'm darting towards the fighting women so fast my feet seem to bounce off the sand. Launching into the air, I wrap my arms around the blonde's waist and throw all my speed behind the grapple. There's a tug as she's wrestled away from the other woman's grip, followed by a sharp crack as my hip hits the ground. Blondie lands on top of me. I suck in air through my teeth.

An arrow whizzes above us, through the space where the blonde was standing seconds ago, and into the shoulder of the blue-crossed woman.

Blondie looks down at me, the incidents obviously connecting in her mind. There's a flash of understanding in her eyes, and she leaps up and turns on the woman, leaving me to flop back to the floor. Side-on, I watch the three pairs of dancing legs which signify the red men are still trying to take down their foe.

I sense, rather than see, Blondie finishing the fight. My right eye is now swollen completely shut, my hip sending biting pain through my side, and my fingers hang limply from my hand. All I can do is lean up on my elbow to recover my breath. The man hurtles towards us—thankfully out of arrows—but I can't respond. I have nothing left. Instead, I involuntarily spit what tastes like blood from my throat.

Blondie steps over me and meets the man head on with a knife she must have stolen from someone else. Once upon a time, I would have been disgusted with anyone prising a weapon from a dead person's hand, but I have lost all sense of that now. All perception of who I was, what was right, how I would act in a deadly situation.

Turns out, I would kill to save myself. The man I murdered still stares at me with bulging eyes when I close my own; his image bright under my lids.

I lean my head back down on the sand. Blondie and the blue man are grunting with exertion. Far across the arena, the two reds have their blue backing away. It won't be long until they bid him goodbye.

Something dashes past my face and hits the sand. It's Blondie's knife. She's unarmed. The crowd's jeers echo around me like the rumble of thunder. The girl's gaze scurries over the sand to find another weapon.

'*Please find one,*' I think in my head but it comes out as a whisper. Blondie backs away, the man slowly advancing, eager to press his sudden advantage. I'm going to die if I don't help, I realise. I try to clamber up, but my legs won't obey, and I stumble. Just as I close my eyes to stop myself from seeing Blondie get killed, there's a sharp tug at my hair. She's leaning over me. When she swings round, my silver hair pin glints in her hand.

With a sickening squelch, the large pin plunges into the man's eye.

He falls. The crowd erupts. This time they don't stop cheering.

I take in the remaining people on the sands. Me, Blondie, William and the two men.

All reds.

My next breath fills my body. It's glorious in my lungs, gliding down my burning throat and running into every swollen finger. We've won.

ve

FIFTY-TWO PEOPLE were chosen to pay the Nation's Debt from twenty-five cities this month. Ten have already gone on to work at the Demonstrator camp. Forty-two battled for their lives. And only five have survived the Demonstrator tryouts!' Ebiere Okiro's satiny voice glides through the Stadium as she steps delicately around the bodies with her head held high. The trail of her elegant purple dress sweeps across the sand in her wake.

'The tryouts will return to Juliet in two years. Meanwhile, enjoy your tax-free month everyone, as I can reveal that one of the winners is from this very city! Ladies and gentlemen, please give it up for your new Demonstrators!' I tune out as she reads the names of the two men, one of whom leans on the other for support up on the big screen. Then the image changes to William's twisted body.

'William Wilson from Echo!'

I want so much to get to him, but my body won't move. So instead I lie here, watching Ebiere weave her magical voice through the crowd.

'Alixis Spires from Alpha!'

A close-up of Blondie appears on the screen. She's still standing near me, and it's weird seeing her silhouette in the corner of my vision, yet her face so huge on the screen. I didn't think the crowd could get much louder, but they manage, shouting down praise and adoration for my fellow team member. Blondie must have fought really well, or maybe they just loved the hair pin ending.

She's looking at the screen, and the camera must be in the same direction because her image is staring straight ahead, her mouth arcing in a sad smile. She nods to receive the applause and I want to slap her. To say, *people have died, you know. You've killed someone and so have I.* But then the sound of the Stadium doubles. I worry that something's happened—that there's a sick twist and we've got to fight again. The spectators are screaming, whooping, stamping their feet. The vibrations run through my body from the ground. What are they cheering for?

'And finally, Sola Herrington from Juliet!'

My own bewildered image is already on the screen, every shade of my black eye amplified to the Stadium. The camera pans out, revealing my matted hair, dusty face and neck, askew tie, and limp arms—one soaked in blood so that it looks as if I'm sporting a lacy red glove.

Ebiere applauds me too, but I notice she stays well back, her team of Herd officers ready to rush out at the slightest sign of danger.

That's almost funny. *We're* the dangerous ones.

I do nothing to acknowledge my praise, and the cheers finally die down. Ebiere wraps up her little speech and waves the crowd goodbye as if she were a queen on her coronation, blowing little kisses here and there.

I lay my head down on the cool sand and stare up at the floodlights.

What happens now?

I'm not sure; I'm just trying to forget that sound of the spear piercing the man's neck. Trying to ignore the way his blood sticks to my arm like some kind of alien organism which will keep spreading up to my shoulders, over my chest, into my mouth, my ears, my nose.

There's a scuffle of footsteps.

I heave myself onto my elbows, looking through my good eye over the dead bodies to where William lies. He's still. Three medics hurry over with a stretcher from one of the gates which line the edge of the arena. They're followed by another cart. I close my eyes a second too late as the first limp body is hoisted onto it.

More footsteps. The clatter of the crowd becomes a low hum. I guess only the most dedicated fans stay to watch the clean-up.

'Sola, you have to stand.' Dylan sounds firm and urgent, as if he were talking through his teeth. I know I should respond, do as he says, but I need to lie down for one more minute. Agony and fatigue claim me as adrenaline flees my body.

'Is she in need of care?' Another voice, this one muffled.

'No. We'll treat her at the camp.' Dylan again, his tone deadly. The word 'camp' breaks through the foggy haze, and I force my eyes open. *That's* what happens now. I go to camp.

'See, she's conscious,' Dylan says to a medic who wears a sanitary mask around her mouth and nose as if she could contract death. The medic runs her gawking eyes over me before turning back and following the stretcher bearers from the arena. Although I would love for my wounds to be treated, for the pain to go, I breathe out in relief to see her leave.

Pushing myself up on my elbows, I catch a glimpse of William. He's been pulled out of his foetal position to lie down straight on the stretcher. His hand poises over the edge in a half curl, like he were beckoning me closer. If I wasn't so exhausted, I would run over and hold that hand just like I did before, but I don't, and soon William is hurried off the sand and his body disappears under the great archway.

I cry out as Dylan hauls me onto my feet. He loops his arm around my waist and calls to Blondie, who's wandering around the arena, peering down at the bodies as if she had nothing to do with the carnage. The two men follow with their heads down. With Dylan's help, I manage to limp over the sand, ignoring the four pumped-up looking Herd officers which flank us. We march through shadowy corridors and out through a small, back door. None of us speak. I'm glad; hobbling is taking up all my energy.

Stepping onto the familiar streets seems wrong. Everything should be different. *I'm* different. With each distant cheer, I startle, sinking away from excited passers-by who eye the group hungrily. For the first time in my life, I'm glad that no one will mess with a Herd officer.

I grit my teeth against the pain which comes in pulses now that the fight's over. My hand is the worst. It's as though someone has injected pins into every nerve ending. I'm almost glad when we turn into city Juliet's hospital, but then I remember what Dylan said about treating me at 'camp'. Why are we here?

'Dylan—what?' I manage to get a few words out as the lift we're all huddled into passes the 23rd floor and keeps going up, up, up. Blondie, or Alixis as I should say, looks at me, chewing on her bottom lip. The medicinal scent makes me feel faint.

Dylan doesn't respond, but I think his grip around my waist tightens for a second. Then the lift beeps and the doors fly open and we're not looking at a ward at all but we're high in the night sky, the roof of the hospital spreading ahead of us like a desert.

And just like a mirage, Dad stands at the far end, next to a huge metal spinner which I've only ever seen miles high in the air before. I can't help myself. I wrestle from Dylan's hold and attempt to scramble over to my father. My shouts must be stifled by the spinner's whir because he doesn't respond, just stands there stoically, un-loving and unknown. The blades slice through the air, casting a foggy wind around the vision of Dad. It wavers for an instant, and I pause, blinking away grit from my one open eye. The image begins to distort, as if the atmosphere is manipulating itself, and I see him. Not my father. Only needles and pain. Mr Winters stands in his Liaison's coat, looking at me through grey-ringed eyes.

All my instincts tell me to run, but my body and mind have disconnected. Dirt crisps away from my face as my

45

hair whips at my cheeks, the wind urging me forwards then pulling me back. Alixis strides past me, followed by the two men. Then Dylan passes with a tap on my back, his silent way of telling me I must follow. It might be my imagination in hyper drive and tainted with delirium, but I imagine there's a warning in that tap. A threat. So I move.

Mr Winters follows me with his eyes. I wonder what will happen to Dad now; whether Mr Winters will sack him; whether he struggled to get to me in the Stadium; whether—a flurry of self-loathing battles in my stomach— he saw me spear that man in the neck.

Clambering onto the spinner, I sit next to Dylan and strap myself in with a wince. The machine only seats seven so the Herd officers stand back, shielding their eyes with their hands while Mr Winters climbs beside the pilot in the front.

There are no windows, just huge gaping holes on either side—open doorways which I'm still hoping will close even when the engine roars louder and I know we're about to ascend. Dylan places cool, soft pads over my ears. I catch his eye. It's the first time we've really looked at each other since before the tryouts. I want to smile, to do anything so he'll show a flicker of emotion about the fact that I've survived, but he gives me nothing. Those never-ending blue eyes have become hard pools of frosty water. Without warning, Dylan darts his attention to Alixis.

We're setting off. The aircraft lurches upward, swaying as though we're dangling from a piece of string before we rush into the sky. The force pushes me against the back of my chair and my fingers whiten as I cling to my seat with my good hand, convinced I'm about to topple out and squish on the hospital roof. One of the men who sits in the back of the spinner lets out a 'whoa' as we ascend.

I've heard people say that when a bomb detonates, you feel the impact before you hear the explosion. Well, right now I'm feeling that bomb, waiting for the explosion to catch up with us. The constant roar of the engine rumbles into one long continuous noise.

Despite the lurch in my stomach, I inch my face closer to the gap in the side and gasp. The city is below us, expanding and yet shrinking with every passing second, as if I'm zooming out on a camera lens. The wind stings both eyes in different ways but I strain to keep one open. I want to drink this sight in. I've never noticed just how beautiful Juliet is. I see now why the Shepherds are so proud of this city. It's a place worth fighting for.

The many pavements twine around each other, lit up by the street lamps like illuminated grey letters scribbling words around tall buildings. Through the blanket of night, the bull's eye image I always pictured when thinking of the rail has vanished, replaced by moving light from the rail carriages. They run circles around the city, each one a giant glowing insect guarding a section of Juliet, which gets smaller, and smaller, and—

We're leaving the city.

I don't know where I thought we would go. I've seen the spinners flying around before and knew Demonstrators came in from other cities, but I thought it would be through some kind of mythical guarded gate somewhere around the border. Despite everything, *this* is what panics me. It goes against years of instinct. Wherever I go, I won't be welcome. No one is.

It's all explained in the Book of Red Ink. With each city trying to pay back their Debt, competitions arose. People began fighting. Now, we're only safe in our own city. With our own people. The Shepherds protect us from each other.

Unfortunately I've learned that being afraid of something doesn't stop it from happening. I lean farther out of the spinner and as we rise, I see it all. My breath is stolen by the sight and the choking wind. The night above us is pure, untainted by the thick mist of pollution. I swear I can taste the clouds. Everything is salty. Cold and crisp and clear. It's as if I've been cured of cataracts, or tuned the digiscreen so it's no longer fuzzy around the edges.

For that second, I'm hovering in the apex of the world. It's one of those moments where everything stops and the city inhales, about to wish me goodbye. I suddenly see Juliet as one big, puffy cheek; a cheek which blows me away with a great huff as the spinner angles and zooms higher.

I'm thrown sideways. Alixis nearly falls through the gap on her side and our eyes meet in joint terror. Thankfully, we straighten up, and by the time I can breathe again we're no longer in Juliet.

Even as we fly away, I look back, straining to keep the city in view. When it finally disappears into nothing but a collection of sparkles in the distance, I breathe out a long, slow breath. I know it's time to look ahead. But I'm scared. Because I know that once I stop staring at the world through a layer of pollution, everything will become clear.

six

HOURS INTO THE JOURNEY, I spot the first clues of sunrise. Time has gone all too fast, and I've spent most of it peering out of the side of the spinner. My face is pretty numb right now, which is exactly the opposite of how I am inside. Everything has come alive; each sight sending waves of excitement right down to my toes.

I'm the only person who seems to be enjoying the view. Alixis has somehow managed to fall asleep, her head occasionally lolling onto Dylan's shoulder. He ignores her, spending the whole journey staring ahead. When I notice another city on the landscape, maybe Bravo or Foxtrot, I can't hide my excitement. I tap Dylan's shoulder ferociously until he turns to look. He nods a stony acknowledgment, but when he glances at me I see a sudden, genuine grin. I'm aware that my expression is probably similar to an astonished monkey, and I think he's laughing at me, but I don't care. It's the first time I've seen him smile since Coral's party. It's enough to make me feel as though I've drank a hot drink. It's like that second before your body gets used to it and the heat travels right down your throat.

After that, I become acutely aware of how close we are sitting. Our shoulders are practically squished together, and my crushed hip aches from being pressed into his side.

Part of me knows I could blame him for all of this. Our kiss brought this on, after all. Yet I can't hate him. His eyes change so frequently; one second they're cold—hard around the edges—but then he looks at me, and all I see is a warm intensity. Anyway, Coral is to blame, not Dylan. Even her name makes me want to spit on something. I contemplate spitting into the air and chuckle when I visualise it coming straight back at me. That would *really* impress Dylan.

I catch sight of another city in the distance. It sits like a globule of phlegm on the charcoaled landscape of what used to be England. After everyone relocated to cities, the Shepherds burnt a lot of the countryside to stop us from travelling so we would be protected from each other. At the time, there were a few rumours that the fires were to massacre anyone who refused to move, but Dad said those thoughts were quickly quashed by the threat of becoming a contestant in the Demonstrations.

I don't really understand how people can be so different in each city. Just as I don't know why the Shepherds have to raise money by charging people to see others get killed, but it's that kind of thinking which gets someone in the Stadium in the first place. So I try to remind myself that there's a reason for it all. That the Shepherds are right and *there cannot be order without sacrifice.*

As we head over the sea, the air begins to change; a shy, pink blush creeps over the cheeks of the sky while red freckles of light streak through the clouds. Then the tip of the orange sun peeks into the world. It hovers momentarily, as if deciding whether to surface or not, before rising with such strength it's as though it never wants to take its sight off me again.

I always imagined a sunrise to be slower than that, like a quiet creak. Instead it's a sudden rush—urgent and painful and beautiful.

I don't breathe or speak or cry or move. My pain disappears. Like an addict from the times before the Shepherds, now I've breathed the fresh morning air I want more. I need the warmth on my skin—in between my toes and inside my ears.

The sun throws its early light onto the sea, and a patch of un-burnt land reaches into the water. We're flying so low over the greenery I see patchworks of old fields. The hedges have grown so wild they're like fabric hems where the thread has jumbled and snagged. Morning shadows stretch awake, and I sense the world turning, changing.

All too soon, I recognise the grey terrain which signifies we are nearing a city. The spinner slows as we reach the border. It's way smaller than Juliet and I can't see a Stadium. This must be it then. Camp.

As we descend, a sinking claustrophobia chokes me. I imagine the border of the camp growing over my head, encapsulating me and stealing my air. I stare out of the gap to try to ease my breath. Right ahead are three identical, tall constructions which look like metal plants growing from the ground. They each have one large shaft in the middle, and jutting from those are dozens of strange, translucent pods. We swerve through them. There are a few more buildings, but most of the camp is oval-shaped fields, with grooves in the grass reminding me of the how the rail circulates around Juliet. We land just after passing an open-topped building—giant and extending into the sky like a stretched egg. Inside, some of the floors are filled with either smoke or steam, and others are murky. I swear the roof is made of water.

Three Herd officers wait for us on the landing pad. I'm yanked from the spinner with the care given to a bag of old clothes and it's all I can do not to collapse straight onto the tarmac. I rip the softening pads from my ears. My stumbles feel unnaturally slow, and the camp is weirdly quiet. Managing a few steps, I peer through the prongs of a metal gate which separates the landing pad from one of the wide fields I saw before. Those strange buildings sit farther in the distance.

'Sola.' A slow voice whispers in my ear. It's too close, and a shudder tells me that it is Mr Winters' hot breath on my neck. I turn, stepping backwards so that my back's up against the cold bars of the gate.

Mr Winters smirks down at me.

'I'm sorry you were chosen. My daughter was *ever* so fond of you. Do you forgive me?'

I don't know what game he's playing, so I shrug, not taking my eyes from his.

'Good, because I noticed your sword out on the Stadium today. I wasn't aware tryouts had such elaborate weapons.' He smiles again, his glare intentionally moving to Dylan, who hangs back, pretending not to watch us.

Eventually Mr Winters turns to where Alixis stands, darting her head around as if she expects something to fall out of the sky and land on her at any moment. Mr Winters curls a finger and she cautiously walks over, followed by the two other tryout survivors from the back of the spinner.

'Alixis Spires. You are from city Alpha, I believe. I'm sorry we have not been able to get more acquainted. And I've been informed you two are brothers.' He doesn't give either of the men time to respond. 'I'm Senior Liaison for Juliet. Please cast your eye over city Zulu—the "training camp" to you.'

Mr Winters indicates past the fence to where I've just been looking. Alixis inhales a long, broken breath next to me.

'How long will we be here?' The taller brother asks, staring Mr Winters in the face.

'Until you finish your tour and have paid back your Debt. Your trainer will explain this tomorrow. I'm merely the deliverer.' Mr Winters seems unfazed by the man's confrontational manner.

'But how will long will that be?' Alixis asks, although the brother had opened his mouth to reply. The urgency in her voice is undeniable. She claps a hand over her mouth, and for a second, I wonder whether she's going to be sick. I wouldn't blame her; Mr Winters' attempts to be humble are revolting. He whirls his hand through the air in a vague way.

'Weeks . . . months. It depends on how good you are. Of course, we can't wait forever, so if you're taking too long, you'll start fighting anyway. Those Demonstrations aren't very entertaining, however.' He states the last part like it's an afterthought. 'Now, I have business to attend to. Your Demonstrator will take you to the Medic's Cabin for examination. Please, don't try anything. There might not be the amount of Herd officers here as you're used to, but there are *no* second chances.'

To me, the Medic's Cabin sounds like paradise. I swear I'm about to pass out from my injuries. Mr Winters waves his palm over a small scanner in the fence and a gate farther down clicks open. Before I know what I'm doing I'm shouting after him.

'What happens after the tour?'

He pauses, then looks back over his bony shoulder.

'You return to your father, of course. Just don't die in the meantime.'

His lips curl downwards, and I wonder if that's his way of laughing. Then he's through the gate and striding down a path around the perimeter of the field. The Herd officer who pulled me out of the spinner guards him.

'Come on, you four.' Dylan speaks softly from behind us, before leading the way through the same gate as Mr Winters, but down a different path.

Alixis and I limp side by side, heads down. The brothers fall behind us, and I hear them communicating quietly to each other. I wonder if it would be better or worse to go through this with someone you love.

Around us, the camp gently awakens. Identically dressed men and women shuffle out from the bottom of the shafts. Some head straight to the fields, others towards a flat, one-storey building in the other direction. We head over a large, tarmac area where a woman begins dancing around, whizzing two plastic swords above her head, then jabbing the air like part of some ritual drill. Two Herd officers stand close, looking bored; I can practically sense the dust on their gun belts.

I don't want to see anymore. I don't want to be here. All of a sudden the crushing reality of what is happening hits me, absorbing my energy and leaving me a shell full of nothing. I need Dad. I miss Mum. I want to be six again and playing in the bath while she sits on the counter and hums. I want her to laugh at my hair when she tries to pull it into a braid. I want to sneak past the kitchen just to see my parents kissing, wondering what it would be like to love someone as much as they love each other.

Dylan approaches a one-storey cabin, and through the windows, beds stretch out in strict lines. Everything is stark white and blinding, except the blades which sit upon short wheeled tables.

I vaguely hear Dylan tell us that when we wake up, we'll be fixed. Doesn't he understand that's not possible anymore?

When I wake up, I won't be fixed.

I'll be a Demonstrator.

seven

DYLAN LEADS US through wide double doors. Five beeps echo through the white corridor as we scan in to the Medic's Cabin, one by one. I count four sealed doors before we turn a corner, which is when Alixis starts hyperventilating. She stops walking, staring ahead with wide eyes.

'Hey,' she calls to Dylan. 'What's going to happen? In there? What are they going to do to us?'

'They'll just check you over, that's all. Mend any injuries, make sure you're okay after the fight.' Dylan speaks slowly, quietly, before offering Alixis a sad smile and continuing to lead us.

Alixis doesn't move, just chews her thumbnail, her eyes darting to each of the closed doors. When the brothers pass her, the taller one touches Alixis' shoulder gently. For some reason, the gesture brings me comfort. It says *we're all in this together*. I follow the brothers down the corridor, and soon enough, Alixis' footsteps tap slowly behind me.

The medics ignore us while we pile into the long, rectangular room. There are four beds on wheels laid out next to each other, each with a number on the headstand and surrounded by various instruments. In between beds one and two, and also beds three and four, is a plastic test-tube holder. I swallow when I see around a dozen empty vials sitting in each holder. I don't even want to know what liquid will fill them.

Dylan goes over to one of the medics, has a brief chat in low tones, then leaves, avoiding my eyes as he scans out. Well, thanks for that, Dylan. No comforting words? No 'Don't worry, I've been through this all before and it's nothing to worry about'? My breathing quickens until I'm aware that, between Alixis and I, we probably sound like we're giving birth or something. At least it gets the medic's attention. She guides us unceremoniously over to the beds. I'm lumbered with the one farthest away from the door, next to the taller brother. As soon as we've all lain down the medic pulls her sanitary mask down to her chin and addresses us.

'We have to take the blood sample before you're affected by any drugs so Patrick here will do that now.' She sounds bored, as if she's said these words a hundred times before. 'Then you'll be sedated. Depending on the extent of your injuries you'll be in here for a few days or you'll be transported to your pod while you're asleep. Any questions? Great. Let's get on with it.' She turns away before anyone can speak.

Patrick is an older-looking medic with fairly kind eyes and a gentle manner. Yet that doesn't stop my rising dread when I see him sit between beds one and two and stick the needle into the arm of the shorter brother. The vial attached to the needle turns red. My arm goes a bit funny, as though it's already happening to me. I wish it was because at least it would be over. Patrick removes the vial, places a bandage over the brother's elbow and gives his upper arm a quick jab with a separate needle.

Then it's Alixis' turn. Patrick carefully slots the blood into the holder I saw earlier before turning on his chair so that he's facing her. Behind Patrick, the brother slumps asleep. I squirm as Patrick cleans Alixis' skin for the needle.

'Don't you like blood?' the taller brother asks me.

I start at the question. I had been looking straight past his bed and didn't even realise he was facing me. He offers a grin and cocks his head towards Patrick.

'Blood's fine. It's what causes it that I don't like,' I reply.

'Needles. Got you. It will be fine.'

'So you and your brother aren't scared at all then?' I ask. It sounds more accusatory than I meant it to. To my surprise, the man chuckles.

'Actually, we're terrified. We were saying earlier that we're quite glad you girls are here because we've had to act tough. It makes it easier, get me?'

I find myself smiling too, not a proper smile but it's better than nothing. 'I wouldn't bother. I think we can all handle ourselves.'

'Except when it comes to needles.'

'Right,' I say.

'Got you. Well, see you on the other side.' He takes a deep breath in as Patrick walks around Alixis' bed and over to us. I'm just about to answer when a movement catches my eye. Alixis is leaning up in bed, reaching over the test-tube holder by her side. She moves her hand quickly and I see a flash of red before she flops back onto her bed, just in time for her arms to sag and her lids to flutter.

No one else seems to have noticed anything; most of the medics have their backs to us, fiddling with the machinery lining the room, letting Patrick work his magic before beginning. The brother next to me has his eyes closed already, taking deep breaths as Patrick works to find a vein.

It was probably nothing. Maybe she wanted to check the amount or something . . . That's so obviously not the case that it almost makes me laugh. But not quite. Because soon, a shadow dims my vision. The brother I had just been talking to is now unconscious, and Patrick stands over me.

I hold out my arm, take a long breath, and wait for the dark.

SUDDENLY, it's the middle of the night, and my throat is screaming for a drink. Straight away, I know I'm not in the Medic's Cabin. That antiseptic smell has all but disappeared, replaced by a dusty scent, like when Dad put down a new rug in the flat. I'm staring at a low ceiling which is as foggy as my thoughts, and for a brief moment I think I'm floating under the layer of pollution back in Juliet. Then I see the trigger camera hanging from above the door and I realise I'm just lying on the top bunk in one of those translucent pods I saw earlier.

The only light comes from the red dot of the door scanner, but it's enough to show a small room—scarcely long enough to fit the built-in bunk, which curves to the shape of the oval, and wide enough for the bedside table. Someone has even thought to lay an open Book of Red Ink on the surface, yet hasn't bothered to leave us with any water.

Clutching the edge of the bunk, I kneel and swing my head over the side. Alixis sleeps soundly beneath me, her bright hair spreading around her pillow as if she were underwater. Each one of her breaths makes me thirstier, like the sound of air whistling through hay. At the sight of her, I remember that moment in the Medic's Cabin right before I went under. I'm not sure what she was doing with those vials, but it didn't seem right. Then again, no one's asking me to trust her.

I clamber down the ladder, now really wishing we did have a new rug because standing on see-through glass is kind of freaky. However, I can barely make out another pod underneath us, let alone the inside of it, which makes me feel slightly less on-show. At least I'm clean and my fingers stretch out as good as new. I'm also kitted out in a white T-shirt and some pyjama bottoms which don't quite touch my feet. I wonder where my school uniform has gone—incinerated probably, seeing as I'll never need it again. There's a fresh scar on my hip where it was smashed into the ground, and I touch my face tentatively, wondering how much of it is purple.

I search the bedside cabinet and find two digipads and some clothes. No water. I bang the door shut too loudly, then glance to Alixis to check I haven't woken her. Another deep breath tells me she's fine.

After one step I'm at the side of the pod, leaning my palms against the smooth surface. The camp lies about sixty feet below: dark and lifeless. Frozen still like the abandoned countryside I saw on the way here. Even the Herd officers sit snoozing on the steps to a low gym-like building.

Actually, the layout reminds me of my old school: the cabins, gyms, and tall pod shafts. The buildings are separated from the vast fields with an area of tarmac which looks like a playground. Of course, no one plays here. They train so that they might survive their next fight and get to see their families again.

I sigh, blowing a wiry piece of hair from my face; if someone gets to go home when they finish their tour, why has no one ever returned to city Juliet in my seventeen years?

I curse in the darkness. I'm so thirsty. My old school might not have had such beautiful fields with a lining of willow trees at the far end, but at least it had a water dispenser.

As I'm about give in, closing my eyes and leaning my forehead on the surface, a light flickers outside. It radiates from a small hut built on thin legs suspended above the tarmac. The way its glow skims over the camp reminds me of watchtowers in old films.

They'll have water.

Without a second thought, I pad over to the scanner and run my palm over it. The door slides open to reveal a tiny, dark shaft, illuminated only by the scanner light. I glimpse at Alixis—still sleeping—and step in.

Then I'm falling. The ground moves beneath me and I'm zooming down. My insides lurch upwards as I try to grab the sides—but they're moving with me. Trying to ground myself in this stupid thing is about as much use as the privacy setting on Debtbook. Eventually the floor jolts to a stop, and the door glides open.

I'm crouching on the floor, my chest heaving as I stand before the expanse of tarmac. Thankfully, the Herd officers are asleep because otherwise they'd think I was insane. After I've stepped from the shaft, the door whirs quietly as it slides back into place.

The 'playground' is kind of eerie. It smells almost familiar, like an allotment or vegetables growing in a humid greenhouse. The light from the watchtower shines across the tarmac in streaks. Even though it's silent, the quiet seems to rage in my mind like the buzz of white noise. Now the need for a drink has passed from my throat to my stomach. Each time my head thumps it's shouting 'water, water, water!'

Here goes. I dart around the yellow glow, my bare feet tapping on the ground as I stick to the shadows, one eye on the sleeping Herd officers. When I reach the steps to the watchtower, I grasp the cool handrail and take a moment to recover my breath. I wish my heart would stop pounding so hard in my chest.

The steps don't even creak as I climb. The silence tells me I'm being sneaky, and right now I'm not sure this is such a good idea. Maybe my thirst can wait. I'll go back to the pod and try to sleep.

'This is absurd!'

That voice. Clipped anger has replaced the usual slow, pronounced tones of Mr Winters. My body goes cold, as though all my blood has run for its life. I don't dare move, fearing one moan from the stairs will be enough to alert him that I'm here.

'Nonsense, Albert! We have to look into all of these matters. There's no need to worry yourself over a small investigation.' This cheery voice I don't recognise. It's male, and I'm so scared I need to giggle at Mr Winters' first name. I'm not even sure if Coral knew it was Albert. I ease myself up the last few steps, holding my breath while inching closer to the door.

'What happens then?'

Is it possible, Mr Winters sounds almost—frightened?

'It will all get brushed under the carpet, of course. You've been loyal to us for over twenty years; my father had great ties with your family. You can trust us to look after you.'

'I can assure you I was only thinking of securing the Shepherds' power, I—'

'Great stuff, great stuff, and I know all that, I do. Trouble is, you can't go around cherry-picking people without some consequences. You know the system for choosing people for the Debt. There's a quota we must abide by and city Juliet is all over the place. It's all very boring, I know, but it has to be done. More tea?'

I hope that Mr Winters is better than his daughter at picking up on nuances, because the other man's friendly tone couldn't be more unsettling if he were shouting.

'Very well. I look forwards to when this is all sorted out.'

He almost gets away with it, but Mr Winters' last word goes up like he's asking a question.

'Great stuff. Goodnight, Albert.'

Crap. I pause, searching for somewhere to hide. It's too late to run down the stairs, but there's nowhere else. The scanner beeps.

I crouch in the corner of the platform just before the door slides open.

Please, shadows cloak me. . . .

Light escapes out the door and Mr Winters emerges. By some miracle, he's concentrating on his digipad, and within seconds he's half way down the stairs and the door has slid shut once more, trapping the light back in with it.

I exhale so slowly it's like I'm not doing it at all, blowing the air over my bottom lip so that it's noiseless. When I bring my hands to cover my nose and mouth, I realise I'm shaking. Mr Winters hits the last step and rounds the stairs so that he's nearly underneath me. I follow him with my stare, every muscle in my body screaming as I hold them still.

He stops and takes one last look towards the watchtower.

His eyes meet mine. They widen a fraction. Then, his courteous smile is back—the one which makes my insides crawl. He gives me a slow nod, which seems to say *this isn't the last of me,* before disappearing from the watchtower's light and into the shadows.

nine

THAT NERVOUS FEAR must have taken up permanent residence in my bones. I stand on the playground the next morning, chewing my thumbnail relentlessly.

'I don't feel very well,' Alixis mutters beside me. She woke me this morning completely unaware of my midnight adventure. She also discovered our digipads in the bedside cabinet, but this time our Debtbook had been updated with instructions to be dressed and outside by seven. The clothes I found turned out to be our uniforms. They're practically identical to our sleeping clothes: white T shirts and sweatpants that don't exactly keep out the cold. I wrap my arms around my shoulders and do a few jogs on the spot to warm up.

'Try not to think about anything,' I reply. By *anything*, I mean everything. The tryouts, the tour, the fact that we're both killers. . . . 'That's what I'm trying to do.'

'I just wish we could speak to our families through the digipads,' she tells me for the fourth time this morning. Our pads have been altered so that we can't comment on anyone else's Debtbook profiles. We can only update our own statuses. Unlike before, where only my contacts from Juliet could write on my profile, now anyone 'following' me can comment. I already have pages of praise from the tryouts. I sigh.

'Yeah, I know. Anyway, you had a good look at everyone who died, didn't you? That's probably why you feel sick,' I say without looking over. Okay, I'm being mean, but I can't try and be friendly with someone who has no regard for what she—what we both—did. Alixis' brow furrows for a moment. She shakes her head.

'I was saying prayers for the deceased,' she mumbles.

Oh.

She doesn't need to say any more. We both know why she was being discreet. The Book of Red Ink replaced the Bible long ago. My family were never religious, but I know some people still pass the teachings of their faith down in secret. Dad said that when the Shepherds first came to power, they even tried to ban words like 'god' or 'lord', but they had been adopted so readily into language that the Shepherds had to give up. I bite my lip.

'Sorry. Um, Mr Winters said you were from city Alpha. What's it like there?' I ask, trying to ease the tension as we wait to be greeted by whoever wanted us out here. Of course I've heard what people are like in Alpha—totally elitist and close to paying back their Debt—but I don't have anything else to ask her about. I take another grateful sip from one of the many water bottles Alixis found underneath her bed, along with two first aid packs and some extra blankets. If only I'd thought to look there last night.

Alixis smiles, looking to a place only she can see. 'It's home. I've been away for so long, I'm worried I'll forget what it's like, but I'll always know that it is home.'

Something doesn't add up.

'So long? It's only been two days.'

'Maybe for you. I was held with the rest of them in that dingy cell for a week. The tryouts are at the end of the month so if you're chosen before that, well, they have to keep you somewhere, drugged up and unwashed. A few of the others had been in for longer.'

'I'm sorry. That's awful.'

'It was. Although, it made me really want to survive.' She gives me a sly smile. 'Thanks for saving me from that arrow by the way.'

I shrug in what I hope is a *think nothing of it* way. I can't work her out. She looks older than me, but acts younger and seems more than a little wary. Then again, neither of us is exactly showcasing our personalities right now. It's been a rough few days. I'm still surprised Mr Winters didn't sneak into our pod in the night and inject me with poison after he realised I had overheard his conversation. 'Cherry-picking'—that's what the other man accused him of. Did he mean the way Mr Winters picked me?

'Our new Demonstrators!' A cheery voice greets us from across the tarmac. It's as if I summoned him from my thoughts or something because I instantly recognise the mystery voice from last night. He looks around Alixis' age, maybe twenty-two, and strides towards us in a pale blue shirt and black jeans. He brings the smell of coffee, and it mixes in with the earthy scent of the camp.

'So it's true then. Two ladies! Apparently, you lovelies caused quite a stir at the tryouts.' He stops a metre in front of us. 'I usually don't greet the newbies, but I had to meet you for myself. Half of Juliet is already following you on Debtbook! I don't blame them, a pair of absolute beauties, both of you.'

He meets my gaze confidently, and it's hard to believe that this is the man who struck fear into Mr Winters—possibly the creepiest guy on the planet.

'You have to be the infamous Sola. Very clever tactics saving that young boy's life.' He winks at me before grabbing my hand in a firm shake. 'And I won't ask where you got that sword from, but you owe me one, okay?' He elongates the *okay*, like he's giving a drum roll. I just stare.

'Which makes you Alixis? I've heard all about that pin in the eye. Great stuff. Great stuff. Well, I'm sure you have lots of questions but save them for your trainer. I merely wanted to welcome you to the camp.' He nods the whole time while he speaks; his brown hair so gelled it doesn't even waver. I get the impression he wants us to respond.

'Thanks. Um, who are you?' This comes out slightly more offensive than I mean it to, and his smile falters.

'Shepherd Fines, of course.'

Alixis jolts her head up.

He's a Shepherd. A real, honest-to-life Shepherd. The government is only made up of seven and the only way to become one is to be born into it. We're taught about them in class but we never see their faces. They are spoken about so reverently I had begun to think of them as some superior force, hovering above each city, listening to the trigger cameras and organising the Debt.

I certainly didn't expect this lively, almost good-looking guy.

'Oh. Wow.' The words come out before I even know what I'm saying. It seems to make up for not knowing who he was because his grin swings back.

'Indeed. I'm in charge of the Demonstrations so spend most of my time here in Zulu. Well, if you need me, my office is up there.' He points to the watchtower. My stomach clenches in protest of last night's memory. Shepherd Fines continues, 'I hope you settle in well. Your trainer should be waiting for you in the first field. Train hard and your tour will be over before you know it. Great to meet you ladies.' He clicks his teeth at us twice, as if he were calling over a horse, then turns back the way he came.

I make a face at Alixis and can tell she's thinking exactly the same as me: *what the hell was that about?*

The other Demonstrators eye us curiously as we make our way to the field. A figure I recognise is running laps. Dylan.

Right then it's like I've passed through some invisible wall and into a land which makes my palms sweaty, causes my heart to hammer painfully and evaporates any kind of moisture from my mouth. The memory of our kiss illuminates in my mind as if I've walked into a room, switched the light on, and there we are, lying on the trampoline, our lips touching.

It was so much easier to see him with the tryouts distracting me. Why didn't I make my hair look nice this morning? My eye doesn't hurt anymore, but I haven't actually looked in a mirror since we arrived here, and for all I know a nasty black circle could be making me look like an old pirate.

Why do I even care? It's not like I really know him . . . but I do know how his lips taste and how his laugh is low and soft and how everything about him reminds me of calm, cool music.

'Hey!' Alixis calls, waving her arm in the air to get his attention. He looks up, nods, and jogs over.

'Morning, you two.' He speaks to Alixis, ignoring me. His matching uniform is marked with sweat.

'Are you our trainer then?' Alixis asks, looking round. Dylan nods a confirmation. He keeps his eyes down, scratching his back as if he's trying to hide behind his elbow.

He's embarrassed to see me. I urge the heat which is flushing my face not to show.

'You training those brothers, too?' Alixis asks, and I swear there's an edge of hope in her tone.

'No. I haven't seen them since the Medic's Cabin. Right, let's start.' Dylan points to the grooves in the ground which mark lanes.

'The first, and most important, part of training is getting your fitness levels up, which means running laps. Keep up.' With that, he sets off again. Alixis looks to me once before sprinting after him in the next lane.

Complete with an unhealthy amount of self-consciousness, I run to catch them up and slide into the lane next to Alixis.

'We'—Alixis huffs in between breaths—'were promised answers.'

'Ask away.' How is Dylan's voice still so perfect when he's been jogging all this time?

'What's this tour everyone keeps talking about?' Alixis asks.

'The tour is how you pay back your Debt. You fight one Demonstration in each city around the country and end with a final fight in your home Stadium. Tickets to this fight are always expensive—so the Shepherds give the audience a twist. The worse the twist the less likely you'll survive.' He glances over to check we understand.

'However, the more followers you get on Debtbook as the tour progresses, the more likely you'll be given a fair last fight because the public won't want to see you killed. Legs up, come on! If you survive your home fight, then you go back to your families,' Dylan says as though it's oh-so-simple.

'Okay.' Alixis is more than a little out of breath. 'But everyone outside of Alpha will hate me. Is there protection for that?'

There's a pause.

'You might be surprised,' Dylan says, 'but yes, Herd officers accompany you everywhere, and when you're in the Stadium you've only the contestants to worry about.'

'And there's twenty-six cities right? That's twenty-six fights,' Alixis says.

'Twenty-five fights. There's no Stadium in Zulu,' Dylan corrects.

Alixis continues to ask the questions I'm desperate to know the answers to. 'So this is the only training camp then? And who decides when we're ready to start?'

'The one and only camp, aye. As for who decides, well that would be your trainer.' This, Dylan says with a grin, and his eyes even flicker to me as he speaks. I look straight ahead, hoping he'll think my cheeks are red from the running.

'So, how come you aren't still touring? Why are—you putting—it off—training us?' Alixis pants.

Dylan loses his grin and looks out into the distance, his answer nearly getting lost behind us.

'I've finished my tour. I've paid back my Debt.'

To that, neither Alixis nor I have a reply, so we keep running. Around and around in futile circles, wearing ourselves out, getting nowhere.

❧

AT LEAST ALIXIS throws up first. I'm not sure how many laps we've done, but my T-shirt is soaked with sweat and I keep wiping more away from my eyes. Well, if I was worried about how I looked earlier I can now rest assured knowing I resemble a frizzy-haired lobster having some kind of heart attack. My mouth, throat and lungs all burn from gasping.

'Getting tired yet?' Dylan startles me by calling across the space which Alixis' absence has left. I risk a glimpse over.

'Are you?' I ask. Our heavy breaths lap over each other's, providing a steady rhythm to our steps.

The side of his open mouth curls just a fraction and he shakes his head.

'Me neither,' I say. Nothing could be further from the truth, but there's a bud of defiance growing within me. Straight away, he picks up the pace. My legs scream in protest, and I push them harder to match him. That smug look on his face tells me he's in his element.

'You like running then?' I ask casually, as if this is *so* easy. As if my whole body isn't begging for me to stop.

'It's grand.'

That lilt in his voice reaches over the space and grips my heart; it's so—perfect.

'Actually, it's my favourite part of being a Demonstrator,' he says. That's when I see it. A flash before he speeds ahead. His blue eyes narrow in a tiny smile and, in that second, I know he's thinking about our kiss.

Those words are an exact echo of what he said at Coral's party. The joke I quoted back to him.

He's surging forwards. I can't match him and he knows it. My legs tumble to a stop and laughter rolls from me.

He remembers.

Best of all, he wants me to remember. My energy floods back and I want to whoop and punch the air and twirl about. Then I remember where I am, that my life is basically over, that Dad is on his own in city Juliet, and that I'm a murderer. Instead, I finish the lap, jog over to where Alixis lies and help her up.

'You feeling okay?' I ask.

'Yep,' she says, brushing the grass from her clothes before giving me a strange look. 'Are you?'

A giggle escapes. I blame the high from exercise for behaving like a little girl.

'Yeah. Turns out, I really like running.'

⊂℞

'PERSISTENCE AND RESISTENCE!' Dylan repeats over and over again as we kill ourselves at fitness drills. 'Those two things will save your life!'

My high has quickly evaporated and every inch of my body aches. It's as though there's a great big hand gripping every muscle, squeezing them until I can't move. I cradle my stomach, which is as tight as a drawstring bag.

'We get a gun, don't we?' Alixis asks as I ram down hits on her punching gloves. 'So it's not like we can *really* die.'

'Aye you can die all right. You only get one bullet throughout your whole tour. Most try to keep it for their last Demonstration, and they're right to. If you need to use your gun before that, you might as well give up there and then. So: *persistence and resistance*. Persist through the fight, resist the pain.'

If it's possible, my body tenses further at the mention of a gun. I never thought I would be in a position to carry the same weapon which murdered Mum. If I picked it up, would I be like him? The man who shot Mum? It was random, her murder. Just a crazy guy who overpowered a Herd officer and killed the first person he saw.

I'm not trying to be noble, pretending there's a difference in killing people with a sword, or a dagger or a hair pin, to a gun, but I'm just not sure I could do it. Shoot someone and see their expression. Wonder whether it was the same expression which Mum had when she died.

I keep my mouth shut, because I'm basically incapable of saying anything around Dylan. Yet thoughts of the gun linger in my mind. I know one day soon I'll have to decide what's more important: Mum's memory or my own survival.

When the sun begins to set, Dylan leads us over the field, towards the semi-translucent building I saw on the way into the camp. It's the only place set apart from the playground.

'Spend at least an hour in here. It will ease the cramps in your muscles,' Dylan instructs. He fishes two keys out of his pocket and inspects them in the diminishing light. 'Here're your locker keys. In there you'll find your, um, swimwear and anything else you'll need for the Wetpod. And don't worry, there aren't any trigger cameras.'

He passes the keys over.

'Dinner's in the refectory from seven till nine. That's the long, flat building right next to the Medic's Cabin.' He points over the field, to where the lights are beginning to flicker on in the pods. 'See you both tomorrow.'

As he turns to go, Alixis calls to him.

'What's happening tomorrow?' She's still out of breath and her voice comes out as a hoarse whisper. Dylan pauses.

'The same again. I'll meet you at seven for morning laps. Get breakfast at six if you want it.' Right then it's hard to believe he's even got a playful side. Alixis lets out a dramatic sigh.

'You'll get used to it. If you don't, you'll die on tour and that's just the way it is,' Dylan says. His 'th's sound like

71

hard 't's, making the sentence seem less angry somehow and more manner of fact. With that, he's off. I watch as he walks a few paces then breaks into a jog, cutting a diagonal across the field.

After spending all day with him, I suddenly miss his familiar scent. It's fresh, like bedding which has been left to dry outside. A hollow emptiness creeps through me. It's as though I'm on a sinking ship watching the rescue boat float farther away. But that's ridiculous. Dylan's not my beacon of hope; completing my tour and getting back to Dad alive is. I clench the key in my hand and head inside the Wetpod.

Dylan's right. There's only one way of getting out of this. I train. I kill. I go home.

ten

DYLAN IS IN LOVE with Alixis. I'm sure of it.

For the past week, I've watched him run over to her every time she falls, vomits, or has to lie down. Fitness doesn't exactly come naturally to her; her womanly curves are still as evident as ever and she can't even finish one lap more than the day we started. Yet I see exactly why Dylan would fall in love with her, because in two short weeks, I love her too.

She moans nearly all the time, but when she finds something funny, she laughs so loud and for so long you can't help laughing, too. I've never spent so much time with anyone in my whole life. We train, eat, and sleep in the same space as each other yet she hardly ever gets on my nerves. I also know that if I told her how much I like Dylan, she would be loyal to me, which only makes me feel worse.

Why can't I stop thinking about him? I've only spoken to him alone once since I've been here. It was three days ago, when I had decided to stay in the Wetpod longer than Alixis because boy, is it amazing in there. I've never seen a Herd officer near it, and when I'm there I'm safe, hidden by the steam and depths of the pools.

Anyway, I had been swimming in the warm pool as usual before heading down to the steam tubes to hydrate my body. This level is literally full of steam, with various tubes running from floor to ceiling, big enough for about five people and teeming with aromas and heat dials. The moment I was about to leave, I noticed a figure approaching through the mist.

This doesn't happen much. Occasionally, I'll meet people in the pool levels or the hot baths but at that time of night the steam tubes are always empty. I was pretty startled, so I darted to where I'd left my towel.

'Oh, sorry. I thought it was—'

I didn't get to hear what Dylan was about to say, because he stopped cold as soon as he recognised me. We stood about two metres apart, letting the steam drift between us like smoke in the wind. I was glad I couldn't see him properly; the men's swimming trunks are long and loose, but just knowing he had his top off was enough to make me blush from my chin to my hairline.

'You're usually finished by now,' he muttered, finally breaking the silence. I went to reply, but had no idea what to say.

My mouth worked for a moment, before I settled on, 'Yeah, well training hurt today.' It sounded a lot like an accusation, and I was worried it didn't exactly make sense, either. I could make out Dylan nodding slowly.

'You're doing well, Sola, but you need to train harder. You never anticipate other people's moves.' His blue eyes darted to mine just as the mist began to clear. He cast his gaze downwards—sideways—anywhere but on me.

I could have giggled at how panicked he looked, but instead I was reminded of how he acted after he had kissed me. I sighed.

'If I train harder, do you really think I can complete my tour?' It's a question that had been tugging at me since the first day of training—each time Dylan shouted for me to go faster, for ten more push ups, my knees to go higher.

'There's a chance you can, aye.'

'So how come I've never met anyone who was chosen before? They disappear and never come back.'

He ran his hand through his hair as if he were trying to pull the answer from his mind.

'There are so many reasons. Those people who never go into the tryouts, the older ones chosen to work at camp, they never pay back their Debt so they can't come home. It's just like being relocated for later life, really.' He shrugs. 'People like you and me, well, you've seen what happens. A lot of them die in the tryouts, if not they go during their tour. Folks can complete it, but the last fight is tough. After you finish the tour you—you don't exactly feel the same. Some people return home under a different identity, some choose to stay here, working at the camp, or even continuing to demonstrate.'

I wondered which one of those is his reason for staying.

'So, people have returned home then?'

'Aye. Maybe just not in city Juliet or in your lifetime.' He shrugged, still looking to the side as though I wasn't standing right in front of him.

'Okay. Thanks,' I said, although I wasn't really sure what I was thanking him for. 'I'll see you tomorrow then. I promise I'll work harder to guess what other people are going to do.'

'You do that,' he replied, his lips barely moving.

'I knew you were going to say that,' I said, and even now I can't help but cringe with the rubbishness of it. Note to self: don't joke when nervous. . . .

Then we moved away. He went farther into the steam room, and I almost ran out to my locker. As soon as I got outside, I took a gulp of fresh air, wondering if I even breathed the whole time I was talking to Dylan. My skin was hot and tingling, and I was trying to persuade myself that my joke wasn't *that* bad.

That was three days ago, and if I thought this encounter would progress anything for us, I was so wrong. It only makes it harder for me to watch him tend to Alixis in our training, while shouting at me to 'put some effort into it'.

Yet even Dylan's attentiveness towards her hasn't lifted Alixis' spirits today. As we walk across the darkening field having spent another evening in the Wetpod, she seems quiet. I towel dry my hair, and shudder as the cold blow gently across the nape of my neck.

'Is everything okay?' I ask.

'Mmm?' she turns to me, broken from whatever daze had taken her over. 'Yeah, I'm fine. You've lost weight you know.' She sighs.

My cheeks flush and I curl my arm around my tummy.

'I didn't really notice.'

Now she's mentioned it, my stomach does feel different, not exactly smaller, but harder. It's not a surprise seeing as Dylan has been forcing me to do two hundred sit ups in the morning and at night. Also, as stupid as this sounds, things have started to seem lighter. Like the other day when I pulled a refectory table closer to my lap. It was kind of *easy*.

'You've really toned up this week too,' I say, guessing the reason for her melancholy. 'Anyway, we've got loads of time to get fit before our tour.'

'I doubt it,' she grumbles.

Just then we pause instinctively as Shepherd Fines waves to us from the path which leads to the spinner landing pad. Alixis groans, repeating, 'Please don't come and say hello,' underneath her fixed, fake smile. I laugh and beckon him over.

I don't mind him at all. He's always the picture of cheery hellos and bad jokes whenever he wanders over during our training; his favourite is pretending he's scared of us. I still fake laugh, although Alixis turns away whenever he approaches which, come to think of it, actually makes me laugh for real. No wonder Shepherd Fines thinks we're friends.

This time, he points to the gate and raises his arms in an over-the-top, *got to go over there; can't do anything about it* kind of way. I mimic him and wave again as he heads down the path, an even bigger grin now on his face.

'You're a lucky lady, Sola, because if he had taken one step towards us I would—hey what's going on over there?' Alixis stops mid-rant and points at the playground. A group of Demonstrators have dragged chairs to the centre and are staring at the side of the watchtower—which I now know is actually Shepherd Fines' office. The Herd officer I've seen pretty much every day stands near the throng of Demonstrators, looking agitated.

I shrug, and without speaking we change our direction from the refectory to the playground.

As we approach, a square of the watchtower's wall unhinges and swings around to reveal a large digiscreen. A man of about twenty years paces in front of the screen, head down, chewing on his lip.

I scrutinise the small crowd for those familiar blue eyes, floppy dark hair, and that occasional smile which makes me hope he's never looked at another girl the way he's looking at me, but Alixis spots Dylan first.

'What's happening?' she whispers, taking a seat next to him.

I plonk myself down at the end of the row, envious of her easy way when she's around the man I'm obsessed with.

'See that guy at the front?' Dylan motions towards the pacing man. 'That's Gideon. His partner begins the tour today, so we're watching the Demonstration on the screen.'

At this, I lean forwards. Although I should be chomping down my carefully portioned dinner right now, I need to know what to expect when my own tour starts. And if I'm honest, I want to say something so Dylan will acknowledge I'm here.

'Do you think she'll win?' I ask.

Dylan looks past Alixis at me and raises a strong eyebrow. It seems as though he's trying not to laugh.

'I think *he* will win, aye.'

Oh. Gideon has a boyfriend. Great, the only thing I've managed to say makes me look like a total idiot. I manage to mumble, 'That's good' before leaning back, eyes firmly ahead. A tiny, selfish part of me is pleased that Demonstrators dating Demonstrators is obviously allowed, but then I remember that this man might be about to watch his boyfriend die, and it doesn't seem so great after all.

There's a fanfare of noise from the screen and Gideon darts into his chair. The screen flickers yellow and a red banner swirls across the middle. It reads:

Demonstration in city Yankee. Dao Zheng vs. criminals convicted of breaching Act 03: strictly no conspiring against The Shepherds.

After a brief profiling of Dao, where certain stats and background information are typed out on screen, the camera cuts to a sweeping view of the Stadium before broadcasting live from the arena.

Ebiere Okiro appears, stunningly fashionable in a daring blue evening gown, her black hair knotted to her head. She gives an evocative speech about the virtues of compliance, praising the audience for their good sense and condemning the criminals for their ingratitude. She asks so many rhetorical questions about the Debt and how the audience is in danger because of other people's stupidity that my head spins. Thankfully, she wraps up her soliloquy and announces Dao before long.

A slight Demonstrator armed with a sword and gun belt enters the arena. When the camera zooms in on the boy's composed face, so close I can see the cornflake-shaped birthmark on his cheek, Gideon moves on his chair as if he were about to jump up. Yet he must think better of it as he stays seated, his wide shoulders heaving with a deep breath. I wonder what, in his mind, he's telling the person that he loves, and whether anyone will care that much for me on my first fight.

Without warning, I'm staring at an arena gate clicking out of place. It slides up, just like it did that day for me. . . . That electronic ticking is so loud I swear I'm back there.

That room. That stench.

William next to me, alive and not stabbed.

Suddenly, I can't see clearly anymore. I'm in the Stadium. About to kill. I can't tell whether the gate's clicking is coming from the screen or inside my mind.

Can't breathe. I'm drowning in the vision: so close and real I smell the blood in the air, choke on the dust in my mouth, taste the sweat which drips down my face. Rasping breath fills my ears; I think it's mine. I close my eyes and when I open them I'm still on the sands.

There's blood on my hand and over my wrist and please stop staring at me! The man's eyes bore into my own. His freckles spell out murderer. His sweat stinks of the deceased.

The gate carries on clicking until suddenly, all sounds are extinguished. It's like my head's underwater. My face is hot yet my lips are freezing. My breaths desperate and suffocating.

The sands fade. Dylan's face shines for a brief, glowing second. Then everything disappears.

 eleven

HAIR DYE AND ANTISEPTIC. The horribly familiar smells of the Medic's Cabin drag me to consciousness. Edges of my vision blur and re-align before sharpening into focus. The ceiling stares down at me, along with an IV pole to my left. The tube sticks into my arm like a finger underneath my skin.

Then, fresh bedding. Is it crazy that I recognise Dylan's smell before I clock him, hunched to my right with a hand nursing his forehead? His eyes are sharp and intent, staring at nothing.

'What happened?' I ask, though my throat is thick and foggy. Dylan jolts his head to me, his serious expression narrowing.

'You passed out. When I brought you here the medic sedated you so your body could rest.' He does that flick of his hand again, as if he were dismissing the medic away from his thoughts. He's wearing a polo shirt today, I realise as I stare at him. The shape of the collar redefines his jaw bones and even in this stark white light he looks so stunning I want to rewind time and replay our kiss over and over again.

The thought makes me dizzy so I lean my head back down.

'Wow. They even treat being unconscious with sedation. Do the medics actually know any other treatments?' I know it's a rubbish joke, but there's no one else in the small ward and the silence between us is unbearable

'This isn't funny, Sola. What made you faint?' Is it possible his accent makes him seem angrier than he actually is? I sit up and meet his hard look.

'I think it was the noise of the gate. It's the last thing I remember. Who's winning, by the way?' I think of Dao and Gideon. While I've been passed out, Dao's been fighting for his life. It's a weird feeling, knowing that life and death continue, whether I'm there to witness it or not.

'Dao won. The fight's over although he had to use his gun. He won't get many followers now.'

More silence. I inhale, and the sound whispers through the ward, highlighting that we have nothing to say. Well, that isn't true at all; there are a thousand things I want to say to him, but they're trying so hard to get out it's like they've jammed up the door and nothing can escape through it.

'Do you think this is going to happen again?' Dylan eventually asks.

'I hope not. I don't think my body can take much more "resting".' I add a little laugh to make it obvious I'm joking.

'I can't believe you.'

Huh?

'You understand if that was you on the screen tonight, you would have died?'

Dylan stands quickly, his disgust so tangible I can practically taste it. 'If this happens when you're out there, then that's it, Sola. No jokes, no second chances. Just you, dead. Is that what you want?'

'Hey, I didn't do it on purpose.' I sit up straight, my skin tingling as though I have raised hackles. Who is he to question what I want?

It doesn't stop him. He carries on, as if he's been wanting to rage at me all week and now's his big chance.

'You have to survive twenty-five Demonstrations. It only takes one of those to kill you. I've seen it before! If you don't push yourself, if you delay for one second, you're dead. *You couldn't see a move coming even if your opponent gave a running commentary as he fought. Now this!*

'You don't seem to get it. You might be trained, but there're more of them. Three, four, sometimes five against one. They want to survive just as much as you. You know that if they kill you, they get to become a Demonstrator? They are fighting for their lives. Don't you want to finish your tour? Don't you want this all to be over?'

'Of course I do!' I shout, but he doesn't stop. His lilt gets stronger and stronger, the irritation pouring out of his mouth and right at me.

'You laugh this all off like you can laugh your way out of the Stadium. Like you haven't got a parent waiting for you at home. You did well in the tryouts, Sola. You have a chance to get out of here. To fight and to win.'

'So I can come back here and train other people to kill, like you do?' I shout.

He freezes.

I've gone too far. I want to suck the words back in, but it's too late. He gives me one more look and I can't work out whether it's anger or hurt or hatred. A second later, he turns and strides out of the room, the beep of the scanner as loud as if he had slammed the door behind him.

twelve

A HORRIBLE, SLOW MOMENT PASSES. It's as though the whole ward is recoiling from me, rolling away in waves, and soon it will all cascade off a cliff top and pull me down with it.

That antiseptic smell intensifies. Do they use it as air freshener around here or something? I need to get out. Now.

I rip the IV tube from my arm then stifle my own scream. I wasn't expecting it to hurt that much. Ignoring the sting of tears which burn my eyes, I slam my feet against the cold floor, leaving the bed sheet to sweep away behind me. I bang the ward door with my fist.

Why won't it open? I'm not sure what I'm going to say to Dylan when I catch him, whether I'm going to shout or apologise or demand he tells me what's going on between us, but I need to do *something*.

In a moment of clarity, I realise I haven't scanned out. I bring my palm across the scanner. It glows red. The door doesn't open.

I want to yell, but all that will come from my mouth are sobs. Hot, heaving sobs which take all my energy to quash. I've never given up on anything in my life. I didn't give up on happiness after Mum was shot, I didn't give up on our farce of a life desperately staying on the good side of Mr Winters, and I'm not going to give up on getting out of this ward.

I lay into the door as if it were another person—Coral, maybe. I slam my fists down again and again, the crack of my hands against the plastic like a whip in my ears.

Eventually someone scans in from the other side and the door slides open. The medic's old eyes widen above her sanitary mask.

I don't hesitate. I push my way through the gap and hurtle down the corridor. Darkness pools in from the main doors which are open, amazingly. Muffled shouts chase after me, but I sprint away, reaching for the freedom I know I won't find outside. I break through the exit and throw myself into the unlit playground.

Straight away, I clock Dylan walking across the field. I take off again, words cramming into my mind as I try to figure out what to say. How can I explain why I've just broken out of a place which was trying to fix me?

Something soft bumps into my arm. I jolt backwards, but it's too late. A firm hand takes hold of my shoulder, and I'm turned to face whoever it belongs to.

'Sola? What are you doing out here so late? What's happened to you?'

I look up to see Shepherd Fines' concerned face. Dylan strides out of the corner of my vision.

'I-I—'

Thankfully, I don't have to explain because the medic bursts from the cabin. She runs straight towards me, pulling her mask down. I flinch as she brings her arm up, but then she sees Shepherd Fines. Just as though she had walked in on someone naked, she leaps back. Her grey hair shimmers on her ducked head.

'Sir, I'm so sorry to disturb you. That girl. She's supposed to be on an IV drip until the morning but she barged past us and—'

Shepherd Fines holds up a hand, his eyes still on me, and the woman falls silent.

'I think we can give the IV a miss, this once. Don't you?' He turns to her. His charming smile is back.

'Of course. If you say so, Sir. We only wanted what was best.' She teeters, glancing back to the safety of the cabin. There's a slight squeeze on my shoulder.

'Come along, Miss Herrington. I think you need a hot drink. Not to mention some shoes,' he says, guiding me forwards for a few steps before dropping his hand to his side.

We walk in silence past the medic, who doesn't seem to know whether or not she's been dismissed. When we reach the metal stairs leading to the watchtower, Shepherd Fines gestures for me to go first.

I creep up the steps for the second time since I've been here. My anxiety warns me I'm treading on forbidden territory. He joins me at the top and opens the door using his finger on the scanner, not his palm. As he heads into his office, I sneak a look at his hand and my suspicions are confirmed; Shepherds don't have scan chips.

But wow, do they have nice offices.

Once I step inside, I gasp. The place smells like ink and that sulphuric scent which a candle leaves once it's been blown out. It's incredibly bright, lit by half a dozen exotic, tongue-red lamps. They cast pink and orange streaks on the teal-coloured maps which stretch across the walls. The digiscreen I saw earlier tonight has been switched back to the inside, now deactivated. Apart from the desk towards the back of the room, there's no other hint that this is an office. A red throw depicting dark outlines of elephants and camels covers a sofa to my side, and my feet are warmed by the tasselled orange rug beneath me.

'It's beautiful,' I say, staring at the artefacts which litter the room. Shepherd Fines chuckles.

'I'm glad you like it. Now, what can I get you?'

'You really don't have to—' I trail off. Shepherd Fines wanders to where a large globe stands on cedar wood legs. Underneath the globe, five glasses sit in holders. The Shepherd removes two of them and balances them on a mound of papers on the desk. A second later, the globe has split in two, opening up to reveal an army of bottles huddled inside.

'You're still only seventeen, aren't you?' he says slowly, not leaving me time to reply. 'No matter, we'll have something non-alcoholic. Let me see.' He waves his finger over the tops off the bottles, as if he were doing a magic trick, before finally settling it on the lid of a purple bottle. A silhouette of a tree decorates the side.

'Great stuff. You'll love this one, Sola.'

After pouring the liquid into two glasses, he clicks a switch underneath each glass which makes the purple drink steam. I remember when those glasses came out; only the richest people in Juliet could afford one. Naturally, that means I've never seen one up-close before.

The vapour swirls around the room. It smells warm and homely. Like cranberries and cinnamon. Shepherd Fines hands a drink to me and sits on the sofa, closing his eyes as he sips his.

'Thanks,' I say quietly, and also take a seat, mainly because I have no idea what to do.

The panic that grabbed me in the Medic's Cabin is beginning to wear off, and now I'm uncomfortably aware I acted like a crazy person—storming out of the cabin in the dead of night with no shoes, tears dripping from my chin and a splatter of blood in my elbow where I ripped out the IV. Now I'm sitting in one of the most powerful people in the world's office, sipping on a drink which tastes as amazing as it smells.

'What is this?' I ask.

'Gekruide tea. It's from a place you've probably never even heard of.' He nods to me and laughs. 'Do you like it?'

'Mmm-hmm,' I mumble through a mouthful of tea. 'How have you got all of this stuff?'

As soon as the words are out, I grimace. Totally inappropriate or what? I haven't exactly got a good track record of dealing with people in power; Coral and her dad have shown me that. Surprisingly though, Shepherd Fines seems excited by the question.

'My dear, I collect an item from everywhere I go. Travelling is one of the perks of the job, and I *always* find the best wine, or dish, or'—he indicates to the floor and grins—'rug available. Anyway, enough about your humble Shepherd! When are you going to tell me why you were running around the camp crying?'

I hesitate, wondering what the answer is. Because of Dylan? Because I'm going to faint if I hear that gate again? Because I'm here? I look into my drink.

'I don't really like the Medic's Cabin very much.'

'No. I wouldn't exactly go there for a pick-me-up either,' he replies before taking a long sip. That's strangely funny for him, but he doesn't laugh like he usually does at his own jokes. 'However, they know what they're doing and we need to keep our Demonstrators fit and healthy, don't we?' He raises his forefinger from the glass and points it at me.

His answer causes a jolt in my chest, like when I'm on my way out and remember I've left something really important at home. *Fit and healthy . . .*

'Oh, Sir, do you know what happened to William?' I ask, realising what his words reminded me of. 'He's another red tryout who survived, I think. The medics took him, but he should be fixed by now. Will he come here?' The words tumble out in a less than graceful heap. Shepherd Fines looks into the air, an overly confused expression on his face.

'Was he one of those two brothers?'

I shake my head. 'No. Well, yes, them too, but William first. He was the boy I helped survive.' I add the last bit quietly.

'Aha! Yes, I remember. The boy. He's still being treated, I do believe. Yes. He will come to train as soon as he has recovered.' He smiles as if the matter is closed.

'Um, and the brothers?' I ask, sensing I'm pushing my luck although I'm not sure why. I haven't seen either brother since my first day here, when one of them told me he would 'see me on the other side'.

'How worrisome you are! The brothers are being taken care of, no need to be troubled. Now, how about you concentrate on yourself for a while? Reach that twenty lap landmark.'

Something niggles at me; it's as if I've returned home to find the important thing, but totally forgotten what it was that I needed. I dismiss it. Shepherd Fines has a point: I need to forget about everyone else, Dylan especially, and I need to train harder if I want to get home anytime soon.

I drain my glass and set it on the floor next to my feet.

'Well, thanks for the tea,' I utter, feeling more awkward with each passing second. Thankfully, Shepherd Fines stands, which means I can, and claps his hand onto my shoulder.

'Absolutely no trouble, my dear. I've got to look after my Demonstrators, I wouldn't want to be like Dr. Frankenstein!' He does an odd, pretend roar and sticks his hands out in front of him, like a possessed demon or something.

I just stare.

'Ah, the books ban. Of course. Never mind,' he says, looking slightly deflated. He runs his finger over the scanner, and the door behind me slides open.

'Right then, run along. And next time I see you, I want you wearing shoes, okay?'

I nod. As if the floor were scorching hot, I scamper down the stairs, pausing at the bottom when I hear my name again. I look up to see Shepherd Fines standing at the threshold of his door, silhouetted by the glowing lights from inside.

'Oh and Sola, I watched your tryout. You were good, possibly one of the best.' A pause. 'Great stuff. Good night then.' With that he turns. The door slides shut behind him, leaving me in the shadows.

I'm totally imagining things, but I swear there's similarity in what he's just said and the way he described his collections.

I look around. I'm alone in the middle of the playground. At least I no longer feel as though I'm about to be dragged off a cliff top. In fact, all around seems still, secured and unmoving. I wonder: if I wanted to fall, would I even be allowed?

thirteen

I'M ALREADY DRESSED and ready to grab breakfast when Alixis wakes.

'I thought you were going to be in the Medic's Cabin all night?' she asks, turning on her bunk so she's lying on her side, hands folded beneath her face. When she yawns, she doesn't cover her mouth, and I see all the way to her tonsils.

'They let me go early,' I lie. 'You ready for breakfast?'

'I'm always ready for breakfast. Oh, you might want to close your eyes, I sleep naked.'

Before I can even register what she's said, she's pulled back the covers. I yelp, just to realise she's dressed in the usual white pyjamas.

'Ha, ha,' I say although I doubt she even hears me amid her cackling.

Over our breakfast of grapefruit, sugar, and the mushy brown stuff which is served en masse every morning, I tell Alixis about my evening with Shepherd Fines.

'Well, I'm happy that William's doing well,' she says through a mouthful of mush. 'He's the boy you saved, right?'

I nod, suddenly uncomfortable. We haven't spoken about the tryouts. Even thinking about that night causes the man I killed to surface in my nightmares.

'That would explain why you have so many followers on Debtbook. You've overtaken me by a mile. How many people did you kill?'

Her question takes me by surprise. I look up, open mouthed, before digging my spoon rather ferociously into my breakfast.

'One,' I mumble.

'I killed three. You'd think that would get me *more* followers. Maybe I should've tried saving someone else.' She sighs, before finishing off the last of her grapefruit.

I wish Alixis would stop obsessing over our followers. She's so preoccupied with the theory behind Demonstrating—getting followers for an easy twist, reading up on those who have completed their tours in the past— that she's forgotten our best chance of surviving is to be able to fight. Also, it seems horrid to talk about the people we killed as though they owe us followers.

'Alixis,' I whisper into my bowl. 'Do you ever regret what you did, you know, at the tryouts?'

She ponders this for a long moment, so long that I almost think she hasn't heard me. Until I see her swallow. She meets my eyes.

'No, I don't. Because I'm still alive. Do you?'

Shame creeps over me. I shake my head.

Alixis doesn't comment, just looks around and takes a deep breath. 'Talking of the tryouts, I don't suppose you've seen the brothers who fought with us, have you?' she asks, her casual tone sounding forced.

'Actually Shepherd Fines mentioned something last night. He told me not to worry about them. Why?'

'No reason, I just don't know why they've *both* disappeared.' She rubs her forehead, practically speaking to herself.

'Why would even one of them disappear?' I ask. Heat forms blotches of pink on my friend's face.

'Don't ask me. Anyway, it's great news about the boy.' She smiles widely.

'Yeah,' I reply. 'Great news.'

Why do I feel as if I'm lying?

We head straight to the field. In the distance, a lithe figure leans against the oak tree. Even from here, I can tell he is missing Dylan's easy gait and strong frame. I check my digipad. 7:00am. We're bang on time for training, so where's our trainer?

My stomach flips continuously as we walk towards the person, as if any second Dylan will jump out from behind the tree. The man—I now recognise him as Gideon from last night—doesn't even look up from his digipad when we approach.

'Come back after twenty laps. You know the score by now.' He speaks plainly, punctuating his words with little clicks from his digipad. I lean in to see the Debtbook profile of the boy from last night's fight, Dao.

It takes a few seconds to notice Gideon scowling at me.

'Twenty laps. Now.'

⊂℟

THE LAST TWO LAPS ARE KILLERS. Alixis has bowed out as usual, but I push my body forwards. It's as if I'm running through thick goo, forcing each muscle to work five times as hard. I wonder if invisible hands have sprung up from the earth, pulling on my arms and legs. My lungs strain to keep me breathing, and each gasp sends sharp cold pain into my stomach, like the air's full of tiny needles.

I keep going because I'm going to finish the twenty laps today. Dylan thinks I don't try. Well, how is *this* for trying?

As pain screams up my body, I push. Stretching out my legs, I leap rather than run to the finish line. And then—

Twenty laps.

I. Did. It.

I'm still laughing when my knees buckle. The grass is all dewy and it cools my burning back. For the first time since I've been here, I get a tiny flicker of hope. I could actually do this. I could complete my tour. I could stay alive.

'That's better than I was expecting, fainter. I want twenty-three laps tomorrow. And you'll be wearing these from now on.'

Gideon's feet appear by my head. He throws down four black L-shaped things so that they land on the grass next to me. When I go to grab one, it pulls my hand down.

'Weights,' Gideon explains. 'They go around your wrists and ankles.'

That's it. That's all I get. I strap them on angrily, yanking off my boots, scowling and thinking unpleasant thoughts about how this is all Dylan's fault . . . somehow.

At least Mr Motivator over here has managed to put his digipad away. He calls to Alixis and waits in silence as she stumbles towards us. My legs are like empty shells as I drag the extra weight up with me.

'Where's Dylan?' Alixis asks, at last.

'He has a Demonstration in city Sierra. I'll be training you this week. Although I'm not very impressed, Dylan usually has the newbies fitter than this by now.'

Something—aside from the insult—squirms at that. I don't like the thought of Dylan training other people and not me. How long has he been doing this, I wonder? Mental note: try and find his Debtbook profile after training. I don't know why I've never thought of it before.

Gideon paces in front of us, arms folded behind his back like the army general I saw in a historical film once.

'Anyway, we need to move on from basic training. You'll still participate in your endurance drills morning and evening, but this week you're on defence. Next week you'll learn to attack with precision and how to give the audience a good show. By your fourth week here, you should be able to combine all of these to conduct yourself appropriately within the Stadium. You must not kill too fast, or too slow. You must read the audience well, judge when they want brutality. Then, you'll be ready.'

I take a sharp breath. *Only three more weeks.* I'm not ready. I'll never be ready. I feel as though I'm picking the petals off a flower; like a damsel trying to decide whether or not somebody loves her: I want to live, I don't want to kill again, I want to live . . .

'So we could be home really soon then?' Alixis asks, her eyes glimmering.

'In theory. Although *you'll* die in your first Demonstration unless you get very good, very fast.' His eyes rake the field behind us. He's not even paying attention. Alixis' mouth opens as if to protest, but she looks away, blinking fast. I give Gideon my best scathing look, which must be terrible because when he finally glances at me, he looks as if he's going to crack up. When he clocks Alixis' expression though, he lets out a short sigh.

'Look, don't shoot the messenger. You're not good enough, either of you. Finishing the fight alive can come down to who has the most energy left. If you can't run this field forty times before you go out to fight, you'll lose. Dylan has been soft on you, and it could cost you your life.

'Persistence and resistance, remember.' He finishes his speech.

I hate those words.

'Anyway, let's stop that from happening, eh?' Gideon says, attempting a happy expression. His raised eyebrows and weird, open-mouthed smile is actually quite funny; being upbeat *really* doesn't come naturally to him.

We spend the rest of the day learning self-defence techniques for when you have been disarmed. They run through my head like the recipe to a tasty dish, and I imagine them read out by a woman with a high pitched, cheery voice:

-To escape one bear hug, you bend, put all your weight to the floor, and elbow your opponent in the head until you are free.

-If you find yourself being choked face-on, simply sweep their hands away in a fast motion while applying one knee kick to their groin, proceed to punch them in the neck and face until they are on the ground.

-To evade one sword attack in a downwards trajectory, place yourself between the hilt of the blade and your attacker. To do this you will need to slide the arm closest to the weapon towards your attacker's neck. Use one free hand to punch the face, and mix in a knee kick to the groin.

The drills go on and on until the sun casts a murky grey through the camp and my arms are as heavy as, well, the weights which I carry. Gideon's right, though: the moves become instinctual, almost to the point where I'm worrying about someone so much as placing a hand on my shoulder to say hello. I think I would have them on the floor with a broken arm within seconds.

Annoyingly, though, when Gideon and I parry, I fail to see most of his attacks coming and end up winded twice. Dylan's words from the Medic's Cabin repeat in my ears, but I push them away. What does he know?

I don't want an answer to that.

At least Alixis is better at these than the fitness exercises. She knows it, too. Her melancholy finally breaks around the same time we hear the whir of a spinner in the distance.

We stare as it lands behind the gate. Gideon checks his digipad and takes in a broken breath, his eyes smiling. He darts over the field and down the path just as Dao passes through the gate.

I guess that's the signal that our training is over for today. Without a word, Alixis and I head over to the Wetpod. I imagine we're both thinking the same thing.

In three weeks, that will be us returning.

We hope.

fourteen

THAT NIGHT, as I sit up in bed, I tap out Dylan's name on my digipad. I hit the link to city Victor, and am confronted with a choice of over two hundred Dylans.

Thinking fast, I tap out the name of Coral's 'BFF', Tulia Hurn. Her profile zooms up at me. I flick my finger across the screen to find her 'following' list.

My name is one of the first on the list. I can hardly believe what I'm reading.

It doesn't fit among the other Demonstrators' names and I'm not sure I like it. *She's* following *me*. Me—the girl who couldn't have paid anyone at school to talk to me, and not only because I didn't have any money.

Although I know it's a tiny bit pathetic, I smile at the thought of Coral reacting to this betrayal by Tulia. My finger hovers over Coral's name for a moment, but I clench my fist. The one good thing about being chosen is that she is out of my life, and I won't invite her back in by checking her Debtbook.

I cast my eye over the many male names in Tulia's 'following' list before I reach Dylan's. Blossoming guilt tells me I shouldn't be doing this, but I tap on his name before I can change my mind.

Dylan Casey.

His profile picture is now one of him fighting. My eyes are drawn to the way he holds his sword, angling towards his victim lying on the ground.

He has 100, 681 followers, five times more than me and the most I've ever seen. His latest status reads: *Dylan Casey is the winner of: Demonstration in Sierra. Dylan Casey vs. criminals convicted of breaching Act 11: all persons must comply with regulatory procedures.*

The statuses and comments don't end. I lose count of his Demonstration wins after fifty and flick through them faster, desperate to find his first status as a Demonstrator. Finally, I reach a page which seems different. It has more gaps, and—I realise with a jolt of excitement—comments from non-followers. This is it, before he was chosen.

There's a comment left by someone called David Harpen. He's asking Dylan if he can come over and play on his model rail set. Above it is a status which makes my throat go dry. The words still inject fear into me, even now the worst has already happened.

Dylan Casey has been chosen to help pay the Nation's Debt.

The date next to it shows December 2nd 2088. Eleven years ago. That can't be right. I race back up to the top of his profile and check the date of birth underneath his name. August 31st 2079—that makes him twenty.

So he was nine. Just nine years old when he was chosen.

I think of William—crouched in his own urine, shaking in the corner. Is that how Dylan acted at his tryout? How did he survive? Why hasn't he gone home yet?

Part of me wants to tap out Dad's name, but I'm too scared. What if he's stopped going to work? What if the last status is from days ago, showing he's still in the flat?

He's never written on my wall, and that scares me, even though I know why. He's a profile monitor; he knows the kind of people who watch what everyone writes, knows how innocent comments can get someone into trouble.

Even if he is hurt, I can't contact him directly. I can't help him. So it's easier if I hold his image in my head and carry around the hope that he's okay. That he will be waiting for me when I finish my tour.

I lie back down and think of Dylan. I want so much to be home, so why doesn't he?

fifteen

I WISH I COULD HAVE spoken to Dylan at least once before he got together with Alixis. Okay, I don't know for a fact that they're an item, but they sit together at breakfast and dinner now, talking in hushed tones and looking as forlorn as war-torn lovers should. I've taken to sitting on the other side of Alixis and shovelling my food into my mouth as fast as possible.

Gideon still trains us. Days pass in a flurry of attack drills, parrying with Gideon, and sleep. Even in the dead of night his voice seems to scream, 'persistence and resistance!' right into my mind.

At least I'm seeing a difference. My stomach is hard and flat from the crunches. My arms and legs seem stronger, carrying me and my weights for thirty-two laps before finally creaking and giving up like a broken digipad. Even my flexibility has increased. Gideon has gone onto teaching us the more flamboyant moves, designed to impress rather than to survive. To get someone on the floor, the most practical thing to do would be to kick them between the legs, then attack them until they're down. Now I know to crouch and sweep my leg out, knocking them from their feet. If I need to evade a blow I should try to leap over it rather than just get out of the way. This works especially well coupled with a blade throw right after, so Gideon says.

One aspect of training which I fear is creating our own 'signature move'. All the Demonstrators have one, apparently, and performing it is like a silent acknowledgment to all your followers. As I never followed Demonstrators before, I don't recognise any, but Alixis gets excited at this and starts to talk about this one woman who used to leap in the air and do a ballerina type spin before delivering her final blow.

'You can often draw inspiration from your tryouts. Shepherd Fines will upload the footage to your digipad if you ask to review it,' Gideon informs us after I express my anguish over the move.

At the thought of watching the tryouts, I shudder. I can't think of anything more likely to reduce me to a fainting wreck.

'Shepherd Fines would upload footage of a raging rebellion if *Sola* asked,' Alixis teases, giving me an over-the-top wink. She's in one of her better moods today. During her darker times, she doesn't take my new friendship with the Shepherd quite so lightly.

We've only been chatting here and there, Shepherd Fines and I, but his jokes seem to be getting funnier—or my sense of humour's getting worse—and I kind of like his company. Especially since Dylan's avoiding me.

Two days after Alixis' comment, Shepherd Fines visits me in the indoor gym which perpetually smells of old socks. I'm sparring with Dao, who sets off on the spinner almost every other day now that his tour is in full swing. Dao is the total opposite of Gideon: quiet, unassuming, and gentle. When I'm with him, I want to protect him even though I feel he's protecting me. He's saving me from going insane with his soft laughter and tactile touches.

Anyway, Dao is going easy on me, and I manage to get past his defences to land a hit with the plastic practice sword right in between his ribs.

As soon as I make contact, a booming chuckle sounds through the apparatus. Dao and I whizz around to see Shepherd Fines standing by the spectators' bench, a grin stretched across his face and his light brown hair gelled so thickly to one side it looks black.

'Well done, Miss Herrington!' he calls, beckoning me over. Dao bows his head, taking a few steps backward before darting from the room.

I head over, swiping the sweat from my forehead and trying to catch my breath. Shepherd Fines holds something in his hand.

'I've been hearing good things about your fighting, Sola. Now I see that they are all true.' He looks into my eyes when he speaks, stressing his words as if he means every single one of them. Heat sears through my cheeks, and I look away, mortified.

'I do believe you deserve a gift, or should I say loan?' He chuckles and holds out an old, battered book. I examine the front cover.

'Frankenstein,' I read. It sounds familiar although I'm not sure why. I turn it over in my hands. I've never seen any other book in my life than the one of Red Ink. I heard that they were all destroyed part way through the Shepherds' occupation. We can download approved material from our digipads, but physical books are too hard to keep track of, I think. They could fill our minds with all sorts of ideas, and before we know it we'd find ourselves in the Stadium, fighting a Demonstrator.

I almost chuckle at this thought. Well, I guess I've got nothing to lose now. I take it, grateful and mesmerised.

'I mentioned it a few nights ago and thought to myself, what a shame it is that young Sola can't read this. It's a brilliant book. However, this stays between us, yes?' Shepherd Fines raises his eyebrows, giving me a wink at the same time.

'Of course. Thank you.' I flick through the pages, smelling the rusty, almost paint-like scent which lives between the paper. Shepherd Fines claps his hands together and clicks his tongue.

'Great stuff. Well, I'll let you get back to your training, although—' He looks around the room. '—you seem to have lost your partner.' He makes a face like 'oops' before grinning and heading towards the door. I'm still turning *Frankenstein* over in my hands when he calls back to me.

'Oh, and feel free to pop by my office to discuss anything about the book. I'll be expecting you.'

It's only been six days since then, and I've spent four of those evenings in Shepherd Fines' office of adventure and spice. He is a little presumptuous, I'll give him that, but underneath it I think he's a nice person. We drink steaming Gekruide tea, talk about why Dr. Frankenstein made his monster, and after I ask, he even shows me where we are on one of his maps.

'I didn't even know we were in Ireland,' I say, tracing my finger around the small outline. There are only four cities in Ireland—Zulu, Victor, Whiskey, and Yankee. They sit on the map like dots; if I connected them, I would get a perfect square.

'Well, we're not. We're in Zulu.' He laughs and waggles his finger at me as if he's telling off a naughty child.

'Oh yeah, of course . . . but between you and me, it's Ireland right?' I check. Shepherd Fines seems taken back by this. He surveys me for a minute, then smiles. It's not one of his trying-to-charm smiles, but a real, cheek-dimpled one.

'Well, between you and me, have a look at *this* map.' He darts behind his desk and retrieves a large, rolled up scroll from a drawer. He unravels it on the table and the stacks of paper underneath make a bumpy surface, causing the map to rise and fold like mountains. He places his glass of tea on one end of the paper to secure it.

I inch closer. I sense Shepherd Fines grinning, looking from me to the map.

It's funny looking, the landscape stretched into an oval, and for a moment I think it's a giant pod, but then I think it's more like looking through a camera lens. Realisation blooms, and I inhale slowly, careful that a large breath could blow the paper away.

It's a map of the world.

Not Juliet, Not Ireland, but the whole, amazing world.

I run my eyes over the picture for England. There's a large shape towards the bottom which takes up about a third of the map. I point.

'Is this England?'

Shepherd Fines tries to stifle a laugh. Then he places his hand over mine, guides it about three inches east. I'm left pointing at a small reversed L-shaped dot on the paper.

'Try there,' he says.

The shape is so small that the cities are represented by mere speckles of ink. I look back up to him to see if he's joking. He's not. In fact, his smile is gone, replaced by an intense stare. His gaze darts down, and I follow suit. That's when I'm aware his hand still covers mine.

I jerk my arm away and bring it up to my neck in a pretty terrible attempt at disguising the action.

'I can't believe we're so tiny,' I say to fill the silence. Shepherd Fines doesn't look up, but clicks his tongue once. I'm not really sure what's just happened. Did I over-react? Is that why I've offended him? He probably thinks I'm some stupid girl who assumes everyone is coming on to her because they try to be nice. So why was he looking at my hand like that?

My tongue grapples around in my mouth for something to say.

'So there must be millions of Stadiums around the world then?'

He looks up, his eyes hard around the edges. It lasts scarcely a second before his grin is back and he claps his hands together.

'Right, that's about enough of that!' He begins to roll the map away. 'So, why do you believe the monster acts the way he does?' he asks. It takes me a moment to catch on that he's talking about *Frankenstein*. I launch into my theory, settling back down on the couch and glad of the distraction. I take another sip of my tea, but it has gone cold.

sixteen

TODAY IS THE FIRST without training in four weeks. Every Demonstrator has the day off.

It takes me about three seconds after I step out of my pod shaft to find out why.

Tryouts.

The word is whispered, spoken and shouted through the camp. There's a buzz in the air, like the kind heard crackling in an electrical wire.

Even the Herd officers look more alert than usual, as if when we're not training we're more hassle. It strikes me that they probably know they're more of a placebo than a real policing force. I mean, how much damage could they do against nearly a hundred trained killers? Once they ran out of ammo, what then?

I smile at the thought.

'Come on, I'm starving,' Alixis says. 'So, what did you get up to with Shepherd Fines last night?'

My defences rise. I'm starving after lying in until 10am and really not in the mood for her jibes.

'We just talked,' I mutter.

'He's too old for you.'

'I don't think of him that way, okay?' I stop still. She walks one pace in front before swinging around, her tongue in her cheek so that it looks like she's sucking on a lolly.

'And how does *he* think of *you*?'

I open my mouth to protest, before remembering the hand-on-map incident.

'Leave it,' I say.

'I hope you know what you're doing, that's all,' she replies, and smiles as if it's all sorted. Her arm drops onto my shoulders. 'Oh look, there's Dylan. Dylan!' She shouts over the tarmac to him. My insides freeze. I take a sharp breath.

'Oops, sorry, I forgot you two weren't talking,' she says with a devilish grin.

I don't even have time to hiss *yeah right* before Dylan strides over. I consider ducking away like I usually do, but on a day like today, when people will soon be fighting to survive, it seems a bit childish. So I mess around on my digipad for a bit while wondering what I can say to him. There's no point pretending everything's okay when we haven't spoken in almost three weeks, but how can I acknowledge it?

'Hey, Alixis.' His voice is as low and magical as I remember. His accent comes through even in one word. My eyes flicker up involuntarily.

'Hi, Sola.'

Oh. Wow. My name in his mouth sounds so delicious that I can't help but take a broken breath.

I give him a half-smile and look away, feeling Alixis withdraw her arm. Then with about the subtlety of a propaganda advert, those two start a silent conversation beside me; I can see Alixis jabbing her head towards me even with my eyes cast downward.

Sure enough, when I glance up, I catch Alixis with eyes as round as coins and Dylan shaking his head pointedly at her. He sees me looking, and takes a deep breath.

'Look, there's something I really need to tell you—'

'Sola!' A cheery voice shouts behind me, and I could kiss Shepherd Fines for interrupting us. I wave a little too enthusiastically, ignoring Alixis' groan. I know my unhealthy obsession with Dylan is probably making me imagine his relationship with Alixis, but I'm still worried he was about to break their 'good news' to me. I don't want to hear that, not today.

'My darling, I have the date of your first Demonstration!'

Shepherd Fines beams at me. The words hit home, jarring in my mind like metal clanging together. Date. Demonstration. Me.

'Are you all right?' Dylan's gentle voice is next to me. There's a soft touch on my arm, but it's gone as fast as it came.

'She's fine, of course. This is what she wants! Gideon recommended her as ready.' Shepherd Fines claps a hand on my shoulder. I can't bring myself to react. I just stand still, letting everyone talk around me.

'Have you got my date?' Alixis now. Her voice hopeful.

'No, you haven't been recommended. I'm sure it's merely a matter of time. Anyway, don't you wish to know when the big day is?'

His question pierces through the fog which clouds my mind. I shake my head, look up.

'Um. No. I mean Yes. Yeah, tell me when it is.'

'Six days' time. November 5th. It's in city Yankee against three criminals already detained. I could get some details on them for you if you wish?'

'No! Please, I don't want to know anything about them.' They're not people. They're not even criminals. They're only in between me and getting back home. I try to cast everything I've ever heard about those from Yankee away from my mind.

'Very well. The first three Demonstrations are on this island.' He gives me a sly grin, alluding to our insider knowledge that we are in fact, in Ireland. 'So you'll have a short journey. Anyway, you enjoy your day off with your—' He looks around. 'Oh, I seem to have scared away your friends. Well, I'll be in my office if you need me—or even if you don't!' He chuckles to himself, before giving me a tongue click and turning away.

Six days.

In six days' time, I have to fight for my life, again. The reality hits me like a defibrillator, sending shockwaves through my body. I would give everything I have right now for a hug from Mum. But I learnt a long time ago that that isn't going to happen. So I take a deep breath and ball my hands into fists.

Shepherd Fines was right; Alixis and Dylan have disappeared. I stand, surrounded by excited Demonstrators on the tarmac, totally alone.

seventeen

THE TRYOUTS aren't until the evening so I spend the afternoon hiding underneath the large oak tree way out past the field. After trying and failing to find William on Debtbook—I can't remember his second name or even what city he's from—I cast my digipad aside and settle back into *Frankenstein*. It takes a while, but eventually I stop reading the same line over and over and allow myself to be carried by the book.

It's strange really, that Shepherd Fines would have something like this. A book full of fear and needing and retribution. He's not at all like the Shepherds I imagined. He's real. Not an infallible force which controls all our movements and decisions. Best of all, he's nothing like Mr Winters, who I guess I had inadvertently based my whole opinion of the Shepherds on while I was growing up.

With a shudder, I realise evening has snuck up on me. Goose pimples steal underneath my T-shirt and travel up my arms, making my blonde hairs stand on end like grass reaching for the sun. I glance up and breathe in the crisp grey air. Even from this far out, I hear shouts and laughter drifting over from the playground.

The tryouts must be about to start.

Here goes. I slap my book shut. The grass is so cold it seeps through my pumps. I can't believe it was over a whole month ago that I was standing on those sands. I wonder if the two groups are waking up in that room right now, or if they're already choosing their weapons. How many of them will die?

Right now, all I really want is to cry and run to my pod where I can hide all night. However, I know I have to take a seat opposite that blank screen which has once again twisted from Shepherd Fines' office. Dylan was right in the Medic's Cabin those weeks ago. If I'm going to faint each time I hear the gates . . . well, I need to know.

I manage to find a couple of empty seats right at the back of the layout. As soon as I sit down, Dylan appears from the stream of Demonstrators and does what I'm least expecting in the whole world: he lowers himself into the seat next to me.

And . . . nothing. He doesn't say a word. Well, I'm sure as hell not going to. Dylan stares straight ahead even though the screen in front of us hasn't activated yet.

In the corner of my vision, I see his face, illuminated from the glow of the watchtower. The rays highlight his strong features, casting the rest into the shade. I could trace the line of light with my finger, drawing a perfect outline over his temple, the apple of his cheek, the apex of his chin, and then up that angled jaw bone. As I think it my fingers move involuntarily—a twitch I'm sure Dylan notices despite his fixating ahead.

A fanfare of trumpets interrupts my sneaky voyeurism. Up there on the screen, the red banner swirls across a background of yellow, reading:

October's Demonstrator Tryouts—Two teams, Only Winners Survive! Hosted by city Indigo.

The banner disintegrates, revealing the live sight of city Indigo's Stadium. With elaborate marble pillars circling the outside, it's almost twice the size of the Stadium in Juliet. Electronic lights snake around them like ivy, making the place look like some monstrous fairground ride. I breathe in relief when I see the sands are still empty—still a grainy peach colour instead of that cruel, stained burgundy.

After a good amount of chanting from the audience, Ebiere's tall figure appears on screen. Her hair is plaited with smooth extensions reaching to her waist and her dark skin looks more radiant than ever, complimented with a yellow tribal maxi dress. She brings her hand up in a dramatic manner, her eyes wide. The crowd falls silent, ready and eager to be seduced by her voice.

'Twenty-five cities. Fifty-five people chosen. This month, the competition to become a Demonstrator is fierce. To survive, they must protect their team mates, fight their opponent with wile and cunning. Only a few will be strong enough to become your—'She takes a breath, her coffee-brown eyes running over the masses. 'Demonstrators,' she whispers into her microphone.

'Now, you have mere seconds before you're presented with the most anticipated Demonstration event in Indigo for years! Brought to you, of course, by your loving and protecting Shepherds. Let the tryouts begin!'

The crowd goes crazy. They have these strange handheld devices which, when blown into, emit the loudest, most invasive sound I've ever heard. It's like a baby's scream blasting through a bass speaker, making me cringe from the inside out. Everyone's dressed in elaborate outfits, stuff I would expect to see on Coral and her family. For some reason, that annoys me. Indigo must be way ahead in the race to pay back their Debt.

The gate on the screen clicks and the sound is so familiar that it drains any warmth from my body. The gate slides upwards gracefully, the clicks not stoic and sinister like before but quick, giving the sound of nails rapping against a table.

It's enough to send me back. I try to blink away the image of the sands, but the sight is painted under my eyelids. The picture on the screen blurs and flickers, morphing into my own vision.

I recognise the people in the arena. They're dead, they're all dead. A dagger flies at me. William's squeezing my hand. There's the stench of iron and rust and dirt and death. I want to squeeze back and say I'm sorry, but I open my mouth and nothing, there's nothing. The dagger hits into

111

him, but he dies there and then, and I'm sorry, but I'm glad that it's over and Dylan's sword is weighing me down—

'Sola,' William says, although he was dead but now he's alive.

'Sola.'

The voice isn't William's. I blink again. My head tingles, as though I've stood up too fast. But I'm not stood up at all; I'm slumped against someone.

Those blue eyes look down at me and burn through the fog in my mind. I latch on, using them as an anchor to pull myself back. Choking on the air as if I had drowned, I sway, finally managing to lean up and away from Dylan, getting purchase on my own chair.

'Better,' he whispers. I'm not sure if he's instructing or praising me. I try to look once more at the screen, but the figures are hazy and bright dots keep twinkling around me. It's only when I blink away the fuzziness and my breathing returns to normal do I realise Dylan is holding my hand.

Which of course makes my breathing go crazy again.

As the second team is released, Dylan turns to me, staring unashamedly and intently. I assume he wants me to look back, but my head won't move. So I ignore his gaze and examine the team of blues. Some step out steadily, head raised, weapon firm in their hand. Others are more hesitant, eyes stained with tears and whizzing around as if they too could see the dots in my vision. An overweight man drops his weapon—a four-pronged metal blade in the style of a boomerang—and when he reaches down to get it a redhead from his own team pushes him onto his side and swipes it from the floor. As soon as he figures out what's happened, the man struggles up to chase her, but it's too late. She's scampered away, out of the view of the camera and the reach of the now weaponless man.

Although the red team were released first, they stand huddled on their side like a collection of trigger cameras trying to cover all angles. The blues scatter and dominate the space, advancing slowly. When I see the man from before sweating heavily, skimming the ground for a weapon, I wish Alixis would say a prayer for him. He stares up at the crowd through glassy eyes, but the ones who notice send only jeers and boos his way. He must be thirty, thirty-three tops. Too young to die.

In fact, there's no one who looks over forty. Just like in my own tryout. Everyone older must have been brought to the camp to work . . . although I haven't seen anyone new arrive. I glance around as if any second a spinner might land with a dozen newcomers.

'Are you all right?' Dylan asks. His question is heavy, as if loaded with something else. My head is still foggy, but I nod anyway. Our eyes meet for a second.

We're still holding hands, but our fingers are so lightly entwined I think a breeze could blow us apart. It's as if neither of us wants to admit what we're doing, as though we're pretending it could have happened by accident. Alixis enters my mind, followed by a flush of guilt. There might not be anything romantic between Dylan and Alixis, but kissing Dylan and betraying Coral is what got me here in the first place. Have I learnt nothing?

I pull my arm away. There's a second of resistance from Dylan before he opens his hand and lets me go.

On the screen, I'm about to feel sorry for the reds when a blue girl gets too close. Like a cracked nut, the red huddle breaks apart and a burly looking man rushes forwards with his sword raised. He takes the blue girl by surprise and cuts her down as though she were a crop.

Then it starts, really starts. The spectators' roars double. Their noise-makers feed off the violence. The reds, now having lost the element of surprise, are charged by three blues, who tackle one man like they're playing rugby. When they step away, the man doesn't move from his mangled position.

Watching the fight is like watching water. One moment, the red wave is farther across the sands, rushing in and waning away, then the blues get a surge of energy and seem to wash through the arena. The weaponless blue man is ignored by just about everyone and takes to standing at the edge of the arena, arms wrapped around his waist. Most of me, the real me, wants him to survive. Yet there's a horrible creature awakening which screams at him to fight, which thinks he deserves to die if he stands there like that, letting his team take all the damage. Letting his team become killers while he waits on the outcome like a coward.

I clench my teeth, and shame flushes the creature away. Or silences it, for now.

Men are slain by women, women slain by men. A child is caught up in a flurry of blades, and when they break apart she lies face down on the sands. The spectators don't react to that, and the camera pans quickly away, bringing us the sight of a separate duel. Two men circle each other, hunched down, weapons raised. I recognise a spear in the red's hand similar to the one I gave William. The name makes my chest hurt; William, why haven't you arrived?

The blue holds two daggers, waving them around frantically as if performing some kind of intimidation salsa. The red rushes in on one side, causing the blue to strike out, but the move was feigned. The red ducks, swerves to the other side and strikes, hitting home in between the blue's ribs.

Before he can celebrate too much, the red arches upwards, his mouth opening in a silent cry before he keels over. The camera spins to show his back. That four-bladed boomerang protrudes horribly from underneath his shoulder blade.

When the camera sweeps around the sands, I stare at the person who threw it. The person who stole it from the other man.

And no.

It can't be.

Because Coral Winters stares at me. Her red hair tight in a ponytail, her tired face gaunt, with the glint of cruelty in her eyes I've seen a hundred times before. Her lips are slightly parted to show her teeth.

That girl who sent me here. Who I hate. Who I can't watch die.

But I can't look away, either.

She still holds a double bladed staff, and now she switches hands, raising it in front of her like a shield while her stare flickers over the arena.

There are more people fighting than in my tryout, which mean more bodies litter the ground. Coral's tactic seems to be to watch other people fight, and then stick the victor in the back if they're a red. The whole time I want to stop watching, but I'm drawn to her as if there's a rope binding us together, even through the screen.

At one point I think she's going to save someone's life. She creeps behind a man who has his hands wrapped around a woman's throat. Coral raises her staff and throws all her weight behind it, sending it through him, but it's too much force. It slices through the man's gut and pierces the woman's stomach too, sending them both to their death.

That's it. No more. I can't bear it.

Blinking away swelling tears, I stand. The other Demonstrators' legs are like claws which I have to battle through to get out of the row. There's something rising in me, that creature again. It's like I'm trying to run from my own body. I need to escape before the hatred and anger and frustration bubbles out of me.

A Herd officer watches warily as I hit the field. I sprint towards the Wetpod, knowing he won't follow me in there. Before I get there that thing inside catches up; I lean forwards and vomit over the tracks.

'Sola, please.' A voice from behind me. Wiping my mouth with my arm, I straighten up. Maybe it wasn't the Herd officer I should have been cautious of.

'I tried to tell you,' Dylan says, but I don't turn to him. His footsteps stop a few paces behind me.

'How?' I croak out.

'Earlier on—before we were interrupted.'

'No. I mean, how? How was Coral chosen?' I angle my body so that I can see him in the corner of my vision. He runs his hand through his hair, looks over the field as if the dark space will give him answers.

'Her father has fallen from grace. It happened a few weeks ago after some sort of investigation. Apparently he's been fixing who gets chosen in Juliet. When you were—' He stops then, but I know what he's going to say. When I was chosen it was fix, and an obvious one, at that. I guess if I had died it wouldn't have mattered so much, everyone would have forgotten about me. But I didn't. I killed and I survived.

Dylan takes a step towards me.

'He's going to be executed in a Demonstration along with her mother. They're saying she was in on it. I think they wanted to get rid of the whole family, but they couldn't exactly kill a teen in a Demonstration when she hasn't done anything wrong. So they chose Coral for the tryouts.' He sighs; I hear his breath catch. 'I wanted to tell you, I did.'

We stand in silence for a moment. I can't help but think that any second now Coral, my old best friend, could be dead.

'It's ironic, really,' I say eventually.

'What?'

'The Shepherds have cherry-picked Coral as punishment for her father cherry-picking people for the tryouts.' I deliberately use the word I heard Shepherd Fines use on my first night here. I remember him assuring Mr Winters it would all be brushed under the carpet.

'Aye, it is kind of. I'm not saying she deserved it, but—'

'Don't,' I say, turning properly now and meeting his eyes. 'Just don't.'

He nods, and once again that silence which always swallows us breezes through the field. He closes his eyes, bringing his hand up to pull on a tuft of hair.

It's weird, but I've missed him. I've missed him and our awkward silences and how I never know what is going on in his head. How sometimes he says the right thing, but most of the time he doesn't, and how it seems okay that nothing goes the way it's planned to when I'm with him.

I cross the grass and close the space between us. I step so near to him that my head is nearly underneath his. It's safer here, away from his gaze.

I want to touch him so much. To make whatever is between us real. But all this is tinged with fear. I'm afraid he doesn't feel the same, afraid of hurting Alixis if he does. So I just turn my head so that it's flat against his shoulder. My face burns where it touches his warm T-shirt which smells so perfectly of him. I'm shaking, and I don't know whether it's because of the cold, being so close to the only person I've ever kissed, or because of Coral. My breath turns into mist underneath his chin and each second stretches like it's taking a lifetime. He's not backing away; he's not shrugging me off.

Hungrily, I run my palm over his arm, feeling his hairs stand up on end. Then I link my fingers through his. He responds readily, wrapping his thumb over my knuckles, his grip strong. When he leans the side of his face on my forehead, I wonder who is leaning on whom.

Alixis re-enters my mind, but I push her away; I need Dylan right now. He kissed me that night and started all of this and this moment I have to have his hand on mine, his skin warm against my own. When I look up, Dylan pulls his head back a fraction. Our faces are so close that if I went on tiptoes my lips would land on his in an instant. I sense him looking at me, and know if I meet his eyes, he'll kiss me, but I can't do it. I won't. Not again.

Dragging my gaze down, I take a step back, still holding his hand. He seems to understand.

'Come on,' he says softly. 'Let's see if they've won.'

As we walk back over the field, I wonder who 'they' are. What's worse, I wonder if I even want them to win.

eighteen

I SHOULDN'T BE SURPRISED that Coral survived. She's stronger than me and I somehow managed it. I don't ask anyone to fill me in on what happened, but when I return to the screen, Ebiere is announcing the winners. Coral soaks up the audience's applause just as her clothes soak in the blood. The man who she stole the weapon from, Jamey Kendra, is still standing against the wall, and when his image comes on the screen the audience's noise turns into laughs and heckles. A teenage boy stands on the other side of the arena, face sober, hand gripping his arm. Blood oozes from between his fingers.

Just before daybreak, the sound of the spinner interrupts my nightmarish sleep. Rain splatters into the camp and bounces off the side of my pod. I squint through the little lines in the sky, painted on by some artist who decided the picture didn't look quite right. It's like watching a day of my past as the figures trudge through the fields and towards the Medic's Cabin. I remember thinking back then that I would never again be the same person. I was right, but it wasn't exactly the death of me I had expected.

The three tryout survivors are accompanied by Herd officers and a female Demonstrator I can't make out properly; Coral is striding almost beside her, seemingly unaffected by the rain or the blood caking her brown uniform. Jamey holds back with the other swaying teenager. When they reach the nearest point in the path to my pod shaft, I recoil from the side. I don't know what I'm expecting—for Coral to sense me, look up through the torrent and smile like her father had done, perhaps? But of course they walk past without wavering, oblivious to the girl watching from above.

❧

I DON'T SEE CORAL until two days later. They stay in the Medic's Cabin for a whole day, and I'm so busy with my training countdown that I hardly have time to even think about her.

Five more days, then four. Dylan is back to being our trainer again, thankfully. Gideon was okay when Dao had won a Demonstration, but in between he was cranky and sniping and made so many comments about Alixis' weight that I wanted to take the plastic sword he held and whack him round the head with it.

I still hate those words, 'persistence and resistance,' but as I ran through that wall Dylan keeps talking about this morning it kind of made sense. Persist with your goal. Resist the pain.

I also made it to thirty-seven laps. Yes, it killed and yes, I'm aching but I did it. Also, when I fought Dylan I would have grazed his stomach had I not been distracted by how gorgeous he looks when he's concentrating.

Anyway, I've thought of a signature move, although how feasible it will be on the sands I'm not sure.

Now I'm sitting in between Alixis and Dylan in the refectory, my hair still damp from the Wetpod. There's a flicker of thick, red hair in the entrance.

Coral makes the white uniform look like it was designed for her lithe figure. She stands, hand on hip, assessing the room like it's not good enough. I could almost laugh at her act; where else does she think she's going to eat? I load a forkful of brown mush into my mouth.

Watching from the corner of my eye, I see Coral deliberate over which of the identical foil boxes to pick up, before finally choosing two: one each for her and Jamey. She surveys the hall once more.

I don't look away quick enough.

'Why is that girl staring at you?' Dao asks through a mouthful of food.

'We kind of know each other,' I mumble.

'Did you see her tryout?' Gideon asks from the other side of the table. 'She was one of the best I've ever seen. Good endurance, fast reactions, fights with cunning. How do *you* know her?'

'We're best friends, aren't we, Sola?'

That sleek voice sounds from behind Gideon. I tense, hating my name in her mouth. It doesn't belong there; she's stolen it from me.

When I look up, she glances to Dylan, curling her mouth into a smile. I'm wishing with all my might that she'll get the hint and go away, but she slides her foil box onto the table and sits down delicately next to Gideon. Instead of tucking her legs underneath the table, she crosses them slowly to the side for us all to see. Poor Jamey hovers behind her. There are no more free seats.

'Nice to see you again, Dylan.'

Dylan doesn't even react, simply keeps eating his food as if she had never arrived. I smile inwardly.

'Do you know how rare it is to have people from the same city survive the tryouts consecutively? Not to mention the fact that you're friends,' Gideon remarks with raised eyebrows. 'You could probably get Shepherd Fines to put you in the same pod, you know.'

Alixis looks to me sharply, narrowing her eyebrows.

'Er, no thanks,' I reply. 'Jamey, isn't it?' I speak past Coral, making Jamey start when I say his name. He nods. 'You can have this seat, I'm nearly done.'

'Yep.' Coral continues as if no one has spoken in the meantime, 'Sola and I have loads in common. Now I'm an orphan, too, I guess we have even more.'

I narrow my eyes, unsure what game she's playing. Whatever it is, I'm not going to enter into it. Dao looks surprised. 'I didn't know your parents had died, I'm sorry,' he says to me.

Heat rises in my cheeks. Some of the other Demonstrators are glancing our way. I guess they could pick up on the tension from a mile off.

'They haven't,' I say to Dao. 'Well, my mum passed a while ago.' I pause, the words still hurting even after all this time. 'But my dad is very much alive. He works for the Shepherds, actually. Well, he's not a Liaison or anything but he's working his way up.' I smile. Talking about him feels good, not painful like I expected. Imagining him with his briefcase and that worried face he pulls when he's thinking, I decide that as soon as I get away from this table I'm going to check his Debtbook profile.

Coral's eyes widen, her face changing. The facade seems to fall away, revealing her open, anxious expression. She chews on her bottom lip.

'Oh, no,' she whispers. 'I-I thought they would have told you.' She looks up through her long lashes at me. My body goes cold. I swallow, and the clink seems to echo around the room.

'I'm so sorry, Sola, but your dad died two weeks ago.'

nineteen

HER VOICE suddenly seems far away. Like I've heard the gate again, but much, much worse.

Someone lets out a strangled howl. It starts rich and full of pain, but trails off as a breathless whine. Empty, void of energy, emotion, pain, hatred.

It's mine.

The table is dirty. I see every speck on the white surface like the grainy sands of the Stadium. I think I might be choking because I can't breathe. I hope I am. I want to faint; I wait for the oblivion. Yet the world is still the same around me. Alixis has covered her mouth, eyes wide and full of sadness. Dylan is shaking his head, scrambling around on my digipad left on the table. Coral still faces me, her bottom lip red and raw from running her teeth over it.

Then I'm not thinking about Dad. I see the news report of Mum's murder, interrupting our Debtbook profiles on the screen in the kitchen. I see the body first, before they say her name. Her favourite fur coat draped on the cement. I giggle nervously, and ask Dad why Mum's sleeping outside although I'm old enough to know better. There's the smash of his mug against the kitchen floor.

'Sola!' A hand on my shoulder, shaking me. My head swims as I turn to Dylan.

'He's not dead. He's alive.' I think the words come from my mouth, but Dylan is repeating the sentence, pounding the rhythm into my mind. He shoves my digipad in front of me. Dad's image stares back at me. There's a status underneath his name:

Roberto Herrington is at Juliet Harvest Hall (work)

It's dated today.

I gasp; my body craving air. My senses rush back to meet me. It's like I've woken from a nightmare; I'm in that millisecond when you realise there wasn't a killer in your flat or you haven't seen someone you love fall from a great height.

'Oops, my mistake,' Coral says through giggles. 'I guess it's just me who's an orphan then.' She stabs her fork through the lid of her box.

Silence. My shoulders heave as I suck in breath. Everyone's eyes are on me, and it's like I'm on fire—a horrid heat infecting my face. Anger is spreading through me like a rash, itching and mauling at my skin.

Seconds pass. Coral's deliberate eating seems like the only movement in the room. I know she, too, is waiting for my response, but I won't bring myself down to her level. Wishing I had something to bite down on, I swivel my legs from under the table and stand slowly.

'See you,' Coral says, like it's only natural I should leave. Leave *my* place and *my* food and *my* friends. She doesn't even look up from her meal.

That's when I flip.

That animal inside me claws its way out and I'm not going to stop it.

Faster than I've ever reacted in training, my hand closes around my cutlery knife. At the same time I launch myself onto the table. Skidding on my knees for less than a second, I swing my leg underneath me and give Coral a sharp kick to the shoulder, knocking her to the floor just as I knew it would. Before she has time to react I'm bearing down on her, pinning her arms underneath my knees, holding the dirty knife edge millimetres from her throat.

Gasps surround me. I don't care. Someone yells something about a Herd officer.

'Say one thing about my family.' My voice is practically a growl. 'Go on. Say it. Another trick about my dad. Maybe that my mum deserves to be dead?' The knife is shaking with the force of my grip. Coral's determined eyes stare into mine, and I know she's assessing whether I'm serious or not. As I press the knife closer, her gaze flickers down, trying to see it. A tear which I hadn't noticed lands in a fat splash on Coral's cheek. She flinches. Even now, Coral still manages to seem repulsed by me.

'I'm giving you your big chance. You don't have anything to say?' I whisper, leaning my head down.

It takes a second. Her gaze darts around, mouth open, taking tiny breaths. Everyone is either too interested in what's happening or too scared of startling me to intervene. Coral looks back at me. Her mouth sets, her eyes narrow and *finally*, she makes a tiny shake of her head.

It's enough.

I withdraw the blade, and in the most controlled movement I can muster, slide it across the floor. It skids, makes a clinking noise as it hits a chair leg.

When I get to my feet, Coral leans up, rubbing her shoulder. I step over her.

'I was just having a giggle, Sola,' she calls after me, and I smile at her genuine annoyance. Alixis is by my side within seconds, clapping her hands together in my honour. A protective gaggle of Demonstrators cluster around Coral, but the people sitting at our table give me a mixture of nods and wry smiles as I pass through the refectory. Although I'm desperate to reach the exit without looking behind me, I'm just not cool enough. I bite my lip and sneak a backward peek at Dylan.

The boy I can't help but adore sits watching Coral try to brush off what just happened. He scoops up the last of his food, pops it into his mouth, and chews as if he were enjoying a snack during a good film.

The creature inside me laughs at his devilish grin, and I do, too.

twenty

'DO YOU STILL STAND BY WHAT YOU SAID?' Dylan asks me, his head cocked to one side. We're leaning against the old oak tree after an intense day of training. I haven't even hit the Wetpod yet, although Alixis limped there over an hour ago.

'What did I say?' I ask, smiling. There's only an inch between us; since Coral's tryout, that uncomfortable silence has disappeared. Maybe it has something to do with my first Demonstration being tomorrow afternoon—we've run out of time to be awkward.

'That, she *isn't that bad really*.' He inclines his head towards where Coral trains with Gideon on the other side of the field. When he tries to do my accent, I crack up.

Still smiling, I shrug. It's been easy to keep out of Coral's way since she 'joked' Dad had died; I'm training all day and so is she, albeit a little obsessively.

'When did I say that?' I ask. Dylan grins, that cute, embarrassed grin that gives him a little dimple.

'The night that—the night that I met you.'

'Oh, yeah.' There's silence now, but I kind of like it. We're both smiling and avoiding each other's eyes. I pick at the grass in between us.

'It's hard to explain,' I offer, 'but with Coral it feels like there's . . . unfinished business. Like all our lives there's been something which connects us, whether it's friendship or hatred or whatever. And that's still there.'

I can almost sense Dylan raising his eyebrows.

'Just think about it. Coral's here because her parents chose me for the Debt which happened because . . . well, because of something I did to annoy her, which she reacted to because she hates me and she hates me because we used to be friends, I think.

'So I guess there's always been this link between us since we were really little.'

'Aye, I understand that, but I still think she's a nasty piece of work,' Dylan says.

'Aye, me too,' I try to do his accent but I just sound like a pirate from an old film. He looks over as I laugh, seriously unimpressed.

'How are you feeling about tomorrow?'

'Okay actually,' I lie. 'I completed my forty laps this morning, I have my signature move and—' I sneak a side glance at him. '—I can beat you in a parry. I'll be fine.'

Dylan purses his lips as though he's considering this.

'Hmm. I'm not so sure you *can* beat me in a parry, Sola. But, for what it's worth, as long as you remember to ANTICIPATE, I think you'll be fine. The Shepherds wouldn't have re-done your profile if they thought you'd lose.'

I'm about to ask what the Shepherds have done to my profile when something occurs to me. I grin.

'Have you checked my Debtbook profile?'

Dylan turns to me sharply.

'No. Well, aye, but I have a right to. You know, as your trainer.' He holds his head up a little too high. I can't help it; I burst into laughter.

'I can't believe you're pulling the trainer card on me!'

He holds his stoic expression, a blush crawling up his cheeks, before giving in and letting out a low chuckle.

'I'm just putting you in your place,' he replies, then pauses. 'That sounded a little weird, didn't it?'

Oh no, I think I've got the giggles. I cover my mouth with my hand and cackle, nodding my head. He must think I'm such a little girl, but who cares? He's chuckling too, shaking his head slightly so that his hair brushes his forehead.

'Tell me something,' he says, still smiling. 'Do I make an idiot of myself *every* time I see you, or just on the odd occasion?'

Never, I think, but I pretend to ponder, counting fake numbers on my fingers. I nod, as if I was delivering bad news.

'I'm sorry, but it's every time.'

'Thought so.' He sucks in a deep breath. Coral and Gideon are now nowhere to be seen, leaving us surrounded only by the evening air, grass, and the occasional falling leaf. The sound of Dylan breathing next to me is like a warm breeze, one which carries me to a different, perfect place. He starts to pick at the grass in between us, too, our hands centimetres apart. There's not going to be any greenery left at this rate.

'While we're on the subject, I'm sorry about what I said, that time in the Medic's Cabin,' I say, taking the plunge.

'I was about to say the same thing,' Dylan replies.

'Oh, okay. Well, I wanted you to know that I know you must have a good reason for staying.' Wow, that's a lot of *knows*.

Dylan murmurs, 'I do now.' My heart leaps, but he swallows and gives a small shake of his head. We both stop picking the grass. His blue eyes stare hard into mine and, although he doesn't change his expression, I know he's thinking about something important. His eyes get that edge—angled, yet soft all at once.

'Everyone who stays has their reasons. I'll tell you mine, one day.'

I like that. I like the way it sounds and its implications and the way he's looking at me, head angled to the side.

'Yeah, one day,' I repeat because one day isn't today and it isn't tomorrow. One day is far in the future.

He holds my hand then.

One day.

twenty-one

DON'T THINK AHEAD. That's what Dylan told me before we parted last night, and that's what I'm doing. The trip to the Medic's Cabin is easy enough. The old lady I dashed past a couple of weeks ago checks me over and declares me fit to fight before handing over a pile of clothes to change into. I look at her quizzically: Demonstrators always fight in white uniforms, not this bundle of red, black and white.

'That's what I've been given,' she croaks out before gesturing for me to go behind the curtain.

As soon as I put on the white shirt, I recognise the outfit: My old school uniform. Or should I say 'new' old school uniform. It's an exact replica, not torn and blood-stained from my tryout, but fresh and pristine. The fabric's cold against my skin.

I guess it figures. Shepherd Fines told me that my school uniform was quite a hit in the tryouts. I was such a late choice for the Debt that they didn't have time to prepare me in those brown potato sack things that the others wore.

My Demonstrator brain forces me to think about the pluses of being a novelty act. The crowd will recognise me; I'll get more followers, and as Alixis reminds me daily, the more followers, the less sinister the twist in my final fight.

Don't think ahead! I reprimand myself.

I broke that rule this morning anyway when I tapped out a status update on Debtbook.

Thanks to all my followers for their support. It's you I'll be thinking of when I fight.

Hopefully, Dad will see it and catch on that it's meant for him.

Once I'm in the uniform, a young girl pulls the curtain back and stands there admiring me for a moment. Her skin is puckered with spots which lie underneath a thick layer of foundation. The nude colour smothers her lips too, making her look ill, while her dyed-black hair has been curled all the way down her back. I've never seen her before. She carries a Tupperware box full of paints, grips and bands and if I didn't recognise some of the stuff, I would think she were here to torture me.

'Oh, I like it when they give me a semi-pretty one,' she says to herself before dragging some colours from the box. 'You need a bit of colour in your face though. Maybe some fake eyelashes.'

'I don't mean to be rude, but if you come near with that stuff, I can't be held accountable for what I do in self-defence.'

The girl scowls, but doesn't seem at all surprised.

'Up to you. But if you don't sell as many tickets for your next Demonstration, don't blame me.' She goes on tiptoes and surveys the mess which is my hair before indicating for me sit in the plastic chair next to her.

'I don't mean to be rude,' she mimics my jibe, 'but that isn't a request. I have specific orders to do your hair, and you aren't fighting until I've done it.' She smiles again and I know in that second that I like her. I sit.

Five minutes and a lot of painful brushing later, something scrapes against my scalp like a ghost running its fingernail over my head. I shudder, knowing Mum's four-leaf clover hairpin must decorate my hair.

'How long have you worked here?' I ask, mainly to distract from the tugs at my nape.

131

'Forever. I was born in Zulu, around the back of this place with all the servers and Herd officers. There isn't much to do in this city except work here.'

'What about school?'

She shakes her head. 'Nope. There's the camp. That's it.'

I can't help but wonder if she's drawn the short straw. Out of all the cities, she's been born in the one place dedicated to training killers just so the rest will be happy. She might as well have been chosen for the Debt and been forced to work here.

'So, you're just as much a prisoner here as I am then?' I ask.

'Huh. Except I don't have to kill anyone or risk getting my head lopped off. Anyway, see you for your next fight, if you win.'

Well, she's got me there. She gives me a patronising tap on the shoulder before picking up her Tupperware box and heading out.

At the landing pad, Ebiere Okiro and Shepherd Fines stand chatting. She's laughing and touching his shoulder. When he sees me he breaks away, running his finger over the scanner so I can pass through.

'You look nice,' he says, with a nod to reaffirm his comment.

'Thanks,' I mumble.

I'm not sure it's protocol for Shepherd Fines to accompany someone on their first Demonstration, but he says he has some business to attend to in Yankee and I try to believe him.

Ebiere ignores me, climbing elegantly into the front seat next to the pilot after Shepherd Fines dismisses the seat for himself. He waits until I've clambered in, leaves one empty space between us, and sits down. As the spinner rises, I run my eyes over the camp. I might never see this place again.

So I break Dylan's rule for the second time. I imagine my return to camp. For the whole journey, I keep my eyes closed, trying to picture myself stepping from the spinner. Even in my imagination, my hands are covered in blood.

twenty-two

WE LAND FAR TOO QUICKLY. This time, the Herd officers wait for me to climb out from the spinner instead of yanking me out. There's dozens of them here, and for a selfish second, I think they're all guarding me. That I'm a really big deal over here or something. But they grip their guns tight as they surround Shepherd Fines, each standing about two metres away from him, giving him the illusion of space.

'Good luck, Sola,' Shepherd Fines says, and he actually sounds genuine. 'I believe you can win this.' He shows me a wink before walking ahead, the entourage matching their pace with his. After his majestic departure, it's actually quite funny watching all of them try to cram into the lift.

I'm left on the landing pad with only four officers and Ebiere. We're standing on the top of a high-rise building, with only the ground far below us and the lift as exits. The wind brushes past my neck, making my hair feel even tighter in its bun. Right now, I could really convince myself that I am back home, or even back in time. As if I'm walking on top of Juliet's hospital, towards the spinner after my tryout, having no idea what is ahead of me. As I think it, I ache for that moment. Back then, I had already fought. I had already survived.

It turns out that we *are* on the roof of a hospital. As we descend in the lift, I turn to Ebiere.

'Are all of the landing pads on top of hospitals?' I ask.

Ebiere ignores me, leaving my question hanging in the silence until a Herd officer clears his throat pointedly.

'Oh.' she looks over without turning her body. 'Were you talking to me?' She's not saying it in a nasty way, but her tone gives the impression that her thoughts are elsewhere. I nod.

'Yes, they all are, I think. Not sure why. Do you know?' she asks the Herd officer who had cleared his throat.

'I do, miss,' he replies. 'It's for safety. When our Shepherds were still in talks over how to pay the Debt back to the other countries, they were worried about important people getting bombed and things like that.'

With that, a creak alerts us all to the trigger camera in the lift corner. The red dot, now blinking, might as well be an eye. The Herd officer falters, his mouth working up and down. There's a shift in the space, with the other three officers deliberately looking away.

'Go on,' Ebiere instructs, and her voice is so soft yet commanding that no one could resist it.

'Um. Well, our fantastic Shepherds knew that landing pads kind of spell out that someone important is travelling around, so they built them all on hospitals. It was done in some war ages and ages ago, too.' He looks proud then, head held high with a reverent smile. When no one speaks, he adds, 'No one would bomb a hospital. It's just not done.'

With a beep, the doors slide open. I walk through the ground floor of Yankee's hospital, thinking about the Herd officer's words. I never considered that England and Ireland could have been in danger of bombing. I assumed all the other countries were happy to wait for us to slowly pay back our Debt. In a weird way, I feel sorry for the Shepherds. It must have been scary, knowing you had to come to an agreement soon or endanger the lives of all your citizens. I just wish the agreement didn't involve me.

Soon enough, a shadow falls over our group. The back of Yankee's Stadium looms over us, practically identical to Juliet's. Stone grey, circular and cold. I swallow down nothingness, trying to ignore how hard my heart is beating. We pass into the darkness, through a hidden door in the stone. My eyes dart to all the corridors and stairways we pass, trying to remember the way. I need something to latch onto, some control over this situation.

Ebiere breaks away from the group without a word, heading up a stairway to where light streams in from somewhere unknown. It takes the Herd officers a few moments to realise she's gone, and a smile tugs at me when two of them suddenly start and race after her.

My smile is gone in an instant, though, because the two remaining Herd officers escort me down a separate staircase. With each step, I draw closer to a shut door. It's freezing down here, and I imagine the cold seeping in from underneath the door, like a green slimy fog. When we reach the last step, the Herd officer who spoke earlier motions towards the scanner.

'We can't go in,' he explains. 'We'll be here when you finish, though.'

And that's all he says. My stomach lurches with a hundred things. Nausea: definitely, terror: yes, but also hope. Hearing a stranger tell me with total certainty that he'll be there when I finish, with no other agenda than doing his job, it's all I need. I scan into the room.

Soil sinks underfoot as I step in. The room is horribly similar to the one I woke up in all those weeks ago, except it doesn't have a gate separating me from the arena, just a large, open archway. Natural light spills into the room from the gap, as well as the hum of excited chatter as the audience take their seats. I look away from the sands and towards the plastic table opposite me. There's a small, stocky woman standing in front of it. She kind of looks as though she's been squashed, with all her height being pushed into her middle. It wobbles as she moves over to me.

'Hi,' she says, and her voice is surprisingly soft. 'I know this is your first Demonstration, but there's nothing to worry about.' Her smile irritates me down to my toes. Nothing to worry about . . . apart from the kill or be killed, life-threatening situation, you mean? After asking me if I have any questions, to which I shake my head, the woman moves to the table. She picks up a wide, tan-coloured belt complete with two pockets—one about half a metre long and the other short and curved. Armed with this, she advances on me.

'Here you go. Good girl,' she says as though I was a child learning how to dress or something. Her podgy hands fasten the belt around my hips. Next, she passes me a sword. It's designed the same as Dylan's sword, the one I fought at the tryouts with, except this time when I take it, it doesn't pull my arm down.

'That goes in there,' the woman explains, motioning to the long leather pocket hanging from my belt. I push the sword in and when I turn back, I flinch.

The woman holds a gun. It's lain across her palms. She stares down at it like it's the Book of Red Ink, or the answer to all our Debt. I seriously think there's love in her eyes. I step back when she pushes it towards me.

'I, um, I don't want it,' I say. My words surprise myself, but I can't accept the gun. The sight of it fascinates yet terrifies me. Even the thought of holding it makes me think of Mum and what she went through.

'Love, it's just back-up,' the woman says, her voice now so gentle it's giving me the creeps. She steps towards me, eyes focused on the second pocket on my belt.

'I said I don't want it!' I shout. I back away so far that I hit against the door. The woman's eyes go wide but she nods her head and turns to the table.

'Very well,' she says. Her soft voice wavers, as if she were desperately clinging on to that understanding tone. 'I will inform the Liaisons. If Ebiere finishes her announcement before I get back, step out into the middle of the arena.' She tries to smile, but I get the impression I've ruffled her usually controlled feathers. Leaving the gun on the table, the woman scans out.

Once I'm left alone, everything goes fast. I stand underneath the threshold of the archway and wait. As ridiculous as it seems, I become really panicky about knowing when to walk into the arena. The whole way through Ebiere's speech, I play out all these scenarios in my mind where I step out at the wrong time and get laughed back. When she mentions my no-gun thing, a gasp escapes the crowd, followed by applause. I don't know whether it's for me or for the end of Ebiere's speech, but I don't get to find out. The sands are empty and this it is. This is when I have to walk out.

My hands grasp at each other, my stomach flips and my bladder *really* wants me to go to the bathroom. I've heard when people die they can wet themselves. That thought, above all others, makes me want to cry.

I know my legs should be moving, but I can't make them. Gradually, the applause dies down. The Stadium falls silent. They're waiting. Ten breaths. I'll take ten breaths then I'll go.

One, two, three . . .

A beep behind me makes me jump. The woman is scanning back in. I imagine her pushing me onto the sands with that condescending smile, telling me there's nothing to worry about.

I walk.

twenty-three

THE STENCH IS THE WORST. It wafts over me like thick goo. I wonder if there's already been a Demonstration here this morning because it stinks of blood and smoke, like a spit roast. Through the sand, vibrations run into the soles of my boots. I think it's caused by the audience, who chant my name as I walk into the centre of the arena. Each shout is like the seconds of a countdown which never reaches zero. Eventually, I stop walking and just stand. Clenching and unclenching my fists. I sense the audience is expecting something, so I pull my sword from my belt and hold it in front of me like it can tell me what to do.

From the lowest stalls, the ones closest to me, I hear 'fearless' and 'fair fight' yelled out. I guess they're talking about my empty gun holster.

The gate opposite me clicks. The criminals' entrance. I breathe tightly in and out through a dry mouth.

Another click.

Slow this time, just like the tryouts. I swear all the warmth in my body is draining into the sand. I sway.

And even though it seems like a really stupid thing to do right now, I close my eyes. That falling sensation is like a giant hand reaching from the sands, threatening to drag me down. The audience goes quiet, or maybe I just can't hear them anymore. All I hear is the gate; that clicking getting louder, causing bright spots behind my eyes. I feel William squeezing my hand.

No!

Gasps come from within and around me. If I fall, I know I'm dead, but my legs won't keep me upright. I'm hot and cold and can't breathe and, damn, why didn't I listen to Dylan?

There are footsteps now, tentative, curious. My vision is fuzzy, and nothing is real. Nothing but the sharp hit of the ground against my head and the cries of the audience and footsteps rushing towards me.

Which means the contestants are out. Which means the gate's up and I'm here, and I've got to get up. Get up.

GET UP!

As if responding to a hypnotist's clicking fingers, I snap my body into position. I push off the ground, standing with legs bent, my weight even, the sword hilt level with my hip. My blade's angled up and forwards, and most importantly, my eyes are open and seeing clearly.

If I was expecting angry, crashing warriors, I was wrong. The three contestants surge backwards when I jump up, like a horse rearing onto its hind legs. The hope drains from them, and I see it; I recognise the look in their faces. They were going to kill me while I was down.

The angry, clawing creature tells me what I must do.

I'm a Demonstrator.

I'm a killer.

I *have to* kill.

The only woman grips her sword in front of her with both hands. She breaks from the other two, edging out and around. Gideon warned me that contestants do this—try to ambush you at the same time from different directions.

The two men sidestep so that the three of them form an arc around me. One holds a round shield in front of his body and a dagger pulled back. He has a good stance.

The other boy is younger, around my age and obviously stuck with the short straw. He holds a rope in the shape of a lasso in one hand and a net in the other. I take a deep breath while I formulate a plan.

There's a second of stillness, and I wonder if the entire crowd is holding its breath. Then I move as if I'm going for the middle man, only to leap towards the boy. His eyes widen as I cross the space between us in three strides. His net and lasso come up, but he can only throw them limply towards me.

I'm sorry.

Sidestepping the net, I step forwards, ready to strike. Yet, my arm won't obey. I can't end his life. This boy who's never done anything to harm me.

Then his eyes change just like William's did on my tryout. They flicker upwards, looking at something over my shoulder.

I wish I don't know what will happen if I jump out of the way. I wish I can pretend to myself that I haven't realised that someone is behind me, ready to kill. But I do know. I still duck and leap to the side. The woman's sword cuts into the boy's shoulder, causing a sickening scream from both of them.

My arm finally gives in. Now that the boy's in pain, killing him seems less horrific. Twisting away from the horrified woman, I jab the boy straight through the chest. At least this way, it's merciful. It isn't murder. Not entirely.

The mob does not scream. In fact, as I whirl around to face my other opponents, I swear I hear the low bark of boos sound through the Stadium.

What do they want from me?

I avoid looking at the woman's hateful eyes as she rushes towards me once again. Her points of weakness are like beacons of light. Exposed rib cage. Weight off-balance. Thinking of the audience, I don't take advantage of the moment. Instead, I swerve out of the way and kick her in

141

the pelvis, sending her tall body reeling. In the momentary respite from her, the man goes to swipe his dagger into my stomach. I see the move coming from a mile off and place myself between his arm and his body. I'm about to disarm him, breaking his arm as I do so, when a sharp cracking sound comes from . . . comes from—me.

I'm already launching myself backwards to escape danger when pain erupts from my nose. It spreads into my eyes and forehead. I have to look away from the man who head-butted me to gag, bringing up nothing. When I glance back, my vision is blurry, my nose telling me it's broken with every painful pulse of blood.

I grasp my sword tighter and light-footedly dance away from my foes, keeping a good few paces between me and both of them. Spectators are jeering at my cowardice but I can't care. If I don't survive this, I couldn't give a crap how many followers I've got.

My back hits the arena wall. I'm out of space, and time. Like wolves sensing a weakness in a herd, my enemies rush in. I meet steel with steel as I fend off the woman's random flurry of swords attacks while jerking away from the man's deliberate dagger jabs. With each movement, I inch myself from the wall, forcing them to come at me frontally rather than from each side.

Then, a slice of pain.

It cuts into my abdomen and I know the man has caught me. I clench my teeth against the sting.

Persistence and resistance.

This is exactly like that. The torture is just another wall I have to push past.

Letting out an uncontrolled cry, I drop my sword and barrel forwards, catching both of them by surprise. It's a risky move, and the viewers reward me with cheers and whoops which boom from above. The man's dagger catches my thigh, but I don't pause. My body works on instinct. I twist, so that the force of my back hits the woman as she scrambles to get up. The man wrenches himself onto his knees, and shoots an arm out in a frenzied but precise jab.

As the blade comes towards my throat, I think he's got me. Game over. I lean back just in time, barely registering the pinprick underneath my jaw. Without time to breathe, I grasp his wrist with my left hand, wrenching it away from my body while stepping backwards.

His shield is rushing towards my shoulder so I loop my elbow over his arm and *twist*. He cries out as I break his wrist. I duck down to avoid the force of his shield, swerving away from the fight and watching where his dagger lands on the sand with a satisfying thump.

While the woman regains her balance, I catch a glimpse of myself on the screen. My school uniform is slick with sweat and sand. Where my face should be, there's a mass of reddish- purple swelling. Seeing it makes it hurt even more, and I look away just as the woman rushes at me, seemingly eager to take me down while I have no weapon.

I guess it's time to see whether my signature move works.

I wait two beats. Then throw both arms up and leap forwards into a cartwheel. I close my right hand over the hilt of the dagger lying on the sand. My legs fly over my head, star-fish style, before landing perfectly on the ground. As my feet hit the sand, I twist. My arm follows the arc-like motion, reminding me of a discus thrower.

The dagger I was holding slices into the woman's neck.

Just as I had planned. Just as I—oh—planned.

A broken cry alerts me to where the man stands, his shield held up defiantly despite his other wrist limp at his side. He looks hopelessly from where the woman now lies back to me. It occurs way too late that they might have been a family.

Or maybe it's too early.

He strides towards me, shield raised. He wants it over. If only I was Alixis. I could give him some kind of prayer or nice thing to say before he dies. But I have nothing. So I dodge the sharp rim of his shield and pivot on one foot so that I'm round the back of him.

In quick succession, so that he would barely have time to register I'm no longer opposite him, I stand on the small of his back and grab his shoulders, using them to launch myself upwards. The moment that I'm at his height, I place my hands on either side of his head.

As I break his neck, I've never hated myself more.

twenty-four

'SOLA! MY DEAREST, you did so well!' Shepherd Fines greets me with open arms, a bunch of exotic flowers sticking out of his fist.

'No thanks,' I say, pushing the bouquet away and clambering into the spinner. I don't deserve flowers, or praise. One of the two Herd officers who escorted me to the Stadium asked for my autograph on the way back, and I nearly threw up all of his digipad.

Shepherd Fines gives Ebiere the flowers instead, which she accepts graciously, of course. He climbs in next to me, shuffling up to the middle seat.

I want that horrible thing inside of me to wake up again. At least when it's there it relieves me of my guilt. I don't see the people who I've killed every time I blink. My body's numb, but I want it worse because I can still *feel*. When I'm filled with fear, everything I do makes sense. When that's gone, what do I have left?

I stare out of the side of the machine which takes us upwards, but the scenery has lost its magic. Everything is dull. I think that's why I let Shepherd Fines keep his hand on my knee. After a while, it slowly creeps up to my thigh. I want to tell him to take it away, but I can't let him see my face. It's covered in tears and blood.

ℭℜ

I SPEND THE REST OF THE NIGHT in the Wetpod. Scrubbing and scrubbing every inch of my skin until I have taken off the old, filthy layer, and it is too painful to scour anymore. The shower in the little cubicle is steaming hot, and I gulp in air through the sharp lines of running water. I don't look down to see the water running red down the drain.

The cuts on my stomach and thigh are superficial, but they bleed more than their depth should allow. And despite already having two royal-purple arcs staining both eyes, I don't think my nose is broken, just very, very bruised.

I relish in the pain. It distracts me from the other hurt: the worse, deeper misery.

Shepherd Fines tried to force me over to the Medic's Cabin as soon as we touched down, but I only wanted one thing from him.

'Sir, when is William coming back?' I asked.

'My darling, who?' He spoke in a similar way to how you would address a favourite pet.

'William. He was hurt during my tryout and went to hospital.'

'Oh, of course. Yes, I was told about him before. There were some unfortunate complications with his healing. Don't you worry yourself, Sola. He will be here, but the way you're carrying on, it will likely be after you've gone!'

Now, as I shampoo my hair for the third time to get rid of every grain of sand, I wonder what he meant by *gone*. Back to my father? Or to my—how would Alixis put it?—*eternal resting place*.

Strangely enough, when I get to my locker and find a new uniform waiting for me, crisp white, ironed and still warm, some of my self-loathing lifts away. I'm not proud of what I did today, but this uniform reminds me that I'm here for a reason. That I'm part of a collective who all do the same.

I'm acting like I'm disgusted by it all, and I am, but come my next Demonstration, I will do it all again. Because the alternative is *my* life.

Selfish, selfish, selfish. Those are all the words I have for myself as I sprint across the empty field and head towards my pod shaft. I scan in to find Alixis sitting in the dark on her bed, her hands clasped together in front of her face and her head bowed. She looks up, startled.

'Sola!' Her arms are like welcome wings as she embraces me. I don't move or hug her back, but not because I don't love her. Because I can't seem to do *anything*.

'Let me guess, praying for me?' I ask.

She pulls away, still holding my shoulders, and examines my face.

'Actually, I was praying for *me.*' She smiles. Using the tip of her finger, she eases my face one way, then another. I giggle, which hurts my nose. I guess everyone is a tiny bit selfish in this place.

'Hmm, you got a pretty bad head-butt, but I don't think it's broken. You'll have those bruises for a while though. Huh, it looks like you're wearing a head band and it's fallen down over your nose.'

'Or like I'm wearing war paint.'

'Or like you fell asleep in your breakfast.'

'Oh yeah, that purple breakfast we're always having?' I ask sarcastically but can't help laughing. I sit on the edge of her bed and fling myself back so that I'm staring up at the metal bottom of my own bunk. Soon, there's a dip in the bed. Alixis lies next to me.

'So, are you well and everything?' she asks. I can tell she's trying to make it sound casual.

Still staring upwards, I shake my head.

'Actually, Alixis, there's something I need to tell you.'

'Ooh. Sounds serious,' she whispers dramatically, turning her head to me. 'Go on then.'

I'm about to talk when I look to the trigger camera. The red dot tells me I probably activated it when I said the word 'prayer'.

'One second,' I say, before getting up and climbing onto the top bunk. I pull the sheet from my bed, lean over to the camera and wrap the sheet as thickly as I can around the small screen at the end and the microphone panel. What I'm about to tell Alixis isn't for anyone else's ears.

Alixis gasps. 'We'll be found out. Shepherd Fines is probably being alerted right now.' She's not berating me; in fact, she looks quite impressed. I climb down from my bunk and sit next to her.

'Shepherd Fines had his hand on my leg for an hour today. Right now, I don't care if I annoy him. Anyway—' I take a deep breath. '—I realised today what's important. I want to be a nice person, but I always put what *I* want in front of everyone else. That's what got me here in the first place. I really like Dylan. I mean, I'm totally infatuated with him. We even kissed at Coral's party even though she liked him first. But what I'm saying is. I *love* you, in a different way. And if there is anything going on between you and Dylan, even the tiniest spark of attraction on your part, then I promise I'll never pursue anything more than friendship with him ever again.'

I wait. There's a second of stillness.

'Pahaha!' Alixis claps a hand over her mouth, but it does nothing to stifle her fit of giggles. She shakes her head, rolls over to turn away and through the gasps of air and laughter, I think she's apologising to me.

'Sorry, Sola. That was rude. It's just—'

She laughs again, then makes a straight face so that it looks ridiculous and over the top.

'Right, sorry. You're just so funny when you're serious.' She brings up her hand as if to bob me on the nose, but obviously thinks better of it.

'There's nothing going on between Dylan and me,' she says, her expression finally earnest.

'What about all those times when you were whispering together, making plans, laughing?'

'I don't know when we were laughing.' A sigh, laced with something I can't place, comes from my best friend. I watch her sit with effort, staring at the side of the pod which looks down upon the playground.

'I'm sorry, Sola. I wanted to tell you before but I had to keep it secret, not for me but—' She looks over her shoulder at me, then to the smothered trigger camera.

My stomach lurches. I sit up and allow her to take my hand. The way people do right before they look into your eyes and give you bad news. . . .

She places my hand on her belly. It's hard, but still round as if she's eaten way too much.

'Meet my baby.' She breathes out slowly, her mouth a hopeful smile.

A second of nothingness. I don't think I heard her right. . . . Her *baby*?

'You're pregnant?'

She nods, casting her eyes once more to the camera.

'But who—how . . . how long have you—?' Apparently the power of speech has deserted me. Alixis looks down, smiling now.

'Three months. My fiancé is the father.' She laughs, almost anticipating my open-mouthed response. I know from Debtbook that she's twenty-two years old, but she still seems too young, too near my own age to be having a baby. Not to mention the fiancé.

'Does he know?' I ask.

'Of course, he was there when it happened, you know.' She raises her eyebrows at me.

I roll my eyes. 'Thanks for the sex-ed lesson. Seriously though, what's going to happen?' I don't need to add *with your tour* or *with your growing stomach*.

149

Her smile lessens.

'I need to fight,' she whispers. I can tell she's said the words to herself a thousand times before. 'Fight and finish my tour before I really show. Training is keeping my belly small for now. I probably have another month, maybe two until I can't make excuses about being bloated any more. But, Sola, in the past people have finished their tour in two weeks! I've done research.'

She looks at me with hopeful eyes; soft around the edges and pleading with me to agree with her. I've known her long enough to gather that even if I do point out that those people were probably in much better physical shape, not carrying a baby, and were about one out of two hundred others, she won't give up.

'You'll need to train harder, but you could do it,' I say with a deep breath. 'Find a way to make the crowd love you in your first game, get lots of followers. Maybe I could ask Shepherd Fines to go easy on you?' I'm basically thinking out-loud, remembering what Alixis once said about Shepherd Fines doing anything for me.

'No! You can't get him involved.'

'I wasn't going to tell—'

'Please, not even a clue. He's the one I'm hiding from. No hints, no nothing, even if it will help me. He'll take her away,' Alixis says.

'I'm sure he wouldn't—'

'He will! I looked it up in the Book of Red Ink, and Dylan re-checked. It's in there.' She casts a worried look at the bedside cabinet as if the book itself will tell on us. 'Act 66: All children borne by persons chosen to pay the Debt at a time when their Debt remains outstanding shall unconditionally and irrevocably become the property of the Shepherds.' The words are learnt by heart.

I wrap my arm around her shoulders, drawing her into me.

'We won't let that happen, okay? We'll get Dylan to recommend you to begin your tour and we'll train you harder and you'll survive and go home and raise your baby.'

The words rush out of me. I try my hardest to believe them for Alixis' sake.

'Dylan won't do it though. He thinks it's a suicide mission. Oh, maybe you could ask him?'

'I'll do it tomorrow, I promise.'

As I rub my hand up and down the top of her arm, a misplaced memory triggers. I think back to our first day here, when I thought Alixis swapped her blood test.

'Alixis, what did you do with your blood vial?'

She knows straight away what I'm talking about. I see it in the way her shoulders sag.

'I didn't mean to get the brothers into trouble. I knew they wouldn't test them for pregnancy,' she whispers. 'Now they're gone and I can't help but wonder . . .' Her eyes fill with water and she looks away. Regret pierces my middle.

'You only swapped it with one brother, not both. And we have no idea what happened to them, it might not be anything to do with you. Now why don't we get some sleep, we both need it,' I say, trying to salvage the situation.

'Oh, my Lord, Sola, I'm sorry. I was supposed to be comforting you after today not the other way around.' She sniffs, pulling away so she can look at me. 'Your fight was brilliant. Debtbook is going crazy over your no-gun thing. You should have seen Dylan when you fainted. He nearly burst a vein!'

That thought makes me kind of pleased, despite everything else which is going on right now. Alixis launches into a list of baby names she likes as we get ready to sleep. She even asks if I would like to get into bed with her, joking that she doesn't really sleep naked, but I climb into my own instead. Her presence brings me comfort but, for reasons I can't explain, I need to be on my own right now. My head is full of facts and theories which I can't make sense of.

-I've now killed four people.

-I can no longer ignore that Shepherd Fines wants something from me.

-Alixis needs to start her tour soon.

-I need to finish mine before I go insane.

twenty-five

THE NEXT MORNING, the camp is fresh and crisp. Freezing cold, of course, but the rain from last night makes everything smell deliciously natural and full of promise. All that was once green, the oak leaves, the grass, has been well and truly ravaged by autumn, and a crisp layer of frost decorates the playground. I wonder if you only really notice these things after you've thought you might never see them again.

Dylan's waiting for me at the edge of the field as usual. While I approach, he looks at everything except my face. I stare at him, noticing the lines creasing his forehead, his pursed lips, and the way he breathes through his nose so heavily he sounds like a bull about to storm. When his gaze catches my nose, his frown deepens.

'You should have seen that head-butt coming as soon as he leaned back,' he says eventually, as if we were in the middle of a conversation about my Demonstration. I suppress a grin.

'Not to mention that you broke your promise to try to survive by not accepting the gun. But there's nothing we can do about that now.' He looks out onto the field. 'Forty laps, then we'll work on how to distance yourself from your enemy without backing into a corner.' He says the last bit pointedly. I swerve around so that I'm in his line of sight and walking backwards onto the field.

'Dylan, this, right now, is my favourite part of having to fight yesterday,' I say, half laughing and definitely grinning. I stay for a second on the balls of my feet before dashing away to start my laps.

Alixis might be the pregnant one, but I seem to be having the moods swings. I've pushed all grim thoughts of yesterday away, replacing them with Dylan's annoyed face and the idea of his watching my Demonstration on the screen.

At ten o'clock, Alixis still hasn't joined us. It occurs to me that she's giving me time to ask Dylan about recommending her, but then I assume that she's probably still in bed. I put my hand up for a time out, panting heavily and bent double after a round of counter-attacking Dylan. His bad mood seems to have thawed somewhat, and he nods, discarding his plastic sword and stretching out his neck. Yesterday, I thought I might never see him again. Now, as I watch his body move, hear his strained breathing, feel his presence so close to me, I'm so, so glad I have.

'What are you doing?' he asks, stopping abruptly in the middle of a hamstring stretch. Adjusting my stare so it looks like I was watching something over his shoulder, I shrug and sit on the damp grass.

'Nothing. Anyway, I kind of spoke to Alixis last night.' There's no easy way to broach this. Dylan looks warily at me.

'And?'

'And I know. About her . . . little . . . permanent resident?' I say it like a question, gauging his reaction. He relaxes his shoulders, heaving a deep sigh before sitting next to me.

'Good. You can tell her to stop pestering me about recommending her.'

Ah. This might be harder than I thought.

'Dylan, you have to. It's the only way she'll be with her baby.'

He looks at me, his face stony. I can tell he's annoyed, almost disappointed, that I'm trying to get something from him.

'She won't be with her baby. They will both be dead. She can't fight like that.'

He says 'baby' like 'babby' and although it's cute, I can't believe what he's implying.

'But the Shepherds will take him or her away!'

'Aye, and help another family who can't have kids, most likely.' He sets his jaw, bracing himself for my answer.

'That isn't their decision to make, or yours. That's her *child*. Please, give her a chance,' I beg.

'I won't send her to her death.' Dylan keeps his tone neutral and non-affected, then, 'You need to practise fighting without a sword.'

Without another word, he gets up, retrieves his sword, and stands ready. I moan inwardly; this boy isn't going to give up without a fight.

When Alixis finally joins us, the elephant in the room intensifies. During our drills, she keeps making 'subtle' eyes to me, nodding her head towards Dylan. It would make me laugh if it wasn't so cringingly obvious.

'I'm getting pretty good at defence, don't you think, Sola?' she asks.

Oh dear, she's actually winking at me.

Dylan takes a deep breath, walking around the two of us as we parry. 'Keep your knees bent, Alixis. Sola could unbalance you in a second if she wasn't letting you win.'

'She's definitely getting better,' I lie. Dylan stops still.

'Look girls, give up. I've been fighting in Demonstrations for a long time. I know when I'm being ganged up on.'

Alixis stops our match and waggles her eyebrows at me. 'That sounds a bit rude, don't you think?'

For some reason, I hide my head in my hand, unable to stop my giggle.

'Anyway, Dylan, I've been training all morning, and it's bloody freezing out here. Are you going to recommend me or not?' she asks bluntly.

'Not.'

They stare at each other for a moment before Alixis lets out a huff.

'Well, why the heck am I doing this then?' She chucks her sword on the ground and storms off towards the refectory, leaving Dylan staring at the ground. I can't believe I ever thought they were a couple. When he looks over, I feel so sorry for him that I don't have it in me to be cross too.

'That went really well.' I say, unable to keep a straight face, before ducking as he throws his plastic sword over my head. The throw was far too wide to have actually hit and when I look up his blue eyes are twinkling with mischief.

'I love it when you do that,' Dylan says without warning, his chin jerking up as if motioning to me.

'Do what?'

'Find an excuse to cover your mouth when you're embarrassed.'

I flush and straight away my hand comes up to my face. I catch myself, laugh, and grasp my hands together behind my back.

'I didn't realise I did that. Anyway, stalker, what else have you been noticing about me?'

Dylan steps forwards, tilting his head slightly. 'Only the way you bury your head when you get frustrated. The way your laugh becomes almost silent when you find something really funny, and only your shoulders shake. You stare at nothing sometimes too. You're completely lost, and I know anyone who's near you is desperate to know what you're thinking.'

I open my mouth, but no words come. When did he notice all this? Self-consciousness threatens to take hold.

'Oh yeah?' I try and sound nonchalant although my voice cracks. 'Well I've noticed things about you, too.'

No reply. Dylan takes another daring step forwards. He's looking at me now. Those blue eyes . . . wow. I swallow and force a laugh.

'Like how whenever you're around, there's this strange smell. . . .' I say.

He raises his eyebrows, stops walking. There's about a metre of grass between us but it feels as though we're already touching, as if he's crossed some invisible contact line we'd set for ourselves because otherwise we'd never break apart.

'That's the price you pay for being able to run like this—' He speeds off.

Even from here I can tell he's not trying hard—jogging rather than sprinting across the field. A flourish of happiness turns in my belly and my legs pedal across the grass without consciously deciding to go after him. Once I'm running, Dylan speeds up.

We run for two laps, laughing as one catches up with the other, overtakes and then is overtaken in turn. I manage to burst ahead of him and, wishing to end the race winning, I break from the tracks and sprint to the oak tree, whooping so that Dylan behind me can hear.

I'm still grinning when I lean my back against the cold trunk and close my eyes. The bark scrapes against my hair.

'That smell back again?'

I open my eyes to see Dylan facing me. He's leaning on the tree trunk, his hands either side of my shoulders. That perfect face of his is completely open, his eyes wide and worried as if he may have gone too far.

Yet on his lips there's a daring smile.

I shake my head, not telling him that I actually smell plants and bedding whenever he's near. He inches closer. His breath comes fast on my cheek, and I don't think it's because we've been running. I'm just glad of an excuse to be flustered. He steps closer again, so that our bodies could touch with barely a twitch of movement. There's a sprinkling of freckles on his uneven nose which I never noticed before.

I've wanted this for so long. I lick my bottom lip, not in a sexy way, but because it's so dry and I really, really want to kiss him. I want it so much my body arches up to meet his strong, muscular form.

His head pulls away very slightly, but he doesn't go anywhere. Instead his hand moves from my side. It comes up to my face and after a moment's hesitation, Dylan brushes his thumb across my cheek bone.

His touch is soft although his skin isn't. I hold my breath as he runs his thumb over the top of my ear and slowly down my neck. He's watching his hand, his eyes severe and concentrating. I wonder how someone with the power to kill can so easily touch me this gently. I tilt my head, wanting—no, *needing*—him to carry on, to touch me all over, but he brings his hand away, focusing once again on my face. He leans in. This is it. My lips part and my eyes close and—

'Sola!'

Shepherd Fines' voice breaks through the bubble we had cocooned ourselves in. Dylan jumps back as if electrocuted, causing me to sway forwards.

If I had a word for how much I want to scream right now, I would shout and yell and shriek. I bite my bottom lip hard, curling my hands into fists. Dylan runs his hand through his hair, casting irritated glowers at Shepherd Fines and walking a few paces away, then back again.

'Tomorrow,' I say to Dylan although I'm not sure what I'm telling him. He gives me a wry grin, nods his head once and, with that, I'm away, jogging across the field and over to the Shepherd who likes to have his hand on my leg.

twenty-six

TOMORROW. My next Demonstration is *tomorrow*. How is that fair?

I've spent the evening with Shepherd Fines, who, judging by his good mood, didn't notice how close Dylan and I were getting out on the field. He delights in regaling to me the highlights of my fight, telling me I hold the record for the most pre-bought ticket sales for a second Demonstration. He even checks my Debtbook to see my followers. One thousand more than last week. It's kind of pathetic, but the main reason I'm pleased is because I know it bothers Coral. She's been updating her statuses constantly with tales of me having no friends at school and how no one likes me at the camp, but it hasn't done anything to dampen my reputation. Perhaps Coral doesn't understand that not everyone is like her.

'My dearest.' Shepherd Fines addresses me as he sits on the sofa. 'I've been meaning to ask you about a matter which has come to my attention. I'm sure it's nothing to do with you, but there seems to be a problem with your trigger camera.'

'Oh, actually that is to do with me. I kind of tied a sheet around it.'

There's a pause.

'Right, I see. Of course I understand that it's not *ideal* to have the camera on, however it is the law, I'm afraid. Could you remove the sheet please, for me?' he asks, although a request from the most powerful man I've ever met isn't exactly a favour.

'I was, um, talking about girl stuff, though. I was hoping that maybe you'd let me keep the sheet around it? Talking makes it easier for me to sort out my feelings.' I add the last bit on with a pang of guilt. I don't intend to lead Shepherd Fines on, but I really don't want the camera picking up on anything to do with Alixis' baby.

A smile flickers on Shepherd Fines' face and his body inflates slightly.

'Yes. Yes, okay. Just this once.'

I try to look enthusiastic, but the Gekruide tea is too hot and he's keeping me up too late in this office. I have to fight tomorrow. One tired mistake and I'm dead.

'Sir, I'm sorry, but I—'

'Sola, don't call me Sir—it's so formal! Call me . . . Shepherd Fines.'

I resist the urge to tell him that's far longer and just as formal. He tops up my tea, and I struggle to keep my heavy eyelids from drooping.

'I really should—'

'That reminds me! I never told you about that time I was in Geneva. It's where Dr. Frankenstein's monster went, you know. You'd love it there. The whole place is blue and wondrous, and I was so extremely blissful. I wanted to bottle up the lake and bring it with me.' Shepherd Fines moves over to the armrest of the sofa, where I'm leaning back against the soft cushions.

'How come you were safe there?' I murmur, closing my eyes for a minute. If we aren't even safe from the cities in our own country, how come Shepherd Fines can travel the world?

'Well, it's not like that over there. In fact, never mind. Let me get you a blanket.'

'No,' I think I say. Images are dancing in my mind which I didn't invite. Shepherd Fines' voice is far away, and these cushions are so cosy. My fingers loosen as someone takes my mug out of my hand. Something is placed over me, warm and comforting and smelling of lavender. Maybe I'm home again.

I smile and snuggle down, pulling the blanket up to my chin before serene calmness claims my mind.

CR

'WAKEY, WAKEY!'

An irritating voice infiltrates my dream. I groan and bury my head in the soft darkness. A hand on my shoulder. I jolt awake, grabbing the unwelcome wrist, ready to twist when—

'Ouch! Sola, it's me.'

Shepherd Fines?

I blink, pulling my hands away. Sure enough, the blurry image of Shepherd Fines' office solidifies.

I jump up, the blanket falling around my feet.

'What the—? Am I late? I have to fight! Why am I here?' My head spins round just as my mind spins like a tornado inside it.

'Relax, dear.' Shepherd Fines keeps a couple of paces away from me, holding his hands in front of him like he is calming a wild horse. 'You fell asleep last night, but there's no need for panic. I woke you with hours to go before the spinner comes. There's time to go to the Wetpod, get your clothes from the medic and even have a little extra training if you want. See? I wouldn't let anything happen to you.'

The memory of last night trickles into my mind. How could I let myself fall asleep here? Did Shepherd Fines sleep here, too? That thought makes me shiver. I nod, avoiding his eyes and stand pointedly in front of the door. There's a beep as he runs his finger over the scanner. I've never been happier to see the sight of tarmac.

'I bet you slept well last night, didn't you?' he asks as I'm about to leg it down the staircase. I open my mouth to protest, to recall my nightmare . . . and falter. I *did* sleep well. No horrid visions, no dead eyes, no fragmented dreams.

Surprised, I nod before sweeping down the steps.

As I round underneath the steps and head for the Wetpod, I freeze. Demonstrators who are already training parry and shout screams of exertion. Right in front of them, at our usual meeting place, stands Dylan.

His face says it all. It's as if the seconds which go by count down to the assumption he's making.

I stare back, the cold creeping up on me like a painful realisation, cementing me to the spot. I'm exactly halfway between him and Shepherd Fines' office. I don't need to wonder whether he saw me coming out of there. My hair's rumpled, clothes creased, and my sudden shame must show in my expression.

Dylan doesn't acknowledge me, just turns, kicks the soil in front of him, and sprints away, joining the others. I take a step towards him, then reconsider. Today, the most important thing is to try and stay alive. Thinking of my diminishing preparation time, I run instead to the Wetpod.

Could this day get any worse?

I laugh at my own thought.

twenty-seven

THIS AFTERNOON, we have a first for you, loyal subjects of the Shepherds. Let me tell you a tale. One of hardship and determination. One of a woman who was so desperate to prove her loyalty to the Shepherds that she trained night and day on how to kill. Yet I am not describing today's Demonstrator. Oh no.' Ebiere Okiro lets out a dramatic chuckle amid her speech.

I'm hidden from the crowd underneath the open archway. Ebiere is on the sands, her voice projecting through the Stadium. I wipe my lips with my sleeve, leaving a bright red lipstick stain on my uniform. I had to resist the urge to knock the makeup girl out when she tried to cover my black-eyes with foundation. Someone should explain to her that purple skin equals a lot of pain and should NOT be touched. Behind me, a man stands grumpily by the plastic table. He tried to persuade me to take the gun, evidently afraid his job as comforter, counsellor and all round patroniser was on the line. I can only assume I'll have to deal with the same type of person twenty-three more times before I get home.

'I am describing our contestant! ' Ebiere continues. 'Yes, that's right. Tonight we have only one criminal daring to take on the power of the Demonstrator. This contestant claims she was arrested solely for a chance to prove herself as a fighter. She shouts through the prisons that she will win her fight and with it, her chance to be trained as a Demonstrator. Will she be silenced tonight?

'But first, ladies and gentlemen, please welcome, for her second Demonstration and by choice without the safety of a one-bullet gun, your defender and Demonstrator, Sola Herrington!'

I step out of the archway to city X-ray's silent crowd. The rows of bitter faces glare back at me. I guess it's true that they haven't paid back much of their Debt back. Their hatred of me shows that. I blink them away and watch Ebiere bid the crowd goodbye while gliding over the sand as only she can do.

I watch the gate opposite me, knowing my enemy waits behind it. Ebiere's speech has at least warned me this woman isn't to be messed with. In training, Gideon mentioned that you come across people who actually *want* to be Demonstrators, but never get chosen to pay back the Debt. Some of these train, then get arrested on purpose. The prize for a criminal who kills in their Demonstration is to become trained themselves, so it's kind of a replacement service. Even after knowing this, the idea of wanting this lifestyle is so crazy that I hadn't honestly expected to face one of these hopefuls on my tour.

My feet shuffle on the spot as I wait. Shepherd Fines was right about my sleep. I'm refreshed, ready. It's as if I've peeled all of my senses, taking away the old battered layer and replacing it with alert new skills. I grip my sword and, for once, my hand is dry. The air smells like a mixture of stale water and blood. My lips taste like salt. I only have one person to kill today. That thought fills me with confidence. If I could kill three before, I can kill one now.

I dart my head up.

The gate clicks into life. That sound, it's like a trigger in my brain I can't control. It pulls me from the present and into that dark memory.

Not today.

Not with this woman who wants me dead.

I clench my eyes shut. Breathe, Sola. Breathe.

Stop squeezing my hand, William. You're not here. You're not real.

I pinch my eyes tighter. The first man I ever killed ogles at me. There are more now. Four sets of dead eyes—

My knees hit the sand. *That's* real.

I open my eyes just in time to see the ground sway towards me. My back collides with the floor, but I roll away, using both arms to push myself up. I have to survive.

That final click resonates through the arena. Heavy footsteps of a contestant step out. She doesn't rush me, which is surprising, seeing as I'm still forcing my body up. I'm frail and woozy, yet she doesn't press the advantage; in fact, the footsteps stop.

There's this *whooshing* sound, like the faint howls of the wind. As it picks up its pace, the audience's cheers grow in time with the noise. I open my eyes, a bit annoyed now, if I'm honest.

The woman—or, should I say, warrior—stands facing the stalls, seemingly unconcerned about me. Her hair is shaven, her skin tanned, and she's quite clearly torn her own brown prisoner's uniform to make it look like she's been in a fight before she came out. She's also *big*. Bigger than me in every way: taller, stockier, more muscular.

The *whooshing* comes from her weapon: a short stick which is extended to body length with wide, sharp blades. She's waving it in front of her in some kind of salute to the audience.

They *love* it.

Someone shouts her name and I catch it in the air. 'Bronach.' *Well, Bronach, it was a really stupid thing to do to get yourself arrested just so you could fight me.*

Recovering from my moment of weakness, I drop into my fighting stance, sword over my head. If she's putting on a show, so will I.

Bronach takes her time, stretching her muscles and inspecting her staff before she eventually turns to me. The crowd titters. I stand like I'm about to pounce while my enemy is acting positively bored by the whole thing. To be honest, I'm relieved it's daytime and the floodlights aren't on. If they were, her shadow would engulf me, and the audience would probably cackle themselves to death.

'I thought they would do better than you, after all the commotion I caused,' she says once she's looking down on me. Her 'th's sound like hard 't's, reminding me of Dylan's accent, but its ugly coming from her snarling mouth.

'Come on then,' I say, surprised by my own eagerness.

Her insults uncurl that sleeping monster, and I welcome it. Take me over. Act for me, *please*.

She drops down.

I strike.

My sword cuts into her staff with a chop. It sticks, and Bronach wrenches me towards her with a yell. She aims a kick to my solar plexus.

In a flash, I let go, swerving the kick and sliding out of range. Bronach smiles. She pulls my sword from her staff and launches it across the arena without taking her smug eyes off me. She already thinks she's won.

Maybe I should tell her I'm used to being weaponless. That the sword only slows me down.

Her blades flash as she swirls her stick, taunting me with a grin that's no longer for her fans. Thinking back to my last training session with Dylan, I twist so that I'm leading Bronach in a circle instead of getting backed against the edge.

My breath is coming fast and ragged, my backward steps scuffing the sand below.

I hear Dylan's voice in my head. *Read her.* Use her strength against her. Don't get into close range.

I dart forwards. Bronach is quicker than I give her credit for, and she angles her blade towards me. I drop to the floor, skidding up sand and grit as I slide underneath her. I dart my hand up, still jerking out of the way of her frenzied jabbing.

The blade nips my wrist, but my heart pounds when I grasp onto her staff. She tries to steal it away but that only helps me to my feet.

As soon as I'm up I yank her weapon towards me—just long enough to make her do exactly what I want.

She wrenches it back, and boy, do I let her take it. I shift all my weight and launch forwards, toppling on top of her.

Her eyes go wide with panic as her own force pulls her backward. Those huge feet shuffle as she loses balance.

I twist away, also falling,—but I'm still holding her staff.

Once my hip thuds onto the sand, I roll back up to my feet. She's up in the same moment, but that cocky look in her eyes is gone. Sand sticks to her arms, and her brown uniform is darkened with sweat. I give the double-bladed staff a little swirl before breaking it in half on my knee and throwing one piece behind me. Perhaps that was cruel, but it's worse if she thinks she has a chance of surviving.

The viewers roar, although I'm not sure who it's for. I think Bronach will retreat, but she puffs her chest out and balls her fists.

I swirl the blade one more time before leaping in to close the space between us, eager to finish the fight. Bronach spins, avoiding my jab. I see a wide elbow, but don't have time to react.

I swear I hear my skin split as agony slices into my eye.

Jeez! I reel backward. Why the face? Why is it always the face?

There's the sound of metal on metal, and I barely register that I'm blocking her attacks as they cascade down on me. She must have found my sword because she uses that and her brute strength to force me to the ground. My knees buckle. Her face looms over me.

We both realise I'm losing at the same time. She lets out a strange, guttural sound and her attacks become stronger.

My energy is zapped with every block. I know how this works. It's just a matter of time.

The sound of the onlookers dulls. My arm aches. Her face, contorted with the hope of victory, begins to tunnel in my vision.

Again and again, the sword clangs down onto my half of the staff. My movements become sluggish. Any second now I'll make a mistake and—

I lean back on my left hand. The cool sand is brittle against my palm. A last, desperate attack forms in my mind.

So, so slowly, I curl my fingers, grasping a handful of grains.

I'm still blocking, but now I'm thinking, too. Planning. I summon any strength I have left and wait for my moment.

NOW.

Sweeping my hand up in an arc, I cast the gritty sand into Bronach's face. I don't see her reaction—I've clamped my own eyes shut—but I hear her screech. In that second, I pivot to my right and use the last of my energy to pull myself up. The boos from the crowd coil around us. Hundreds of people scream for my blood.

A sword swings down from ahead. Instead of defending myself I match her attack with a blow of my own. I can't fight her strength; I knew that from the start. But I can go faster than her for longer.

I dodge her blows with my body instead of deflecting with my bladed staff, swerving and tilting out of the way while I try to find a weakness in her defences. Her breath is fast, heavy, and rancid like stale eggs. She groans like an animal as I put all of my training behind my attack, swinging my arms so fast she hardly has time to block me. Like a widening crack in the earth, her strikes dwindle as she tries to back away, but I stay close. I'll stick to her just like the guilt of her death will stick to me.

I lean away. Bronach panics and, as she tries a last ditch attack, her neck is left defenceless. My chance.

Countering her attack with my blade, I jab her, palm up, in the side of that thick neck. She gags, those strong shoulders sagging. Without any more fuss, I swing my half of the staff up. Bronach looks up in time to see me end her life, cutting through her shoulder and into her collar bone.

Another set of dead eyes to plague my dreams.

As Bronach slumps to the ground, jeers wash over me. I let the crowd storm, keeping my head held high as I exit through the open archway.

I didn't want to kill her. She chose this. I didn't. And if throwing sand in someone's eyes is what it takes to survive, then I'll do it. Who needs pride if you're dead?

But I still won't use a gun.

Even in all of this, I will protect that part of who I am.

twenty-eight

'GREAT STUFF, GREAT STUFF, SOLA,' Shepherd Fines says somewhat unenthusiastically as we make our way through X-ray's hospital. Ebiere follows us silently, her mouth moving as she looks slowly around. I wonder if she's practising her next speech.

'She had evidently been training her whole life and you, on your second Demonstration and without a gun . . . well, the crowd will forgive your "little moment" in no time.'

'There's nothing to forgive. I won,' I say, nursing my headache. Please stop talking. *Please.* Coupled with my guilt over killing, I can't stop thinking of Dylan; the way he leaned in to kiss me by the tree, the brush of his thumb against my skin, the look on his face as he saw me leave Shepherd Fines' office. Each second that passes is another moment in which he thinks badly of me, and I can't bear it.

'At least now you have a second chance to win some followers,' Shepherd Fines shouts as we cross the roof to where the spinner's roar awaits us.

'What do you mean?' I yell over the din of the engine.

'My dear, you have another Demonstration booked.'

'When?' I stop climbing into the spinner, afraid of the answer.

'Today.'

CR

WE FLY STRAIGHT TO city Whiskey. Even with ear pads, the screams of the spinner sound like the jeers of the crowd—like they're following me everywhere I go. My arm is stiff, my body exhausted. Once we land, Shepherd Fines jabbers on in my ear about how you have to 'strike while the iron is hot' with someone's tour. Quick exposure means maximum sales. I'm replaceable, but a badly sold Demonstration isn't. Thankfully, he leaves me at the back entrance to Whiskey's Stadium with Ebiere and four Herd officers. Although I'm exhausted, the familiar buzz of survival swarms over me. I'm shown into another room just like the two before: small with an open archway and a 'kind', 'understanding' worker trying to force a gun into my hands.

It's as though I'm playing a digipad game, and can press *save*. I'll save my life the way it is before I step out onto the sands and load it up again once I've made the kill. That would be a lot easier to believe if I didn't have to watch myself in the huge screen. I walk out as soon as Ebiere finishes her speech. It's only when I'm standing there do I notice a dried red patch on my uniform where I let Bronach catch me.

I'm not sure if it's because I've already fainted today, or perhaps because Ebiere described the two men I'm about to fight as kidnappers who stole and hurt a child, but as I watch the gate clink open William keeps away from my mind.

Icy air washes over me and cools my throat. It carries the wild scent of hay and sawdust. As the last of the clicks signify the open gate, I hold my sword across my body as if it were part of my arm.

When the first man steps out, I charge.

The mob's cheers sing to me, joining in with the musical rhythm of blade against blade. The men—barely older than me—are terrible fighters. They don't work together, they panic, and they continuously try to outrun me. I play their game for a while, enticing the crowd by cutting at my enemies. I let them think they have me. Then I swing my sword in a dramatic arc, slicing one of their bellies. I don't

171

know which one, and I don't care. The other one runs away: surprise, surprise.

The crowd is sending me signals so clear I can practically read them. These are criminals they can hate without a second thought. They are positively salivating for their blood.

I hate them too, I realise. What they did to that little girl . . .

As the wounded one lies dying on the sands, I cartwheel over his body, grabbing the knife that rests in his shaking hand. In that moment I feel as though I'm dancing; the vibrations of the Stadium my music. I'm rewarded with whoops; the audience must have seen previous footage of what I'm hoping will become my signature move. When I come out of the cartwheel, I extend my arm, leaning my body back, as if I am blowing the fleeing man a kiss. The knife flies out of my hand. It hits home in the small of the man's back.

I'm not sure those eyes will be joining my nightmares.

There's a smiling, blood-stained girl on the screen and it takes an age to figure out she's me.

One woman in a front stall leans over the barrier, tears running down her face. Her mouth moves, slowly forming a word.

'Beautiful.'

twenty-nine

I LIKE SHEPHERD FINES. I do, but the words 'personal space' aren't in his dictionary. When we leave the Stadium, night has fully descended on Whiskey, a place which has buildings so thin and tall that I'm surprised they're not scraping the hanging layer of pollution. Shepherd Fines tells me we are staying here tonight as there aren't any spinner departures until tomorrow morning. Although Ebiere heads to the hospital for a bed for the night, a host of rather exited-looking young Herd officers escort Shepherd Fines and me through the buzzing town and to our hotel.

The rules are different here. In Juliet, you can't even speak loudly in a public place without a glare from a Herd officer. Here, the officers greet and tease the passers-by. The streets are living things, full of friendly faces and bright lights from drinking houses and open shops despite it being way past 10pm. Delicious food smells drift throughout the paths, making me crave my dad's fried chicken. The men here are supposed to be so chauvinistic that no woman from another city would ever be safe, but I swear there's a female Herd officer on patrol. I've never seen that in Juliet.

No one recognises Shepherd Fines or me, probably because of the tight circle the officers have created around us, but one officer keeps finding a reason to look around him. The next time he 'discreetly' glances at me, I dart my eyes up and scowl.

No one said Demonstrators had to be nice, did they?

We reach a tall, wide building which looks like one of the old cathedrals I've seen in films. Orange light shines from every ground floor window, and just being near it makes me imagine warmth. The officers request Shepherd Fines to scan in. Evidently, his finger is the only thing which will open the elaborately decorated glass doors.

I follow him inside. My boots mash into the thick, cream carpet. A log fire crackles beside an array of empty loungers on one side of the foyer, while a nervous woman behind a polished oak desk obviously awaits our arrival on the other.

After the Herd officer who kept on staring at us speaks to the woman behind the desk, she hands him a card, and the group lead us up the wide, carpeted spiral stairs. Canvass prints of old men dressed in white hang on the pristine walls, and I wonder if they are the first ever Shepherds. They seem to ooze that important, 'wouldn't smile even if it solved all the world's problems' look about them. Then again, what do I know? The only Shepherd I've ever met never stops smiling.

'Wow, business is booming here.' I joke to Shepherd Fines, indicating to the uneasy silence which surrounds us. There's not another customer in sight.

'You're correct actually.' He grins back at me. 'I hired the whole place out for security reasons. It's just you and I tonight, Sola.'

Oh. This is not good. I'm suddenly grateful for the Herd officers who accompany us upstairs.

I cross my fingers by my side. Separate rooms, *please* separate rooms . . .

No such luck.

Shepherd Fines uses his card to open a large door, and after we step in, he slides it shut on the curious face of the young officer. I can't help but think this is going all over Debtbook the second we're out of sight.

'Wow.' I let the word drop from my mouth. The 'room' is actually a living space twice the size of my whole flat back in Juliet. There's a gigantic screen which bursts to life as soon as Shepherd Fines steps in, oozing classical music.

'Welcome, Shepherd Fines.' The warm voice makes me jump but I soon spot the surround-sound speakers in each corner. Shepherd Fines gives me a grin.

I pad over to the full-length windows, entranced by the lights of the city below. Halfway across the room, the screen flickers to my profile, and I see the update solidify underneath my name.

Sola Herrington is at Les Bergers d'Arcadie Hotel with Shepherd Fines.

'How did it know?' I ask slowly, pointing to the screen.

'Oh, do you like it? It's state-of-the-art technology, you know, connecting to your scan chip without you having to lift a finger. Some whizzes are working on it in Kilo. If all goes to plan, the devices should be ready to install around the country in a year or two. Those scanner boxes are so ugly, don't you think, my dear?'

I groan inwardly. Dylan is bound to see this.

Shepherd Fines places his digipad on the circular desk and continues talking despite my lack of an answer.

'Sometimes, people manage to open doors without scanning in. Or they disable their scanners altogether. Soon, that kind of deception will be a thing of the past. This also has the added bonus of connecting scan chips with those around you, meaning less work for profile monitors.'

'I thought you didn't have a scan chip?'

'Oh, I don't! No thank you, not for me, no Sir-ee! I'm rather old fashioned that way, prefer good old fingerprint readings. The hotel has programmed me in manually. I've stayed here before.'

A 'great,' is all I manage. Shepherd Fines shows me the rest of what I can only call our floor, and it turns out that there are two bedrooms attached to the study.

I breathe out in relief. Hopefully, there will be another status when I get to my own room which reads 'SOLA HERRINGTON IS ON HER OWN!' Yeah, I know. Wishful thinking.

Both rooms are amazing, more plush than even Coral's house with double beds, five extra pillows than you would know what to do with, and en suites that are the same size as the bedrooms themselves. It's a bit weird sharing a place with Shepherd Fines, but after the day I've had, I can't wait to lose myself and my conscience in the plethora of duvets. Also, the large bolt across the top of the bedroom door is reassuring.

I change into a set of checked pyjamas found hanging up in my walk-in wardrobe before I hear a knock on my bedroom door.

Shepherd Fines stands outside, still dressed in his black jeans and a dark blue shirt. There's a drink in each hand. He chuckles when he sees my outfit.

'You look sweet in those. Very innocent.'

'Appearances can be deceptive,' I say dryly, taking the drink angled towards me and walking past him.

'Cheers to that!' He catches up to me and clinks our glasses together. 'This is an Irish speciality. A portion of this is probably more expensive than anything you've ever owned.'

I raise my glass, the smile going stale on my lips.

'What film have you put on?' I ask, noticing the screen frozen on some opening credits.

'*Martyrs Rising.* It's a recent one. I thought you might like it.'

I groan. Another 'fictional' film about a group of men who save England and Ireland from rioters. This time they're robot rioters, but the principle is the same.

'Or you could choose one from my library if you wish?' Shepherd Fines slides his finger across his digipad to unlock it before passing it over.

Eager to see what kind of films a Shepherd has in his library, I take the digipad. A small face I recognise stares up at me. The title of the document reads:

Extradition records: William Wilson.

I hardly have time to gasp before the digipad is swiped from my hands. Shepherd Fines makes some high-pitched excuse, fiddling around with the device before handing it back to me. This time his film library folder is open.

There's a moment's stillness as I stare at the titles in front of me. Shepherd Fines watches my face closely. Although I open my mouth to ask about William, a tight sensation in my stomach stops me. I swallow and scroll through the list, picking one at random.

'What's this about?' I try to sound casual, keeping my voice steady.

'Ah, *The Godfather*. Banned in every city since 2094, you know.' He winks at me, the tense moment seemingly forgotten. 'I suppose I could let my favourite Demonstrator watch it.'

That's exactly what we do. Well, during the first half an hour I have no idea what's going on. I'm far too pre-occupied with why William's face was on the digipad and what that title meant. But soon, the Old Italian restaurants and American streets with no limitations draw me in. I like that I don't know how to judge the characters. They're doing terrible things; yet, I'm drawn to them and their exotic accents.

An hour into the film, I reach to turn the heating down and accidentally knock Shepherd Fines' drink over. He's in the bathroom, so after a quick glance towards the door I mop up the spillage with a cushion and slide my own hardly-touched drink over to his spot. When I hear the door open, I bring his empty glass to my lips.

'Finished already?' he asks.

'Mmm, delicious,' I say, wondering what he would think if he knew his ridiculously expensive drink was actually staining the silk lining of a cushion right now.

A few 'I forgot how long this film was' comments from Shepherd Fines later and he's practically lying down on the sofa, his eyelids drooping.

'I've been wanting to talk to you actually, Sola. Let's turn this off.'

'Erm, we can talk and watch?' I offer. The thought of being this close to him with no other distractions worries me.

'Very well.' He yawns. 'In light of our recent—' He pauses, rubbing his eyes. 'Our recent . . . progressions, I have a surprise for you.'

I tear my eyes away from Michael Corleone on the screen and try to act pleased.

'It's a party. At the camp. For you.' He takes slow breaths between every few words. When he looks at me I notice his face kind of . . . sag. It's as though his features are melting: his eyes look up like those of a puppy dog while his lips make a half-drunk smile. 'You're very special to me. I think you know it.' He closes his eyes. 'I think, I think you feel it . . .'

More breathing. This time it doesn't stop. I look down at his empty glass and swallow, suddenly not wanting to watch the end of the film. A tingling sense of dread warns me I should run into my room and bolt my door. Yet a different, daring side is propositioning me.

I take a deep breath and test the waters.

'Sir?' I say, first quietly, then louder. No reaction. I give his arm a shake. He grumbles something inaudible before settling back into his deep sleep.

Every inch of my mind is on high alert as I creep over to the desk and take his digipad. That's it now. I've gone past the point of no return. If he wakes up, there's no explaining away what I'm doing.

It's kind of ridiculous that I'm scared of him. I could end his life in a moment's notice. It's the power he holds over everyone—the whole country, including those I love—which really frightens me. I know deep down that I wouldn't kill him, either. In the Stadium, everything is black and white. The fear controls me and forgives what I'm doing. Kill or be killed. Outside, life is harder to decipher.

I tiptoe back to the sofa. Holding my breath, I take Shepherd Fines' limp hand. The Italian-American voices are talking quietly on the large screen, but I recognise the tone of coercion.

Please no gun fire, I beg the film silently.

Shepherd Fines twitches. I freeze in position, not daring to gasp. It's as if the whole room is counting with me. One. Two. Three. Breathe.

His hands are surprisingly soft. The navy blue cuff of his sleeve hangs over his wrist. Peeling his forefinger straight, I swipe the tip of it across the digipad. The small screen glows white before activating back onto the film list library.

Slowly, I settle Shepherd Fines' hand to dangle over the edge of the sofa and start to navigate around his digipad. The software is completely different than mine; everything I need to use is on my Debtbook—libraries, contacts, download sites—but Shepherd Fines hasn't got a profile, only a blank home screen with separate icons.

There's nothing which hints to William. One icon marked 'November charges' brings up a list of names with various offences attached to them, and even as I'm staring at it, another name appears at the top of the list. I close it down and instead double click on an icon titled, 'October sales'. My breath is fast and shallow, my fingers leaving little moisture marks on the screen. The display shows yet another list of names, this time with titles of countries next to them. I narrow my eyes and tap in 'William Wilson' in the search box. One match . . . The country's title next to him is Greece. I tap on his name feverishly fast.

Damn! It's asking me for a password. I chew on my nail, my chest hurting with how many times it's flipped in the last minute.

Come on, come on. I look at Shepherd Fines, racking my brain.

'F-R-A-N-K-E-N-S-T-E-I-N' I type. I tap enter.

A loud chord strikes from the digipad, telling me I guessed wrong. My stomach and guts leap into my mouth and I start, whizzing around to face Shepherd Fines. He rubs his eyes, groans, and turns onto his side to continue his heavy nasal breathing. I can't try again. I'm out of ideas, and bravery.

With legs like empty, wobbly shells, I replace his digipad on the desk. It rattles with how much my hand is shaking when I put it down. As soon as it's out of my grasp, there's a flutter of relief. Without a second thought I run to my room, bolting the door behind me and dragging my laundry box across the entrance just in case.

As I get under three duvets, hiding my head within the mountain of pillows, I add some factors to my ever-growing mental list of things I know for sure.

-I have now killed seven people.

-As soon as I see Dylan, I'm going to tell him how I feel.

-For some reason, William is in Greece.

-Shepherd Fines tried to drug me tonight.

thirty

IF I COULD, I would hit the ground running. Instead, I wait with agitation pulsing in each fingertip for Shepherd Fines to unlock the gate in Zulu. We've hardly spoken all morning. I've been avoiding him like I would a spider I'm too scared to get rid of, while most of his sentences have started with him clearing his throat. I have to face it: he knows I checked his digipad. I forgot to change the screen back onto the library list, and I cringe to think of him unlocking it to the words 'password needed' when he woke up. To complicate matters, I have no idea where we stand on the whole 'you tried to drug me but fell asleep yourself, do *you* know that *I* know?' saga.

As the wind from the spinner drops, settling my hair back on my shoulders and giving my ears some respite, the gate beeps open. My breath is practically condensing on the metal bars because of how close I'm standing, and I jolt with the impact of it opening. That familiar garden scent welcomes me back.

'Don't forget the party I'm holding for all the Demonstrators on Thursday. I believe I . . . mentioned it last night.' Shepherd Fines tries to force his cheery tone but it sounds mechanical and awkward. I notice how the party 'for me' has turned into one for everyone. Well, perhaps some good has come out of last night after all.

'Yeah, you did. See you later,' I say without even glancing in his direction. I slip through the gap in the gate while it's still widening and sprint down the path, searching the white uniforms on the fields for Dylan's muscular, tall frame. No avail.

I head to the refectory and sweep my eyes over the tables . . . nope . . . nope . . . ugh. Coral leans back on her stool, listening to Gideon speak with his arm around a disgruntled-looking Dao. Jamey's on her right, staring at her with a gooney grin. I've only been away for two days, but it's as if I'm seeing her for the first time since she arrived. She's different. Her body looks strong, with a toned roundness to her forearms and thighs. Every movement she makes is with such grace I wonder whether I look like Jamey right now, staring opened mouthed. She took dance classes in city Juliet, one of three girls in my year who could afford it, and coupled with her obvious strength and conviction in everything she does, even the way she moves her hair from her neck, amazes me.

As though she can sense yet another pair of eyes on her, she turns from her conversation, her half-closed eyes locking on me. In a quick, easy motion, she blows a dainty kiss my way, followed by a swift smile before turning back to her group. None of them react, and in that second I wonder whether I'm going mad and conjured the whole scene up in my head.

No.

She sits there, laughing and joking with her friends. And she almost looks *nice*. Fun to be around. If I was anyone else I might be tempted to think that the kiss was an invitation to join them. The thought of walking over, being part of her group, still mesmerises me.

I hate that.

Anger broils up from my feet, spreading through my legs, stomach and up to my throat. It's not even for her, but for myself. For being so weak. The force of it takes me by surprise and my face flushes hot. I spin on my pumps and storm straight out of the refectory.

I haven't checked the Wetpod for Dylan, so I head over there. The November cold seeps through the blue jumper which I found in the hotel wardrobe this morning. It's the only thing I've worn except my school uniform since I've been here that isn't white. I have no intention of giving it back. I scan in, ignore my locker, and head straight to the hot pool on the first floor. My pumps leave rebellious brown smudges on the wet floor, and I get more than a few funny looks from the swimming costume-clad Demonstrators who lounge around, working out their cramps from the morning.

I take three flights of narrow stairs rather than the busy shaft. I glance up to the next floor. There's only the plunge pool level left. Well, that's not strictly true; there's the open-top level which I've only ever seen from the spinner, but that's no entry except with special authority. I know exactly why—the same reason any high rise buildings in Juliet are jump-proof. Suicide.

I pad up the stairs and slide the door open to the plunge pool level. A wall of cool, misty air hits me. When the door slides shut, it locks out the chatter and splashing noises from the floors below, cocooning me in the silence of the large space. I've not been up here before, preferring the hot water and steam rooms like everyone else. It seems ghostly; a cold, empty parody of the bustling places underneath.

I walk through the wide corridor of showers before coming to the edge of a large, oval-shaped pool. The rim runs all the way around, thick enough to walk on. Splashes and movement tell me there's one person swimming.

Dylan's body cuts through the water like a wave breaking. He's front crawling straight down the middle, his sharp breaths punctuating the splashes from his legs. I draw breath, fighting the twist in my tummy at the sight of him. His white swimming shorts are the only thing he's wearing, and his perfect body shimmers underneath the surface.

Wow.

I pull off my pumps, roll my linen trousers up to my knees and sit at the edge of the pool, near the apex of the oval. The water is *freezing*, so I quickly abandon the plan to dangle my feet in the pool and instead tuck them underneath my bum.

Dylan hits the opposite edge, turns, and begins to swim back. I desperately try to steady my breathing, waiting for that inevitable moment. Why on earth didn't I look in a mirror before coming here? I run my hands over the frizz which is my hair.

Just then, Dylan stops, the water rushing past him from the rhythm he had built up. He sees me. His head bobs on the water about half way down the lane.

My stomach flips as though my whole body is waking up.

After a long second, he swims to the side of the pool. Water cascades from him as he hoists himself onto the edge.

What was I going to say to him again? Speech abandons me. All I do is watch the man I fantasise about every waking moment grab his towel from the hook and walk over, drying his neck in an obvious attempt not to look ahead.

I close my mouth, still staring at his face, his arms, his firm torso. Hopefully my smile will hide my nerves.

'It's freezing in there!' I half laugh/half breathe out.

He pauses about a metre away from where I'm sitting and looks out onto the rippling water.

'I'm not training today.' His voice is as cold as the water.

'I know. I just . . . came to see you,' I say quietly.

'Did you enjoy your time away?' he asks, his tone flat.

'Yeah, my favourite part was nearly being killed by some crazily strong she-wolf,' I reply, seeking his eyes with mine. He nods ever so slightly.

'Yeah, she looked tough.'

'Not as tough as meee.' I make my voice go playfully high, teasing him out of his dark mood. He finally looks at me, the edge of his mouth itching into a smile.

'You were lucky.'

Standing now, I close a foot between us.

'You're the lucky one,' I say, keeping his intense gaze.

'Why?' he asks, and I step even closer, my jumper nearly touching his damp skin.

'Because you know how to swim,' I whisper, allowing a millisecond for what I'm saying to sink in. Then I push.

Maybe it's the high of finally seeing Dylan after the night I've had, perhaps it's the thrill of knowing I could have died so many times yesterday, or maybe I really am going insane. But right now it's as if anything's possible; it's like I'm a kid again, back when pushing someone in a pool was honestly the most hilarious thing in the world. I'm laughing when Dylan resurfaces, shaking the water from his face like a dog. He works to keep himself afloat.

'You're such a rookie, Sola,' he shouts.

I lean down. 'Oh yeah, why's that?'

He reclines in the water so he's facing the high ceiling. The room echoes his words, making them sound quiet and loud all at once.

'Because now I'm wet, it can't get any worse. You, however . . .'

I take a step back from the edge. He doesn't look, but it's as though he senses my movement.

'Aye, don't worry, I won't do anything yet. Nah, I'll let you sweat. Because that's what happens when you have everything to lose.' Why does that sound so flirty in his accent? I giggle, finding what he's saying—how I'm feeling—ridiculous. Then, while he's still facing upwards, I whip my jumper and T-shirt over my head, unzip my trousers with nervous hands and chuck them down next to me. My breathing comes fast, like I'm having some kind of psychotic episode. Maybe I am.

I don't stand long enough on that edge for him to see me.

'I'm not afraid of losing!' I yell as I jump.

The cold greets every part of me, around my ribs and under my arms, gripping my throat. My hair separates underwater, flaying around like seaweed trying to ensnare my face. Shock travels up my body as I lurch upwards. Soon, I break free of the surface, gulping back breaths.

Through the liquid whooshing in my ears, I hear something whole and real bouncing across to me. It's Dylan. He's laughing. Really, really roaring. There are splashes and coughing and what I think is the start of my name then more chuckles. It fills me with happiness, knowing I've made the most serious person I know laugh, knowing our amusement connects us.

With a few strokes, Dylan has swam beside me, all traces of his earlier annoyance gone. His eyes are wicked, full of mischief. He regards me side-on, a brilliant grin on his face. I guess now, neither of us have anything to lose.

Then, the most amazing thing happens.

We play.

It's stupid, twenty- and seventeen-year-old killers mucking around in a freezing cold pool, but that's what we do. At first I keep to the water, too aware of my now transparent underwear. Then, after rounds of who can hold their breath for longest (it's him) and who can reach the other side fastest (mainly me), Dylan pulls himself out before taking a run up and dive-bombing in the deep end. Without really thinking, or caring, I follow suit and as I jump, I yell out the rudest word I know.

Dylan's cackling as I swim up.

'You kiss your mother with that mouth?' He laughs, before taking a sharp breath in. 'Oh, sorry, I didn't think—'

'It's okay,' I say, splashing water in his face. And it really is. It's okay how inappropriate he is, how embarrassed, how we both know he's put his foot in it. For some reason, Mum dying doesn't feel like a secret I should carry alone when I'm with him. It's not good, or cool, it's just okay.

'Anyway, I know a worse one.' He grins again and gets out. When he jumps he shouts a word I've never even heard before, but it sounds disgusting. When I ask him what it means, he says he would never tell a lady, so he can tell me. Obviously, I splash him a bit more.

We head to the shallower end, and he asks me to climb on his back. I do so, fending away the claws of self-consciousness. Our skin is slick against one another. He tucks his strong arms underneath my legs before launching himself upwards. He jumps, leans back and lets go. I fall through the air, screaming until I plunge back into the cold water.

With that splash, it's as though the past two months never happened. I sink, letting my legs, arms, and hair rise. Tiny bubbles jet around me as if I had jumped into a giant glass of lemonade; I peer through the fuzzy, stinging water. I wonder if this is what it is like to die. Then my body lifts up, pulled to the surface by the millions of living particles which make up me. I gasp and flick my hair away from my face.

This isn't dying. It's living.

I turn to Dylan, laughing at the absurdity of it all.

'Your turn.'

thirty-one

LATER, WE HEAD TO THE REFECTORY TOGETHER. I had to change back into my clothes minus underwear and, although I did it far from Dylan, sharing the secret makes me feel cheeky, as if we've done something wrong and no one can know. I definitely have one up on the Herd officer who watches us as we make our way across the field.

The air is even colder than the pool and the camp already looks grey, like night is lying in wait, invading the sun's time.

While it's still just us two, I take a deep breath in and try to keep my voice casual.

'You know, that time I left Shepherd Fines' office in the morning. I'd fallen asleep there. I'm beginning to think I was drugged or something.' I can't let him think something happened for a minute longer. For some reason, I giggle, although it's not funny at all. Dylan looks at the ground.

'Did, did he hurt you?' he asks quietly, but I see his body tense. I shake my head. Dylan lets out a long breath.

'Then it's a good thing,' he replies. 'Not if you were drugged, aye.' He forces a breathy chuckle too, and it seems hollow compared to our real laughing in the pool. 'But that Shepherd Fines likes you. You should keep it that way.'

My 'oh' comes out disappointed. What did I expect? That he would be consumed with jealousy?

'I'm not going to keep it that way, but I get what you mean,' I say, although really I have no idea what he's trying to tell me.

His eyebrows furrow. 'Shepherd Fines can keep you alive if he wants to. As long as he thinks he has a chance with you, you'll get an easy twist in your last game. You have thought this through, haven't you?

'I get that . . . but I'm not going to pretend I'm interested in someone who I'm not.' I guiltily think back to the time I implied that Alixis and I were talking about Shepherd Fines in order to keep the sheet wrapped around the trigger camera.

'So you're not interested in him?'

'No,' I say, although my voice cracks. There's a pause as I stare at my pumps.

'Don't throw an opportunity like this away, Sola. Everyone has to do what they can to stay alive.'

Am I imagining things, or does his voice have that cold edge back?

'Shepherd Fines is not an opportunity. He's a person,' I say, although again, I'm not thinking that at all. I'm thinking, who the hell are you to tell me what to do? What exactly *are* you asking me to do? Jump into bed with the Shepherd because he can help me live? Then I'm not thinking at all. I'm getting hot and angry. I'm wondering what it is that makes everyone think they can make decisions for me.

'Why do you refuse to save yourself? Don't you know how lucky you've been?' he asks.

I think back to our argument that night in the Medic's Cabin. So long ago, yet the same points are being hammered home again and again. Dylan wants me to do everything *his* way, and if I don't, I'm an idiotic little girl who doesn't know how plush she's got it.

'I've done fine so far. I can look after myself.'

189

I'm worried if I say full sentences, I'll never stop. I'll tear into him about how much I hate but love him and blame him but owe him. How much I don't want his advice but need his friendship.

'No! I got you here, Sola.' His eyes blaze into mine. 'It's my fault you're here. If you die, I'll have to live with it.' He jabs a finger into his chest. 'So listen to me and stay alive.'

I stare, open-mouthed. Fury vibrates in my chest, infecting my whole body and mind. I clench my teeth and ball my fists. *This* is why he cares about me. Guilt. *This* is why he's nice to me. I see it all so clearly. Where my invented love affair once stood now lives the clear picture of yet another person trying to use me for their own good.

'Stay away from me,' I hiss.

'What?'

'Stay. Away.' I meet his eyes. He's surprised, I can see it. I wonder if I'm really radiating all the hatred and rage that surges through me. I sense him go to speak, to reach out, but I turn and stalk away. I'm too angry to run. I need to walk with control, sending my wrath down into the tarmac and through the earth with each footstep.

Dylan either doesn't care or actually listens to my request because he doesn't follow.

Lucky me.

thirty-two

I DODGE TRAINING THE FOLLOWING DAY. My next Demonstration is in two days' time at Victor, Dylan's home city. That means I have all of tomorrow to train properly.

I bid Alixis goodbye before we reach the edge of the field, making an excuse about wanting to work on my strength in the gym. Dylan will probably tell her that we've had another argument, but I don't want to get into it right now. I'm still getting to grips with having been Dylan's charity case since I arrived here.

Once I reach the path leading to the gym, I glance back. Coral now walks beside Alixis, as if she had been lying in wait for me to leave. My fists clench automatically, defences tingling for my best friend. But the two girls look happy enough. When Coral jogs away to Gideon, Alixis even flicks her hand to say 'bye'.

My teeth clamp together. I scan into the gym slowly, reminding myself I have no right to be jealous. I can't dictate who Alixis chooses as a friend. Yet that doesn't stop a bad mood taking over. I grab the heaviest weights from the walk-in cupboard, before yelling out as I try to bring them over my head. They throw my balance, pulling me backwards. To stop my arms from breaking I embrace the fall, cracking my coccyx and the back of my head on the ground. My arms judder with the force of the weights as they, too, smack onto the floor.

'Ow,' I say to myself. Suddenly, my eyes are stinging. I'm lying on the floor of the cupboard, crying because my head hurts. Just like a kid. I *seriously* need a break.

'Sola,' a tender voice calls. I swivel my head to see Dao reach me. He crouches down and gently rolls the weights away from my hands.

'What's the matter?' he asks, sitting next to my head. I love him for blocking what must be the most pathetic sight in the world away from the other Demonstrators' prying glances. I sniff loudly, pulling myself onto my hands with a wince.

'I fell,' I say, then laugh at my own childishness. Dao nods, showing me a sheepish grin.

'I can see that. Come here.' His natural voice is so quiet it's practically a whisper. He pulls me into a light hug. Although it hurts my back, it's soothing to have Dao's arms around me. I never used to be tactile, but this camp is turning me into a touch-maniac.

'Is this about your argument with Dylan?'

Good moment: over. I draw back.

'How do you know about that?'

'Gideon and I ran into Dylan last night. He was upset, I think.'

'Oh. What did he say?' I ask, rubbing the last of tears from my cheeks.

'I shouldn't really gossip—'

'Dao, please. I just want to understand,' I say.

He sighs. 'I remember what it was first like with me and Gideon. We didn't really argue, but we tiptoed around each other *so* much.' He lets out a chuckle, looking at nothing but his own memory. His eyes glance to mine. 'I think that Dylan does really care for you,' he whispers. 'But last night he seemed to think that you were selfish. I'm sure he didn't mean it, though.'

Great. Now Dylan's angry at me. Even if Dao's right, if Dylan *does* care for me the tiniest amount, he's still trying to control me. And I'm not ready to forgive him just yet. Looking back to Dao, I try to change the subject.

'Dylan's right. I'm selfish. I haven't even asked you about your tour. How is it? You must be nearing your final Demonstration now?'

'Oh, yeah, I am.' Dao smiles. 'I only have five more left. And, do you know that Gideon and I are from the same cities? Gideon finished his tour ages ago, he just stayed here to train, so once I've finished my tour we can go home together. Isn't that amazing?'

'Yeah, it is.' I mean it.

'Everything is going to work out, Sola. Okay?'

'Yeah.' I try to smile. 'Although I better get to the Medic's Cabin, that fall actually really hurt.' I clamber up.

Dao giggles. 'Perhaps your weights were too light?' he says with a cheeky smile. Although I laugh, my cheeks burn red as I hobble over the gym floor and out into the open.

Once on the playground, I do a slow turn of the camp. Dylan and Alixis train far out on the field, with Coral and Gideon sparring close to them. I won't find any comfort over there. The Medic's Cabin has its doors open, inviting me in to be sedated, hooked up to an IV and prodded with every needle available. Or there's my empty pod shaft, where I can sit alone or dream of people I've killed.

With shame creeping up on me, I turn my back on all of those places, limping my way over to Shepherd Fines' office. He welcomes me with a great smile and wide arms. When I tell him I need a break, he says that just this once he'll arrange an easy Demonstration in Victor. He tells me it's his way of compensating for our stay in the hotel the other night. Really, I know what he's saying sorry for. It's drugging me; lying to me about William.

Despite this, I accept his help. Even though it proves that Dylan was right: I'm selfish and I'll trade affections with Shepherd Fines to help myself. I accept his offer because it means I won't die in two days.

And I really, *really* need a break.

thirty-three

'I LOOK RIDICULOUS.'

Alixis' face is so annoyed it's hard not to laugh. She stares down at her short, blue dress stretched over her slight belly, then back up at me. I wonder if it was made to fit her pre-bump and pre-busty figure.

'How come you got the nice one?' she asks, looking longingly at the full length black thing which she zipped me up in. I shrug. These are the dresses we found laid on our beds about an hour ago and it doesn't take a genius to work out they're what we're supposed to wear to Shepherd Fines' party.

As promised, my Demonstration win yesterday in Victor was effortless. Well, except that I fainted again. Thankfully, my two victims mainly stumbled around the arena in a daze. On the way back, Shepherd Fines hinted that we will arrange something spectacular soon to win back followers, but for now, it was important to rest.

I shuffle my shoulders around, trying to get rid of the itch on my back. I haven't worn a dress since I was a kid, and that was only on Mum's insistence. This one has a cowl neckline and criss-cross spaghetti straps making a string of 'x's up my bare back. It also ITCHES.

'I'd much prefer to be in jeans,' I say, running my hand over my side plait.

'I'd much prefer not to have my boobs popping out,' Alixis replies, before looking through the side of our pod at the party below. I follow her gaze. The Demonstrators are an array of bright colours, lit up by the combined outdoor heaters and mood lights. They mingle around, drinking and eating from the long table spread which has been set out. The screen on Shepherd Fines' wall is switched so it faces outside. I can hear the faint classical music it plays even through the pod's walls.

I can't help but be nervous. This will be the first time I've seen Dylan since our argument. I wonder if he saw my last fight or if he still thinks I'm selfish. Not that I care. I've decided that I'm totally and completely not interested in anyone trying to use me for their own gain.

'Come on then,' I say, scanning out. 'You're going to make a lot of male Demonstrators' days in that.'

Alixis scowls at me and I'm pleased to say, I totally deserve it.

'Hey, what's the deal with Coral by the way?' Alixis asks, catching me off-guard as we step out of the pod shaft.

'What do you mean?'

'She's been really friendly with me recently, and I don't get it. She's like a different person from the girl who writes horrible stuff about you on Debtbook and did that "joke" about your dad.'

I have to stifle my scoff. But then I realise I am being selfish, and Alixis deserves to know the truth if Coral is wrapping her into our games. I touch my friend's arm, signalling for us to stop before we reach the group of Demonstrators at the party.

'When Coral's nice to you, you feel like the most important person in the world. But the more she likes you, the more she'll turn on you later if you annoy her. Alixis, you can be friends with whoever you like. Just know that Coral was the person who sent me here. We used to be best friends and then she tried to get me killed.' I say the last bit with a little laugh, because the truth is so absurd it's quite funny.

'Right, that's it. Coral is officially on my hate list,' Alixis says way too dramatically, eyes narrowing like she was a gangster from that film *The Godfather*. I can't help but laugh as we resume our walking.

'And who else is on that?'

'Just my old neighbour's cat. It always got the better of me.' She carries on in her comical tone. 'Of course, it's dead now.'

'You killed it?' I ask, still chuckling.

'No, it had a heart attack. It was actually really sad,' Alixis says, with a hint of melancholy. I think I murmur an, 'Oh' before Alixis looks around.

'The group's there.' She points to where Gideon, Dylan and Dao stand chatting. 'I'll be over in a minute.' With that, she weaves her way through the crowd. I make my way over to the men alone, who fall silent as I approach.

'Hey,' I say, daring to glance at Dylan. To my shock he's looking straight at me. Instantly, his gaze darts away, his hand running through his hair. No one replies to my greeting.

'Any more news on the big day?' I ask, referring to Dao's final Demonstration. Really, I'm just trying to distract myself from how incredibly gorgeous Dylan looks in his suit and black tie.

'Two weeks,' Gideon replies, wrapping his arm around Dao's shoulders protectively.

Thankfully, Alixis' voice interrupts what I can only describe as four people auditioning for 'the most awkward silence ever' award.

'Get all your laughs out now, come on.' She challenges the men, no doubt in response to Gideon's smirk as he takes in her bare legs, chest and arms. As she berates an

unsuspecting Dao for complimenting her, I turn away, grabbing a glass of coke from a passing server. When the server heads Dylan's way, he too takes a coke before

197

turning back to the group. I guess we are all staying here then.

We chat like this for a while: Alixis making everyone laugh, Dao defending individuals who Gideon makes nasty remarks about, and Dylan and I standing opposite each other, both pretending the other doesn't exist. Eventually an ivory-coloured suit appears out of the gloom. It belongs to Shepherd Fines, his light brown hair slick with even more gel than usual, an embroidered hanky flopped over his shirt pocket.

'Ladies! You can stop looking for me now, I'm here!' He laughs as he approaches, arms outstretched as if we're his loving children waiting for him to return from work. Dao and Gideon share a look, as if to ask, 'are we supposed to be ladies?'

'Sola, may I say, you look breath-taking.' Shepherd Fines places a hand on his heart, like he were struck by some invisible force. Gideon and Dao separate as Shepherd Fines muscles into our group between them. 'And you,' he turns to Alixis, 'I have some great news for you, Miss Spires. The date of your first Demonstration.' He laughs at Alixis' response, which is to stare, then to gasp in delight. 'It's on Thursday, next week.'

'Thank you.' She smiles widely, and in that moment she is so beautiful I understand what they say about how mothers-to-be glow, despite her awful attire. 'Thank you.' Her eyes flicker to Dylan.

'Lowering the standards a bit, aren't they?' A false-innocent voice infiltrates our little group. Coral stands behind Shepherd Fines, smiling as politely as if she had just pointed out a stain on our clothes to protect us from embarrassment.

'Not at all, child. As a wise man once said, fitness appears in many guises.' Shepherd Fines speaks in a reverent voice, like he is announcing the secret to life.

'Who said that, Sir?' Alixis asks. I can tell she's desperate to change the subject.

'Come to think of it, it was me!'

Alixis' laugh is way too loud, although Shepherd Fines doesn't seem to notice; in fact, he nods to himself, looking up to the corner; I just *know* he's remembering to use that joke again.

Another server appears with a loaded tray in his hand.

'Great stuff! Miss Spires, would you care for a drink? You're old enough, aren't you?' Shepherd Fines indicates to the champagne-filled glasses atop the tray.

'No thank you, I don't drink.'

'Yeah right.' Gideon scoffs. 'How do explain that beer belly then?' He raises his eyebrows playfully.

The whole camp seems to freeze. I look to Alixis, whose mouth works up and down but nothing comes out. Eventually she makes a strangled sound which I think is supposed to be 'what the heck,' and reaches for a drink. It's painfully obvious how much her hand is shaking.

'Gideon! You never say that to a woman.' I feign vanity, distracting the attention from my best friend. 'Poor Alixis ate so much of that oat bread they served this morning her stomach practically burst. I was like it last week, too, do you remember?' My laugh sounds mechanical and fake. Alixis shakes her head as if the memory is just *too* funny.

'Yeah, you were on the toilet for ages,' she exclaims.

What the—? I try to hide my alarm with more laughter. Dylan makes a *those were the days* kind of sigh followed by a little tut. Thank goodness none of us ever went into acting.

Shepherd Fines looks positively disgusted. He glimpses over his shoulder at another group of Demonstrators.

'Yes, well.' He clears his throat and looks to me. 'Perhaps I will see you later when you're more—' He runs an eye over Alixis. '—alone.'

With that, he walks off, raising his glass to someone else. I'm not sure when Coral left but Gideon goes off to find her, which leaves the four of us standing there. Dao's the

199

first one to break a giggle, then Alixis and I chuckle, too. As soon as the laughter catches up to Dylan, I stop. I don't want to find anything funny which he does, too.

'I thought she was being nice to you?' I say to Alixis, motioning to where Coral had been standing. She shrugs.

'I found her earlier. Told her that I'm too old and too ugly for game playing and that she'll have to find someone else to recruit into her gang.'

I stare, open-mouthed, and to be honest, a little bit in awe of Alixis. She laughs. 'This does mean that you're my only friend now, so, get used to it.'

'Cheers, Alixis,' Dylan pipes up sarcastically. 'What about me?'

'Sorry, Dylan. But Sola's better.' Alixis is still grinning and she offers me a wink. Heat begins to flush my face when Dylan goes quiet. He glances to me, a familiar mischief back in those blue eyes.

'Aye, she is.'

thirty-four

SIX FISH-AND-CREAM ROLLS LATER, and I'm standing by the snacks table, loading anything I can into my mouth. I've never tasted food this rich. Something tells me it's probably not a good idea considering my next Demonstration could be any day now, but it occupies my time so I don't have to think about Dylan. Or face him. Or try and fathom out what is really going on with us. Reaching for a pastry jam-packed with some spicy vegetables, I hear Shepherd Fines call me over. My eyes narrow at the pastry, sending it a message of *we have unfinished business*, before I catch myself. This place is doing weird things to my head.

Shepherd Fines stands with two women I've seen around the camp. The shorter, older-looking woman leans in to Shepherd Fines, nodding while he speaks. When I approach I swear her face tightens.

'Oh, Sola, how good of you to join us.' Shepherd Fines sounds as if he's forgotten he *just* beckoned me over. I give him and the girls a half-hearted smile, my mind still lingering on the food only paces away.

'You have some cheese on your face.' The po-faced short woman tells me without actually indicating to where it is. I wipe my jaw with my arm as Shepherd Fines chortles.

'Kofi has asked me for some tips on her next Demonstration, but as you know, I like to leave that to you professionals!' He raises his eyebrows as though we're all in on some private joke. 'Have you got any advice for her?' he

201

asks me. It's quite clear from Kofi's face she wasn't hoping for this. To me, it's hilarious that girls fawn over Shepherd Fines. I'm so used to dismissing him as a pest that I overlook how good-looking he is, how most people would find the mix of power and good cheer attractive.

'Well, I'm actually further into my tour than you are so don't worry about it.' Kofi dismisses me with a flick of her hand and a quick smile. Her voice is pleasant enough, so I shrug and look around, trying to find an excuse to leave.

Straight away, someone touches the curve of my back. In this dress, their touch is silky, like their hand might slide off accidentally. Although he's standing right next to me, I'm surprised to find the touch belongs to Shepherd Fines. He leans down to my sight level.

'Are you looking at the lamps?' he asks, and his voice is smiling. 'They're designed from the ones you've admired in my office.'

I nod. Around the tarmac, various free-standing lamps have been erected. They dangle from their hooks, large colourful orbs decorated with copper wiring.

'They're the ones from Egypt, right? When you wound up in a brothel instead of visiting the leader there?' I laugh, referring to a story he told me the other night.

'You know full well that was an accident! Anyhow, I refuse to believe you've never been to Egypt. I'm sure I saw you there.' He laughs at his own joke and so do I. I'm surprised to find that I'm not putting it on. Kofi and her trainer have turned into one another, excluded from our you-had-to-be-there conversation.

Shepherd Fines straightens up but keeps his hand on my back. It weighs heavily, making me feel safe yet like I'm on a leash all at once. When a faint knocking sound distracts us, I turn to it, stepping away from Shepherd Fines' hand. What I turn to isn't much better.

Coral stands on a chair in front of the screen, tapping her glass with the edge of a plastic practice dagger. It makes a hollow noise, like breathing down a tube. Shepherd Fines lets out a 'hmm' to himself as he regards the situation, yet when people peer at him with questions in their eyes, he smiles and nods as though this was all part of his plan.

'Hello everyone.' Coral runs her eyes over the crowd, letting them take in the sight of her. She stands in a one-shouldered paper-white gown while that red hair cascades down her back in sweeping curls.

'I wanted to raise a toast. To all of us. For fighting so hard to pay back our Debt.' The sight of her beaming so radiantly seems to enrapture most of the people here. They nod and murmur their assent, raising their glasses. I accidentally catch Coral's eye.

'Oh, and to Sola Herrington, because we might not be having this party if it wasn't for her.' She raises her glass to me, and for anyone watching it would seem genuine. I nod stiffly in return, the small space between me and Shepherd Fines pressing in on me like an accusation.

'Finally, to Alixis Spires. Sola informed me of your good news.'

What? There's a familiar sense of panic. Alixis looks to me, her expression sending waves of fright down my body.

I step forwards, having no idea what I'm planning.

'How many months are you? Judging by your belly I'd say four.' Coral smiles. The whole world stops.

Alixis stares, lips parted, one hand on her stomach. As if she can't take in what's just happened. Like if she doesn't move, she can pretend nothing was ever said, no one heard anything.

I don't have that luxury. Shepherd Fines brings his glass down, his expression darkening as he scrutinises the crowd.

As if to sweep away any doubt,—and I hate her, I *hate* her—Coral adds, 'I'm sorry Alixis, did you want to tell everyone yourself that you were pregnant?'

People turn, some gawping, some eying Alixis conspiratorially. Within seconds, a gap has opened around her and Dylan. I need to help, but I'm frozen. Caught between wanting to attack Coral and comfort Alixis. What can I do to make it all right?

A nod from Shepherd Fines causes a Herd officer to appear from nowhere. He follows Shepherd Fines through the crowd and when they reach Alixis, the officer indicates for her to follow. It's not a request.

All anyone can do is watch as they walk solemnly up the stairs and disappear into Shepherd Fines' office.

Coral raises her glass. 'Cheers, everybody!'

thirty-five

I'M RUNNING ON HOT RED RAGE when I catch up with Coral moments before she reaches her pod shaft.

'What the hell is wrong with you?' I shout, not caring who hears.

She turns to look at me, rolling her eyes before continuing to her pod shaft. 'Calm down, Sola. There's no need to get so excited.'

'Why would you do that? How did you even know?' I let the words pour out. I can't help it.

'I guessed ages ago. I was trying to help her, and today, she threw it back in my face.' She speaks over her shoulder.

'So you can't handle it that one person doesn't want to be your friend?'

A lamp near me flickers, reminding me of getting caught in an electrical storm. Coral swings around like a threatened spider.

'Sola, everyone wants to be my friend. Even you.' She laughs, her delicate shoulders quivering. 'It's true, isn't it? Despite everything, you're still obsessed with me. It's a shame that I find looking at you disgusting.' She bites her lip and shrugs in a way that says 'oops'.

Her comment washes through me. It's as though I'm reeling backward, but my feet are stuck to the ground.

'Is this all because I kissed some boy?' I whisper, despising that she can see how much I care.

'Oh, honey.' She puts on a high, soprano voice. 'I was only jumping on the trampoline—like we used to.'

I recognise the parody of my own words. It was when I was apologising to her, when I thought all of this was behind us.

'No, Sola, it's not what you've *done*, just who you *are*.' She spreads her hands out, gesturing to me. I fight the shame that threatens to take over. 'The moment you kissed Dylan, I realised you are *exactly* like your mother.'

'What?'

'Well, maybe not exactly,' she says, looking into the air as if she were remembering my mum. 'She was prettier than you, but you're both harlots.'

Red blotches creep into my vision. I have an overwhelming sensation of despair, which, combined with my rage, reminds me of being in the Stadium. That creature seems to wake from within. I don't know who would win in a fight, but I'm willing to take my chances if she says one more thing about Mum.

'We're not harlots,' I say, barely moving my mouth. 'I'd never even kissed anyone before Dylan.' It takes me a second after I've said it to realise I'm actually defending myself to her. How does she do this to me? How do I still care what she thinks?

'Sweetheart, that doesn't surprise me. Yet, now you're giving it out to both Dylan and Shepherd Fines. I guess it's not your fault. Adultery is in your blood.' She gives me a patronising smile, but I can see from her tensed body that she's ready for me if I pounce.

'What are you talking about?' My voice cracks. I'm on the edge of something and suddenly I don't want to fall. I need to run back, retrace my steps. Curl up into someone's lap and refuse to hear the words I've just asked for.

Coral stares at me for a moment, her facade falling as she tries to read my face. She shakes her head incredulously, her features crumpled up in revulsion.

'You honestly don't know?' Her tone is flat, disappointed. 'You're like a child.'

When I don't reply, she sighs, not even ready to fight anymore.

'Your mother seduced my father for over ten years. Why do you think we always had to play together when she came around? What did you think they were doing?' She has her head tilted back, exposing her neck to me. I could kill her right now. Get it all over with.

Her words won't sink in. It's all lies. She's tricking me like a fighter feigns an attack or a weakness. She's luring me in.

The red blotches close in on me. It's as if I'm on the big screen and someone has pressed pause. The creature is frozen inside me too, unknowing whether to take over and attack, or to lie still.

I try to assemble 'they were just friends' but nothing solidifies in my mouth. Instead, what comes out is tiny and doesn't belong to me.

'My dad?'

'Yes. He knew.'

'Your mum?'

'Yes.'

I nod. Unable to stop the pictures which invade my mind: her waiting with Mr Winters outside school; Mum and me getting on the rail to Coral's; asking whether her makeup's okay before we knock on their door. Over ten years. That was longer than I knew her for. *Did* I even know her?

Coral scans into her shaft. Everything's racing. As I watch her, the link that joins us solidifies in my mind. We're tied together whether we like it or not. No wonder I could never let her go.

'Coral,' I call, covering the metres of tarmac between us. 'You might be my sister.'

207

I'm not even sure I've said the last bit aloud until she turns, spinning slowly. Her cheeks are sucked in as she glowers darkly. In that second, I can hardly believe how ugly she is.

My comment isn't new to her.

'You are no relation of mine, Sola Herrington.'

She blows me a lacquered-fingered kiss, just like the one in the refectory a week ago, and strides into the pod shaft. All I see is the ragged rope that runs from her to me, understanding but not understanding at all.

thirty-six

ONCE AGAIN, I spend hours sitting alone underneath the oak tree. Eventually, night swallows the camp whole, and the cold gets too much to bear in my flimsy dress.

I hate Coral more than I thought I could. The picture of my perfect family has been smashed and Mum's not even around to defend herself. Don't people say that once the seed of doubt has been sown, you can convince yourself of anything? That's why you should never diagnose yourself, why everyone's innocent unless proven guilty.

Well, that's what I'm doing now. Re-evaluating every memory of Mum, of her and Dad. Of Mr Winters. As I tread back to my pod, I shudder at the thought of Mr Winters being my father. I imagine every patch of grass is his face, which I stomp with my dainty black shoes.

Alixis is sitting on her bunk when I scan in. She mirrors her pose from when I returned from my first Demonstration. Except this time, she isn't praying. Her eyes are dry and empty. She doesn't react when I sit next to her.

I try to find some perfect words—that magic sentence which will make Alixis and her baby okay, my mum's memory whole again, and me back at home with Dad. But there isn't one. Instead, I twine my arm around my best friend's. We sit like that for a while, staring at the pod's side, watching the cleaners work into the night to dismantle the party remnants on the playground.

'It's a boy.' Alixis breaks the silence, causing me to start. 'They made me take an ultrasound.'

I glance to the trigger camera. It's on, and the sheet I wrapped around it so long ago has finally been removed.

'And what happens now?' I whisper. Alixis' voice is steady—vacant.

'I wait, I give birth, I give them my baby. Then I fight.'

I swallow. No words, again.

'I'm . . . I'm sorry. You know I didn't tell Coral, don't you?'

Alixis nods, speaks slow, vacant words.

'It doesn't matter now anyway.'

When she turns to me, I don't think she really sees me at all.

'Good night, Sola,' she says. She's still smiling that empty smile which makes me want to cry. I nod, untwine my arm from hers and clamber into bed without changing.

thirty-seven

I NEVER THOUGHT I would think this, but the Demonstrations have become welcome in my life. My tour is well and truly zooming past. The fainting seems to be getting better, too, although I now stand a lot farther away from the criminals' gate. My kill count is going up and up and up until there's no more room for dead eyes left in my dreams.

I cut down five elderly people in city Uniform. Drawing the fight out so that the contestants thought they stood a chance . . . all the while thinking about my number of followers. Right now, the thought of surviving my last Demonstration is all that's keeping me going.

Time at the camp has become unbearable. All the life has been sucked from Alixis, leaving her a vacant, bump-growing machine. She stays in our pod all day, reading the Book of Red Ink over and over until she wanders out to the refectory. It's as if she's living in a world of shade, only seeing and hearing the things right in front of her. Every day she falls deeper into her own empty space and there's nothing I can do to drag her up again. Each time I see her purple-ringed eyes, a fear creeps up on me more terrifying than anything I've ever felt in the Stadium.

I've tried talking to Shepherd Fines, begging him to change his mind. He says it's out of his hands. He 'has to obey the rules in the Book of Red Ink like everyone else'. That doesn't make any sense to me, considering I know he

211

has the power to implement change on every single one of those rules. He only has to persuade six others, and it's done. But no, he has his 'father's legacy' to uphold. The baby will be taken, and what happens to the child after is none of my or Alixis' business.

I just hope Dylan was right, that the baby will be given to a family who wants a child.

Dylan and I are still not speaking. Somehow, it's turned from me being mad at him to the other way around. You would think he would be happy—I'm spending more time with Shepherd Fines than ever. Didn't Dylan give us his royal blessing? Yet, now that we lack Alixis to glue us together, we stride past each other at camp with our heads held high and without a sideways glance.

No one ever told me that in order to ignore someone, you had to be painfully aware of everything they're doing *all* the time.

I miss him. I miss Alixis. I miss Mum being my mum and Dad being my dad.

⳽

A FORTNIGHT AFTER THE PARTY, Shepherd Fines and I return to the camp from a Demonstration in Romeo, where I killed two women for conspiring against the Shepherds. The moment I step through the gate, I know something's changed. The air is quiet but full, like poisonous gas has been channelling between the buildings, and no one can breathe or speak.

'Sir, is everything all right in there?' I motion across the empty field towards the camp.

'Of course, my dear. Now you go and get some rest.' He waggles a finger at me.

The Shepherd has abandoned all pretence of having business in the cities where I demonstrate, and I have to admit, seeing his face in the crowd when I fight gives me more strength. It reminds me I have a shot of finishing this thing. Of getting out of here.

I've heard the rumours of course; Debtbook is rife with speculations about the school-girl Demonstrator and her Shepherd. Some people think it's sick and that I'm his favourite pet. Others like to believe it's true love, and we've found it in the least likely of situations. I think it's a little mix of both. Maybe love, on his side, maybe control for both of us.

The wind turns colder as I reach the playground. Shepherd Fines heads down a separate path, on his way to who-knows-where.

A low sob hiccups through the silence. I follow the sound until I reach a huddle of Demonstrators at the bottom of Shepherd Fines' stairs.

Four of them sit tightly together, while one paces behind.

'It's Sola,' I hear one whisper. The pacing boy stops.

'Did you know about this?' he demands. I don't have time to answer.

'Of course she did. She is sleeping with *him*, after all.' The man sitting on the stairs looks me up and down. I recognise the disgust in his eyes. There's a murmur of assent from the rest of them.

'Whatever,' I say. 'I came to see whether you were all right, but forget it.' My fists are little balls as I turn away. I'm not sleeping with anyone, but if I am, what business is it of theirs?

'Dao's dead.'

I stop breathing. Everything inside me freezes. Dao's last Demonstration was today. We said goodbye last night. He was going to win. I knew it.

'Your Shepherd blinded him. What a fun twist,' the boy spits out at me.

'I . . . I . . . I didn't know,' I whisper, still facing away from them. I close my eyes against the image of gentle Dao unable to see in the Stadium, desperately trying to hear

213

those around him. I've been so obsessed with my own fights, my own misery that I didn't think to ask Shepherd Fines to go easy on Dao. I didn't consider his poor count of followers.

The message is simple: if the crowd doesn't care about you going home, you don't go home.

CR

GIDEON DOESN'T LEAVE HIS POD FOR DAYS. From the nasty looks various Demonstrators shoot me as I wait by his pod shaft, I know I'm blamed for Dao's death. I'm just about to give up and head to my pod when someone scans out of the shaft. It's him.

His eyes are ringed with grey bags, his skin practically draping from his cheekbones. I wonder when he last ate.

'You need to leave,' he says. I take a deep breath. For hours, I have been preparing myself for this, but imagining how much he hates me is nothing compared to the emptiness in his voice.

'Gideon, I'm sorry about Dao.' When he doesn't reply, I continue. 'I don't care who else blames me for what happened, but I need you to know that I didn't have anything to do with it. I had no idea—'

'Maybe you could have asked, then.' He interrupts. 'Maybe you could have cared? One word from you, and this wouldn't have happened.'

'That's not true! I don't even have influence over my own Demonstrations. I can't control what Shepherd Fines decides. I loved Dao. I—' I'm rambling now, trying to quell the stickiness in my throat and burning in my eyes.

Gideon interjects. 'Fine, Sola. It's not your fault he's gone. But why do you still cosy up to the man who killed your so-called friend?'

I shake my head. I can't believe what I'm hearing. How any of this can be pinned on me?

'It's his job! And why are you still friends with Coral?' I shoot back. 'She is the reason I'm here. Not to mention how she told Shepherd Fines about Alixis' baby.'

Gideon stares back at me. The hollowness of his gaze, the way his mouth sets, makes me shudder. It's as though he's looking at a corpse.

'Coral didn't murder Dao,' he says quietly. 'You know, Coral's not perfect. She isn't going to be rescuing orphaned kittens anytime soon. But she looks out for those she cares for. Which is more than I can say for you.'

I open my mouth to tell him we must be talking about different people when he speaks again.

'Look, you and I were never great friends to begin with. Let's just stay out of each other's way from now on.'

He turns and scans back into his pod shaft before I can find any words. This was not how I imagined our conversation ending.

℘

I WISH THINGS HAD BEEN peachy since then, but that was two weeks ago, and I've given up on making friends in this place. Demonstrators leave on the spinner every day. Some come back, some don't. I try not to let myself think about stuff too much. That's why I've been fighting non-stop since Dao died, adding a new scar to my criss-crossed body almost daily.

Dylan didn't mention this part in his little plan to keep me alive. 'By the way, whenever anything bad happens, everyone will blame you because they all think you have influence with Shepherd Fines. Thanks to Coral's and various other status updates, the whole camp thinks you're together . . .' I even heard someone whisper Shepherd Fines had given me drugs to make me a better fighter.

The whole way through this month from hell, I keep thinking that I might have a sister living yards away from me.

So, what kind of person does it make me that all I want is to destroy her?

thirty-eight

TODAY IS CHRISTMAS.

Or at least it used to be.

Shepherd Fines told me that since religion was declared illegal, people get restless on December 25th. I know he's approved whatever fight has been planned for me; he's been a mixture of frantic excitement and genuine worry for days. Even Dylan stops tapping on his digipad when he sees Shepherd Fines and I walk across to the gate.

'You don't have a Demonstration today, do you?' he shouts across to me. I nod, but keep my pace up.

'But, it's a tryouts day. We get the time off.' Dylan sounds confused, anxiety flitting into his low voice. Worried about his conscience, no doubt. I let the Shepherd do the talking like my own personal bodyguard. He tells Dylan some speech about how I'll get more followers if I demonstrate when no one else does. I walk away without a second glance.

❧

VERY SOON, I wish I'd listened to Dylan. At city Hotel's Stadium I'm rushed into a different type of room than usual, equipped with not one, but two workers with understanding smiles. The place is oddly silent, with no open archway, just another door.

One of the workers grins. 'Sound-proof,' she tells me, looking delighted. Instead of handing me the usual leather belt, she picks up a long, oval, metal clamp from the table.

She runs her scan chip over one end and it opens up like a jaw. Beaming that condescending smile, she instructs me to put my arms up. When I do, the woman places one half of the clamp over my body so that it runs from my shoulder to my hip. The other side is pulled down over my back, and the two ends join together with definite clicks. I look down to see an angry red circle on the clamp, like the lens of a camera. It sits right over my heart.

'What is this?' I ask.

'Something slightly different. You have to work out the rules when you get out there.'

She nods to her colleague, who I notice is holding a tiny controller in her hands. Her hands move and something buzzes through my chest. I scream out.

'Fantastic, it works.'

I barely register the woman's words. My breath is rushing out of me, my heart going twice as fast. I want to be sick. The electric shock was like a hand reaching into my rib cage and scratching my organs.

'Don't worry. You won't feel that again. And if you do, you won't be around to experience it for long.'

ଔ

THE OTHER DOOR leads out onto a staircase. At the bottom, I'm escorted to the open archway and practically pushed out onto the empty sands by the two workers. I roll my shoulders underneath the clamp. It already weighs heavily, pulling on my neck. No one cheers as I walk to the centre of the arena, but I do hear a cough. It's this that tells me I'm in trouble—people are too excited to speak in case they miss something. Anticipation hangs in the air like a thick fog over my head. My hands are idle and useless without my sword, so I end up fidgeting while I wait for something to happen.

I knew today would be different. People are getting restless with me. My ticket sales are creeping down. They're bored of my signature cartwheel move, bored that I always win. Even my gate-induced fainting has lost their interest. Some have written on Debtbook that I should get a new quirk. They prefer Coral, her deadly dance-like moves, her clear enjoyment of the fight. That seductive lack of compassion.

I'm shuffling ever closer to getting home, and I'm rewarded with disdain.

The gate clicks.

I gulp down ice-cold air. Let my body sway. Instead of panicking and fighting the faint, I clear my mind, closing my eyes and latching onto the smells of this Stadium.

Mothballs, stale rubber . . .

Stay here. Stay here.

My hands hit the ground as sharp gasps rise around me, like the sound a vegetable makes when you chop in it half.

The gate is up. There are footsteps, one set, two, three . . .

I open my eyes wide, terror overtaking me in whelms. Over a dozen brown-uniformed men and women face me, frightened and shaking, clutching their weapons like sacred talismans. I'm stepping back, calculating how I can go about killing that number of people when there are more clicks behind me.

I fight the faint this time, and only my adrenaline keeps me here. Whizzing around, I clock the group already out and the rising gate to my right in swift glances.

More people. They fall onto the sands like white-faced lemmings, lingering at the edge of the arena.

I'm trapped between two groups, crouched in my bracing position. I try to count the heads, but there must be over thirty people against me.

That's it. I'm dead. I'm dead, and I don't want to die, but I will. In this vast space, it's as if I'm shrinking, becoming tiny and useless even though my enemies grow bigger.

Maybe I am fainting after all because on everyone's shirts lies a bleeding 'x'. Just like my tryout. They're painted with blue and red crosses.

Dylan's words come back to me: *it's a tryouts day.*

The December tryouts at Hotel. I'm *in* them.

Up on the screen, my face takes up half of the image with my name at the top and a tally at the bottom. It reads 0/10. On the other half is footage of the contestants. Some of them are inching closer. To me or to the other team? I can't tell.

Sickness glides over me like a mist. For some reason, I know I've not been put in here to stand around and watch the outcome. I try and adjust the clamp over my heart, but it won't budge.

I take a deep breath, swallow, and run to meet the woman closest to me. If this is what I think, I need to act fast. She waves her hand in sloppy slices through the air. Her whole arm is encased in metal and at the end is a semicircular blade. For a split second, I wish that she isn't a red—I guess I still harbour some loyalty to my own team, though not enough—as I wait until she's swerved her arm far out, and then jab her in the nose. There's a satisfying snap underneath my palm. I twist, grabbing her weapon arm and forcing it towards her chest. Her eyes connect with mine moments before they go vacant.

She's left on the ground with her own blade sticking out from her chest as if she has her hand on her heart. I stare at the screen.

1/10.

The audience certainly isn't silent any more. The usual screaming pulses from the stands now that I've given them blood. It's as though my kill gives others permission to do the same, as both teams rush in, colliding like turning cogs.

Each body that falls is one less point for me.

The metal clamp constricts my chest. It's hard to breathe. I just *know* I have to reach that number. Ten kills before the fight is over.

Or the clamp kills me.

Time is not on my side, so I run into the furore of the fighting. No more dragging out the combat. No more pleasing the crowd. That raging monster uncurls, and I gladly allow it to take over. Blades clatter all around, aiming for my body, trying to jab into me. I duck, swerve, teeter backwards, leap and roll to evade the blows. The rhythm of fighting hammers in my head. Music made of clashes and thuds ring through the Stadium; vibrating through the ground and into my boots.

If the teams didn't know the rules of the game, they catch on after I kill three more reds and a blue. It doesn't matter what team they're on. I just *have* to get my kill count.

5/10

A man darts past me, dragging a heavy metal chain. I stand on it abruptly, causing him to topple backwards. Before I crumple his throat with my foot, I make sure I look into his pleading eyes. I don't deserve to forget about these people easily.

Paces away, two blues have teamed up and are executing reds with irritating precision. If they carry on, I'll still be stuck on six kills by the time the blues win. Which means I lose.

I spin round, taking in the scene. Some of the crowd scream my name; others ignore me, watching the slaughter with eager eyes. My lips taste salty and stale. I wipe my face with my arm, trying to clear some sweat from my eyelashes.

Eighteen bodies are still dancing their sloppy fights. A child stands near the gate, eyes clenched shut and hands against the Stadium wall.

I tear my gaze away. I haven't got time to save anyone but myself today.

As soon as I locate the two blues, I take off—

Something clamps around my throat. The hands squeeze, then pull me back. I gag.

Their skin scrapes under my fingernails as I claw at their grip. Useless. My mouth works up and down, panic stabbing at my throat in hot jabs. My attacker's body is pressed against my back: strong, desperate, determined.

The chain clatters as it falls from my hands. I watch my scrambling legs as if they're not mine.

Can't breathe. Choking on vomit. My mouth is slowly opening, tongue flopping out. I can't see. I'm just falling, falling.

I freeze.

Panic: one of the biggest killers in the Stadium.

It only takes a millisecond to clear my head. Get my bearing. I force my eyes to focus, pull up the last of my ebbing strength, and *lean*. Not forwards but backwards into my assailant. At the same time, I reach behind me, cupping my palms between their wrists before pulling with all my remaining strength. The force is enough for their hands to jolt, losing their grip and allowing me that beautiful, god-sent breath. I strike out with my elbows, battering their head while I twist to face them. My throat scorches as if I have a flame in my belly, and I'm 99% sure I'm about to faint. Yet I still find enough strength to kick them in the groin, knocking them backwards. Almost as an afterthought, I flop on top of them, pinning them to the ground before using both hands to jab my hairpin through their throat.

There's some cheering, but I hear a low wave of disappointment from the stalls. Maybe the whole point is that I don't have a weapon. Oh well. I take a moment to re-gain my breath, relying on luck that no one stabs me in the back while I lie on top of the man I've just killed.

Something near me moves. That's my cue to roll away and jump up, meeting my next assailant face on.

Another man. I use his own sword to cut his arm before knocking his legs from underneath him and seizing the weapon. I clock his green eyes, slice into his chest, and look up to the screen.

8/10

What a waste. Lying by the side of the young girl I saw earlier is a fully loaded crossbow. If I could get to—

Something jabs into my calf. A woman with dirt smeared over her face rears up the side of me, pulling her knife from my leg and moving to strike again. I cry out, but even with my injured leg, she's no match for me. In the seconds before I run my sword through her stomach, her jaw sets in resignation.

One more. One more.

Ten survivors scatter across the sands in three groups.

The two blue alpha males have recruited another man and three women. They stand ready, weapons sturdy in their hands, their uniforms soaked in blood and grit. Three reds have come together on the other side of me, while the girl still faces the Stadium wall, preventing anyone from seeing her coloured cross.

I have to kill once more before the blues exterminate the reds, else it's all over. For me, at least.

Just as I've made the connection, so must the blues. They rush in with war cries to meet the reds. The pain in my thigh is becoming unbearable, but I grit my teeth.

PERSISTENCE AND RESISTANCE.

I dive into the furore.

Hands grab my arms. I look round, and there are so many blues—*too* many blues— grasping at me, holding me down. I struggle, writhing around like not-quite-dead rail-kill. One of the alpha blues comes towards me with his mace raised high. Undeniable intent fills his wild eyes.

I squeeze mine shut.

No. Can't die now.

I force my eyes open. The mace rushes to meet me. I lurch my neck backwards and push both my feet from the floor, relying on the pair of blues who hold my arms to support me. My boot collides with the mace with a crunch.

I hit the ground as one blue drops me. Straight away, my feet find purchase. My forehead rams into someone's nose as the mace again rears upwards, ready to bite into my shoulder. I swing around. Grab the man still holding my arm. Heave him in front of me . . .

Even I wince as his back makes a chewing sound. The alpha who dealt the blow stares, mouth open in shock as he tries to pull the weapon out of his comrade's back.

I take long strides backwards, glancing around as if my next assailant could come from anywhere. Damn! The screen still reads 9/10. The kill doesn't count as mine. As I reach the side of the Stadium, the young girl runs from behind me to join the group now forming. The group which, I realise with a sickening clarity, all don blue crosses painted on their chests. It's over. The blues have won. I didn't meet my target.

So how come I haven't been shocked into oblivion, thanks to this clamp?

My boot hits something hard on the floor as I back up. The child's discarded crossbow. I pick it up with shaking hands. The sounds of the arena heat the air, confusion twirling around me. No one knows what's going on. Why hasn't it been announced that the fight is over? Why aren't I dead? Why aren't the medics and Ebiere coming out here to wrap it up? All eyes turn to the screen. I'm still on one side, the huddled group of blues on the other.

Ticker tape runs across the bottom of the screen.

One of the blues is realy a red. They switched their shirt earlier in the fight. The tryouts are still live!

There's a spelling mistake, as if someone's typed it out in a hurry.

223

That tiny flicker of hope is all I need. I speed towards the group, seizing my chance before anyone can steal it away.

The five survivors step away from each other, panic and fear now rife in their faces. They're trying to work out who the red is. I raise the crossbow.

I can shoot anyone. One more person, and I'll be saved. My aim hops from one face to another. If I choose a true blue, then the mysterious red will still have to be killed. With both hope and anguish, I realise that if I manage to kill the hidden red, I can save one person's life tonight.

I rule out the alpha blue I've seen all game. Then there's the woman whose nose bleeds from my head-butt. Not her. Another woman who I'm sure I saw earlier with the blue men. That leaves the other male and the child. Was the girl wearing red when I spotted her earlier? Why was she hiding her cross against the Stadium?

Like an echo of the beginning of the fight, the audience falls silent. This unexpected twist tantalising them more than blood alone could. I lean on my good leg, heaving breaths, holding the crossbow as steady as I can manage. Adrenaline pumps through me, pushing away the edges of exhaustion and pain.

'Only one of you has to die. Which one switched? Tell me, and you can save someone else's life,' I half-shout, half-gasp out to the group.

More shuffling. The child looks to the floor, hiding her face.

The man I couldn't place steps forwards and pushes the child towards me. She squeals and tries to rush back into the group, but they all stand tight.

'It was her,' he shouts shakily. 'I saw her switch but didn't want to say anything. Please.'

I'm not sure what he's pleading for. The worst part is, if the girl had used her crossbow, her team might have won.

'Okay,' I say, but I'm thinking *I'm sorry.* The girl hides her face.

I let the arrow fly.

It cuts straight into the man's heart.

There's a second of quiet. Then—cheers. The audience erupts. They're screaming. The game is finished. My clamp opens with a click. I haul it off my chest and as far away from me as I can manage. Urgh, my shirt is saturated with sweat where the thing was secured.

The child looks up at me, her wide eyes questioning.

I don't have it in me to explain. I didn't know it was him. I'm still not sure it was. I just knew the crowd would love it if the snitch died. No one is going to prove the crowd wrong, not even the Shepherds.

The girl scurries over to me, clinging onto my leg with tight arms.

'Happy Christmas,' I whisper.

thirty-nine

AFTER THE FIGHT, I spend a day recovering in the Medic's Cabin. They fix my leg, and only a small mark remains where I was stabbed. In the bed opposite lies the child from the tryouts.

I hadn't noticed during my fight that the girl had been injured, but the medics had come around with their little stretcher and tried to load her onto it straight after I shot the man. Immediately I thought of William, how I had saved him only to send him to who-knows-what life somewhere else. I told them she was fine, gathered her up in my arms and limped out of the Stadium with her on my hip.

I'm not sure whether it was this or the way I fought that tipped me back into the lead for followers, but either way, I've overtaken Coral and have reclaimed my title of 'best Demonstrator with a live Debt.'

When I check my digipad, there's another scathing status from Coral about my fighting. She makes a joke about how it was obviously the little girl who switched.

I can't help but wonder if Coral's as scared as I am that this is the beginning of our twists.

'That red-head seriously has it in for you,' makeup girl says as she fiddles with my IV.

'You a medic, too?' I ask, hoping she can detect my sarcasm.

'We're trained in pretty much everything. Apart from killing, of course.'

'Of course,' I repeat. 'I don't suppose you could train her as staff? Make her work as a server instead of a Demonstrator?' I ask pointlessly, indicating to the sleeping child.

Makeup girl smiles.

'She's clever enough. She'll survive for a while. Anyway, Shepherd Fines visited, wants to see you in his office when you're better.' She sounds as though she's trying not to giggle. 'Go on. Tell me.' She crouches down to my level and whispers, 'What's going on with you two?'

'I can trust you, right?' I ask, lowering my voice and shuffling over.

She nods enthusiastically.

'We're planning on taking over the world. We're going to get rid of all the city borders and rule the earth as King and Queen like in the old days.'

I'm pleased to say it takes her a while to catch on that I'm joking. As I watch her storm off, I laugh harder than I have in a long while. I swing my legs over the side of the bed, pull the IV from my arm with a wince and try to stand.

'Where are t' others?'

It's a voice so tiny I think I've imagined it. I peer around suspiciously. Now is not the best time to have voices in my head. But my gaze settles on the little girl from the tryouts. She's still lying down but has opened her grey eyes. She peers over the side of her bed at me.

'What others?' I ask, lowering my voice to meet hers.

'Ones what were chosen from my city.' Her forehead wrinkles just above her eyebrows. I swallow. Teaching kids the facts of Demonstrations was not on my to-do list today.

'I'm sorry, but they're gone. Who is it you're looking for?' Why did I ask that? I can't help her.

'All of them,' she replies. 'Ones chosen this month. What happens to t'others?'

I wish she would stop asking that. I scramble for a delicate way of telling her they must have died in the tryouts.

'Do you remember the big fight we had? That's where everyone chosen from your city this month would have been. You're very lucky; you survived.' I speak slowly as if she were hard of hearing. Her eyes narrow; more lines appear between her brows.

'But what about t'others? The ones what weren't in't tryouts?'

'Oh, the older ones? They must have been chosen to work here.'

'I haven't seen them!' Her voice goes high-pitched, worried. 'I've been lookin'.'

I'm pretty sure my frown now matches hers. I get up, pad around to her bed.

'Hey, it's all right.' I try and sound soothing. 'I've got to go somewhere, but I'll come and see you later, okay?'

She nods.

'Now, don't repeat what you just asked me to anyone else. That's really important.'

Another nod. She pulls the covers up to her chin. 'What's your name? I like rememberin' people.' Her voice is muffled through the sheet. I smile.

'Sola. And I like to remember people, too—maybe I should have yours?'

'Tabby.'

I grin and follow a medic out of the ward without scanning out. As I head across the playground to Shepherd Fines' office, Tabby's words dance in my mind. While I lived in Juliet, around three people were chosen each month. If that's the case everywhere, then there should be an average of seventy-five people in each of the tryouts. From the ones I've seen and participated in, there's been between thirty or fifty. So that means that every month, at least twenty new workers should be arriving at the camp. I haven't seen one new server since I've been here.

I take the stairs two by two before banging on the watchtower door. It slides open.

'Sir, I need to—'

'Sola! My dearest, I've been *so* looking forwards to seeing you.'

Shepherd Fines opens his arms wide before sliding one behind my back and guiding me through the door. His coffee breath follows his eyes over my face.

'Hardly a scratch on you.' He looks amazed. 'I knew you were going to become the best, and you're so nearly there. However, we don't have much time alone, I'm afraid.'

Did I imagine it, or did Shepherd Fines just squeeze my waist? I watch with wary eyes as he walks to the other side of his desk. He throws glances my way, his mouth turned up into a proud smile, his eyes wide with excitement. Each look makes my skin tingle with awkwardness. It's as though I've transformed into a butterfly in front of his eyes or something. When he sits, I gladly take a seat on the sofa.

Seconds later, there's a slow, deliberate knock on the door. Shepherd Fines opens it from his remote control system.

'You wanted to see me, Sir?'

I would recognise that sickly sweet voice anywhere. I straighten up, anger already burning hot in my belly. Coral beams even wider when she sees me.

'Hey, Sola. How's Alixis doing?' Her expression is full of pretend kindness but her eyes are laughing at me. Shepherd Fines prevents me from replying.

'Come now, don't hover in the doorway, take a seat! I have some great news for you both,' he rotates his wrist in a flippant way towards the sofa. Coral lowers herself gracefully into the antique-looking carver chair by the door.

'As you might know, Miss Winters here has overtaken you, Sola, in her number of Demonstrations.' Although Shepherd Fines is talking to me, he nods to Coral, evoking

229

another smile. 'She kills well, but the spectators can get bored easily when a Demonstrator shows no emotion. So we've had to speed her tour up. Strike while the iron is hot, so to speak.'

I resist the urge to snicker, but it's hard.

'In any case, her final Demonstration is coming up.' He continues to talk as though Coral weren't present. 'By a stroke of genius, Miss Winters here has dramatised a rivalry between you pair widely on Debtbook. In fact, the whole country is talking about it. So, what better way to boost ticket sales and followers than to have you fight side by side?'

'What?' Coral practically jumps out of her seat. Shepherd Fines raises his eyebrows and leans back slightly, daring her to question him. There's a shuffle as Coral settles back into her chair.

'I just mean. Well, Sir, this is embarrassing but—' She ducks her head, changing tack.

I sigh exaggeratedly at her attempt to be shy.

'I don't want to fight alongside Sola,' Coral says. 'She's too good. She'll get all the credit in my final fight.'

'Nonsense, my dear! I've seen you in combat and you're giving Sola a run for her money!' He chuckles. 'Nothing will be more spectacular than the best two female fighters with a live Debt putting their differences aside for the sake of the Shepherds. Also, it benefits both of you. Miss Winters, you'll have far greater chance of winning your final fight and returning home, and Sola, it will count as one of your Demonstrations.' He smiles, claps his hands together, and clicks his teeth at Coral.

'Right then, now that's settled and you can run along. I'll meet you at the gate in three days. I wouldn't miss this for the world!'

Coral looks deflated as she leaves the office. Sharing her glory with me must be the worst outcome she could imagine for her final fight. The door slides shut behind her and the air lightens, if only for a moment. Shepherd Fines is next to me before I can even stand, an eager arm wrapped around my shoulder.

'So, what would you like to drink?' He looks suspiciously happy. There are so many things I need to ask him about: what Tabby said about the others; where the brothers went; why William is in Greece. If we were truly friends, I would be able to come out and demand answers. But I have to face facts that we're not. Although we get along, I've known for ages that he sees me romantically. And I've manipulated that, in my own way. I've given him some control over me in exchange for protection and comfort.

That fight on Christmas day has made me realise that I need to start taking control of my own situation.

It might mean giving up answers, but it's time for our fake romance to end.

'I'll have tea,' I say and watch carefully as he pours the Gekruide tea. No pills in it this time, at least not that I see. When he brings them over, I point to the glass he holds closest to him.

'I'd prefer that one.'

His gaze flickers down, heat showing on his cheeks. I guess it's the first time I've made it obvious that I know about the drugging attempt. It's also the first time I've ever seen him blush.

'Of course,' he mumbles and holds his glass out. 'I apologise for what happened . . . before. You just looked tired . . .' He trails off, his voice small.

I wave it off. In truth, I never thought he was trying to hurt me.

'Do you forgive me?' he asks. I nod as I take the glass.

'Yeah, I do. But we need to talk.'

'Great stuff, darling. I want to talk to you, too.' He reclines in the middle of the sofa, evidently pleased I've accepted his apology. Something tells me he won't be happy for long.

231

'Look, I—I can't help but notice that you're . . . interested in me in more than a friendly manner. Or that of a Shepherd and his subject, perhaps,' I say, drawing breath while I stare at the red sofa throw, the plush carpet, the sleeping lamps hanging behind his head—anywhere except his eyes.

'Unfortunately I'm unable to return your affections,' I say.

There. I've said it.

I wait.

'I understand,' he says.

My relief must be obvious. My shoulders sag and I breathe out slowly. Shepherd Fines makes his clicking noise.

'It's the age gap, isn't it? I've been thinking along similar lines.' His face is grave. He clasps his hands before his neck, just like I've seen Alixis do in prayer. His forefinger extends out to touch his lip. 'Well, there's no need to worry,' he says eventually. 'I can simply change the law, if you wish. Make it so every relationship must have at least a five year age gap?'

The room is getting smaller, I'm sure of it. I wriggle my shoulders and shift so that I'm sitting on the edge of the sofa. 'No, that's not it. Sir, you've formed this attachment way too quickly. I mean, you don't even know me! Perhaps it's borne out of my fighting abilities more than anything else? But we could still be friends?'

I have no idea why I'm speaking like I've walked right out of *Frankenstein*. Diplomacy was never my strongest point.

Shepherd Fines slaps his hand onto his chest and shakes his head slowly, as if I've shot him in the heart. 'My dearest, I'm so glad you've spoken to me about these concerns. There *has* to be communication if this is to work. I only wish you'd expressed your anxieties sooner! I understand now why you might have been holding back your desire for me.' He stands and paces in a leisurely, almost comical manner.

I lean back on the sofa, eyes on the door. My mind is racing for what to say next.

'I admit that from the second I saw you fight I was enticed by this "school-girl protector of the weak",' Shepherd Fines says. 'However, since then we've formed this *connection*. You don't pander to me. You don't tell me what I want to hear. I like watching you fight, yes. I like that you're the best, yes. But I like *you* the most.' He jabs a finger in my direction, stops in front of me. His eyes lose his smile suddenly, his lips going tight.

'As for just being friends, well, my dear, that would never happen. With a connection like ours, it's either all or nothing.'

I'm not sure if I'm open-mouthed from shock or because I can't find a reply. All I can think is *this is not good.* Over and over again. My hands fidget in my lap. I stare at them, trying to form words.

He sits next to me, his arm pulling me nearer. For a fleeting second, I get the real urge to kill him. I could do it, right now. I know how.

Yet, this is exactly what I was afraid of—that training would make me remedy everything with violence. I don't hate Shepherd Fines, I don't want to hurt him, not really. But I also don't want his hand on my leg or to detect a threat in the way he said 'all or nothing'.

Instead of killing anybody, instead of confronting Shepherd Fines about Tabby's concerns, I sit, nodding along to whatever he is saying into my ear. My eyes are on the bottom of the door, hoping that if I stare at it enough, it will slide open and set me free.

forty

THAT NIGHT, I hold back Alixis' hair as she throws up into the toilet bowl. We're in the bathroom at the bottom of our pod shaft and, between sickly heaves, Alixis tells me to go back to bed. She says it must have been something she ate. When I tell her it's probably the baby, she looks away quickly. 'Maybe it was the yoghurt,' she replies, before throwing her head over the bowl once more.

❧

AFTER FORTY LAPS, I run one extra for each person in my life. I forgot to go and see Tabby last night despite my promise to her, and when I saw her this morning, she asked more questions that I couldn't answer.

Sweat tickles my eyelashes. I blow mist from my mouth in time with the pound of my boots against the mud. In and out. Left, right, left, right. The field is tipped with white. Ice crackles up each blade of grass, weighing heavily on any remaining leaves and biting into the tree bark like a disease.

Lap forty-one: for William. Not in my life but far, far away, all because I saved him in the tryouts.

Lap forty-two: for Tabby. A cautious child who's seen far more of life than she should have. Who in my dream last night whispered to me, 'Where are the others?'

Lap forty-three: I run this one fast. It's for Dao. Blinded and murdered after twenty-four Demonstrations.

Forty-four: my legs start to burn. For Alixis and her baby. For my best friend who has given up on everything. For her child who I already love but blame for taking Alixis away from me.

Forty-five: the pain in my calves is welcome through this one. For Shepherd Fines. Who has written on my Debtbook that we are in a relationship. Whose secrets I need to discover.

Forty-six: red hot anger sears up my legs and through my arms. This. One. Is. For. Coral.

Seven: Dylan. My mind is going to mush. My vision is blurring, lungs are bursting. Legs are going to cripple. Dylan. Who thinks I'm selfish. Who tries to control me just like Fines. Who I hate.

Who I love.

Eight: I can see them at the end of the lap. For a dad who might not be my dad. For a mum I never knew. Not really.

My legs go from underneath me. I fall to the ground, the ice stabbing me the moment I touch the floor. I don't know when I started crying, but salty tears mingle in with sweat. I grab my numb legs up to my chest and curl into a ball on the field.

I need to get up before the cold claims me completely.

Ș

'SOLA!'

My body freezes as I limp my way towards the Wetpod.

I've trained by myself once again. My fight alongside Coral is tomorrow. And for some reason, Dylan is calling my name for the first time in over seven weeks. He jogs up by the side of me.

'I'm headed this way, too,' he says by way of an explanation. My feet hit the ground faster, my gaze unwavering from ahead.

'Big fight tomorrow. I saw your practice drills.'

If this is his way of making conversation, he can forget it. Maybe he thinks I'll die tomorrow and wants to ease his conscience by making up beforehand.

'Fine. You don't want to talk' he says. 'I only wanted to say you need to keep your arms in; you're exposing your sides too often.' He sounds annoyed now, as if he's tried oh-so hard. I reach the entrance to the Wetpod, but I don't want us to be trapped in there together, so I stalk past it and across the next field.

'Thanks for the heads up. Will you go now?' I snap once I realise he's following me.

'I'm trying to help!'

'You can help by leaving me alone.' A fallen twig snaps underfoot as I stomp ahead.

'You hate me, I get it. Maybe you've finally caught on that this is all my fault.' He speaks as if he's being sarcastic, as if he would be annoyed if I really did think that. Yet, I'm not sure. My mind is fried, and I can't deal with stupid Demonstrators who want to mess with my head.

'Just don't let it get you killed,' he adds.

And that's it. Something inside me explodes.

'Who do you think you are?' I ask, spinning around. 'Going round, telling people how to feel? How to act? How to stay alive? I'm sick of it, and I'm sick of you!' I step forwards. His face flashes surprise, then resilience. He stays where he is. 'So I'll fight with my arms waving in the air,' I continue. 'I'll fight without a gun. I'll fight without Shepherd Fines' help and I'll fight without you even if it *does* get me killed!'

Silence. We're inches apart. I embrace the heat which flushes my face, my chest, my tummy. He nods.

'Throwing another lifeline away. How unlike you,' he says quietly and turns away. I hate him for not shouting at me. I hate him for being calm and disappointed and only caring about me out of guilt when I love every inch of him.

After he walks a few paces, I catch up to him and grab his shoulder, spinning him round.

'Fight me,' I say.

'What?'

'You think I can't handle myself. So fight me. Don't hold back. Whoever gives up first loses.'

'I'm not going to hurt you.' He says it as though it's an answer. He's already turning away.

'I know you're not. Come on; if I win, you don't get to tell me what to do ever again. And if you win . . .' I scratch around for something which he might want.

'If I win, you wear a gun tomorrow,' he says slowly, angling himself to face me once again.

Mum flashes in my mind. I don't think I could pull that trigger . . . then again, I won't lose this.

'Deal.'

forty-one

THE NEWLY-TRODDEN GRASS crinkles under my boots as I steady my crouching pose. We're far out, near the fence that runs around the fields. I keep my eyes locked on Dylan. Gone is the awkward man I've seen run his hand through his hair so many times. Now a warrior stands opposite me. His eyes are intense, his jaw set and firm.

He'd tried to get the plastic swords. I told him no. No weapons. Just you and me.

His head cocks to one side. He raises his eyebrows. It's an invitation.

Fine by me.

Like a swimmer on their marks, I crouch lower before blasting myself towards him. My bones throb with renewed energy.

I try to jab him in the stomach. He hits my wrist out of the way again and again. I change to attack his side, but he's ready and he deflects my blows lazily. Each time I fail to make contact, frustration bites at me. Grunting, I desperately try to land something home. My top is damp with sweat, and yet Dylan stands there, moving only to block me.

Next time he grabs my wrist to deflect, I swirl behind him and grip his arm too. I throw him away from me and leap backwards, putting some much-needed space between us. My short gasps send shock into my lungs.

No more playing by his rules. I try to encourage the rage inside me, feed the creature like I do in the Stadium. I close my eyes and breathe in the frosty air.

When he comes for me, I'm ready.

He goes for the most obvious move to get me on the floor: a leg scoop. I jump over his leg, and land my right foot onto his thigh. Instead of kicking, I take hold of his shoulders and launch myself onto his back. Wrapping my leg over his shoulder I tip my weight forwards. He's pulled down with me, and I ignore the thud of the ground as I try to find his arm in the heap of our bodies. Dylan's too fast. He rolls away swiftly, and I'm glad to see he's breathing hard.

I charge once more, aiming to jab his neck with my palm. He sidesteps. I recognise too late I'm about to collide with his outstretched arm. It hits my neck, choking me. My legs swerve forwards and I land on my back, struggling for breath. The idiot winded me. I hardly have time to curse before he goes to pin me down. I roll away and clamber up.

We've travelled even farther away from the camp now. Behind Dylan, the ground slopes before it dives, meeting a collection of willow trees at the bottom of the hill by the far side of the gate. I wonder whether Dylan's noticed; if I can unbalance him onto the slope, I might have the advantage.

He steps towards me. Within moments, we're back into the fight, and I aim a side kick to his head, but he ducks and pushes my leg forwards, throwing me off-balance. I spin like a dancer, swerving out of his attack before raining down a combination of elbow, palm, and knee jabs. He blocks, grabs, even tries a head-butt, but I see it coming and land an elbow on his neck.

That's when I hear a cheer. White speckles appear in my vision. At first, I think I've got concussion but then I realise Demonstrators are cheering us on.

The world twists upside down. I'm rolling, tumbling through the air. Dylan has blocked my attack with a jump and hooked his leg around my waist. As he tumbles, I go with him, over his body and landing with a painful crack.

Somewhere around me, Shepherd Fines cheers my name.

Our misty breath mingles together now. We tussle on the floor, trying to get on top of the other. My chest is bruised, my lungs are straining, my hip and sides are screaming out, but I won't give up.

I go to grab one of his attacking arms, and with the force I fall over his body—

Grass then trees then sky then grass. I'm rolling. My fingernails scrape through soil as I try to stop. We've tipped over the slope and now we both crash over one another, still fighting as we flip down the hill. I scratch flesh semi-by-accident. A knee smacks my jaw, and my own teeth jam into my lip. Something bony collides with my head.

We roll onto even surface. I pummel my arms into what I think is Dylan and try to get hold of myself, to figure out what's sky and what's ground. My shoulder slams into a tree trunk and suddenly we're underneath the willow trees. The falling ice is welcome on my body as the tree shivers to life.

It takes a moment for me to recognise I'm on top of Dylan. Holding his wrists in a vice-like grip with his legs pinned underneath my knees.

Neither of us speak. Just catch our breath together. Blood streams from his nose. There are two deep scratches on his forehead and his clothes are soaked from sweat and frost. I swipe my eye with my shoulder. Crusty soil rubs off onto the white T-shirt sleeve. There are no cheers from the spectators; we're hidden away under the crescendo of willow branches.

After an age of breathing, Dylan croaks out, 'You win.'

'I can take care of myself,' I say back to him, pushing down on his arms. Despite the blood which flows over his lips, he grins.

'You can.'

I scowl. Somehow I think he's getting the better of me. I tentatively bring my hand away and, when he doesn't move, I swipe the blood from his mouth.

'You look disgusting,' I explain.

'You look beautiful.'

Huh? Before I can open my mouth, I feel his hand snake around my neck. He leans up, still pinned underneath me, and presses his lips against mine.

Hot explosions erupt in my chest. Instinct yells at me to push him off, but I don't.

I part my lips slightly and kiss back. First urgently, then softly. His blood tastes just like mine, and I don't care. I just keep kissing, letting him explore with his perfect tongue and lips and—

His palm's at the back of my neck, his fingers extending into my hair. I slide my knees from his legs and he tips me over gently, still holding me tight. My back meets the cold, hard ground. Dylan is leaning over me, lying on his side but with one leg wrapped in between mine.

Every touch is a lightning bolt, and I crave the electricity. His fingers are like silk as they caress my neck. From his desperate touches, I can tell how long he's wanted this. Each kiss erases a separate doubt I had over how Dylan feels.

He goes to pull away, but I wrap my arms around his neck and kiss him deeper. He tastes like iron and sweat and sweetness.

Eventually, he breaks free, and I open my eyes. His face hovers above mine. When I go to speak, Dylan gives me that mischievous smile I've missed so much.

He's beautiful. *Beautiful*, and he's kissing *me* and it feels so right and so natural. There's a burning flourish in my tummy which spreads up to my throat. When he leans down, my breath catches, and I think he's going to kiss me again, but instead he winds his way up to my ear.

'I don't want you to die,' he whispers, 'because I'm in love with you.'

His words find purchase deep within. Everything tingles, as though my body is crying. I lean my head against his, wrap my arms around his neck and savour being this close to him. We're holding each other so hard I wonder if he can even breathe. Then we're kissing once more, our lips meeting, nibbling, exploring. I want all of him, *need* all of him.

We only have seconds longer.

Footsteps are making their way closer. Down the slope and into our hidden cavern. Dylan leans me back onto the ground once more, continuing to kiss me as he places his knees on my legs. He traces the lengths of my arms with his fingers and entwines them around my own.

Just before the willow branches are pulled back, Dylan drags his hands so that they're grabbing my wrists, and draws away from me.

'Who won?' asks Shepherd Fines, peering in through the parted branches.

Dylan doesn't turn to look. Just stares down at me, his smile gone. Yet I can trace happiness in the lines around his eyes, the curl of his mouth.

'I did,' he replies.

forty-two

THE NEXT MORNING, as I make my way to the spinner, Dylan catches my eye. We don't dare say a word. Our gaze plays out a conversation that in my mind goes like this: we kissed last night. Let's kiss again. Don't die so we can kiss some more.

Even when Shepherd Fines tucks my hand into the crook of his elbow and guides me away, I turn back, watching Dylan. I'm smiling and wishing and loving so hard that my chest feels full and on fire.

The spinner is already waiting for us on the landing pad. Coral stares out of the gap as Shepherd Fines climbs in beside her. He taps the other seat next to him, and I pull myself into it. Even knowing I have to fight alongside Coral today won't extinguish the excitement that tingles through me. I'm still imagining my and Dylan's next kiss when the spinner hovers over Juliet.

Home.

We descend onto the hospital roof. After two months, I breathe in the smell of my home city. The sights rush back to me, familiar and crooked at the same time. Everything looks askew, as if it's been knocked down and rebuilt wrong. Was it always this small?

Scaffolding leans against new buildings like climbing frames. Something's different. The place seems less like home and more like the cities I've visited since being chosen. . . .

A glance at Coral tells me she's noticed too. She breaks her cool facade to lean out of the gap, gasping at our home. An unwelcome pang of jealousy hits me. Coral gets to go back today. Everyone knows the Shepherds are going to give her an easy twist. In the lead up to this final fight, Coral's followers overtook mine, and no one has bought tickets to see her die. The crowd want their hero rewarded.

It will be me soon. Just seven more Demonstrations before my final fight. I'm not sure if that thought delights or terrifies me.

Coral's out of the spinner faster than if her seat were alight. We don't say one word to each other as we're led by a thick group of Herd officers through the hospital and the city streets. I'm too busy standing on my tiptoes, desperately searching for Dad. People stare back, and a crowd slowly forms, following us to the Stadium with whispers and squeals of excitement. I catch sight of a new digital billboard I've never seen before.

To my surprise, both my and Coral's faces fill the pixels. We're smiling. I recognise the pictures as school photos taken before we were chosen.

I look so . . . young.

Underneath our faces reads: *the heroes of Juliet, chosen for you by the Shepherds.*

Then I understand. The scaffolding, the vibe that something has changed. It *has*. *We've* changed it. Two of the most popular Demonstrators and both from Juliet.

To me, *heroes of Juliet* equals *we're making people rich.*

I don't look up again until we're led through the depths of the Stadium. I've gotten accustomed to the interior of these places; each one's built the same. So my suspicions rise when we walk past the usual room with the archway. I recognise soundproof walls as we scan into our waiting room. If it's anything like the room in city Hotel, that door opposite us will open to reveal a staircase to the archway.

Thankfully, the Stadium workers don't strap any clamps onto us, just hand us the usual leather belt, sword, and for Coral, gun.

As we wait for the workers to open the door, Coral lets her hair down. Right then, I wish I had let the makeup girl work her magic on me, too.

The stuff plasters Coral's face; she has dark liner rimming her eyes and stark powder bronzing her cheekbones. Her long hair has been curled at the ends. The red ringlets bounce down her back and contrast with the white uniform, which sets off her crimson lips.

I, on the other hand, am dressed in a tighter version of my school uniform. My face is untouched, and my hair's scraped back into a pony tail with the pin sticking out of it like I've been caught in a game of darts.

It's a good job we're on the same side. Otherwise, I know who the crowd would be rooting for.

I wonder how many people from school will be in the stands tonight. Not that it matters now. That life belongs to someone else. I'm not Sola 'tease me and laugh and pretend you can't hear anything I say' Herrington anymore.

I'm a Demonstrator.

The thick silence is punctured by the workers scanning the door open. Coral stares ahead, shoulders back, head up, sword ready. Tall, toned, and beautiful. The loaded gun on her belt sways with her hips. Before we step out of the room, she looks over her shoulder at me.

'I've got your back, sis.' Even though her tone isn't sarcastic, I know she's laughing at me.

I grip my sword, breathe deeply, and follow her out into the open.

The Stadium has transformed since my tryout. Yellow lights lick the edges of each stand, barrier, and gate. Dramatic music blasts as we enter, and outdoor heaters droop over the crowd like super long walking sticks hanging from the ceiling. Through the incoherent screams and general buzz blurting from the stands, I hear the audience chanting, 'Ju-li-et, Ju-li-et!'

In all my visits, I've never seen the place so packed. People squeeze into every available space. The steps are no longer clear aisles that run up and down the stands but seats to anyone who can fit onto them. It reminds me of the cash machines in old arcades. One more penny and the people leaning over the barriers would spill onto the sands and never stop falling.

Coral looks up at her fans through thick eyelashes, smiling and drinking in the applause. I turn to the gate, crouching with one foot forwards. Let's get this over with so Coral can go home, and I can finish my tour in peace.

The familiar clicking sound causes the audience to hush and the music dims. Up on the screen, Coral bites her lip and grins at the gate. I may not agree with the Shepherds' way of enforcing their power, but right this second, I see that Coral was born to do this. To kill others and make herself feel good. I put another step between us and calm the raging fuzz that overtakes my mind.

More clicks.

Breathe, breathe, breathe.

Iron, death, dirt—the stench of my tryout comes rushing back. I look to Coral, but I see William. I didn't want this today. Not when I have to be ready for whatever comes out of that gate. After my last Demonstration, I *know* there'll be a twist.

I say William's name and feel him squeeze my hand, reminding me he was stabbed on these very sands.

I swear, and the sound of it pulls me back. I'm swaying forwards, listening to Coral scoffing beside me.

My vision clears in time to see the gate finish its upward slide. Just before two opponents step out onto the sands.

My mouth goes slack.

I stare at Mr and Mrs Winters.

forty-three

THE FOUR OF US stare across the arena in silence. I gasp, and it sounds like a can being opened. The colour slips from Coral's face. She drops her sword, takes two running steps towards her mother, but stops.

Seconds go by so slowly, the stillness so tangible that I can taste the excitement emitting from the crowd. They take in the scene greedily and in their expressions is knowledge. I wonder how many bought tickets purely for this moment.

Mr Winters straightens up. He's thinner than before. His skin so grey it's almost see-through. He doesn't drop his scythe. Coral's mother looks to her daughter, then to her husband. She grips her staff, holding it in front of her chest like a baby.

That's when Coral begins to back away. Without taking her eyes from her family, she bends down and gropes around in the sand for her weapon.

Even seeing Coral's face—desolate and empty in the screen—I can't bring myself to feel anything less than loathing for her. But no one deserves this. Not even her.

I walk over, breaking the stalemate.

'Coral, I can do this. You don't have to,' I shout. It seems to travel through the whole Stadium.

She turns to me, venom in her eyes.

'You'd like that. Kill my parents while I watch? Take all my glory? Go stab yourself, Sola.' She spits at me, and I jump back to avoid it. The audience hiss and boo but I don't know who for. Perhaps it's just because no one has died yet.

Coral advances. A thin lipped determination settles onto her features. Her mouth moves as she talks to herself. They form the same words over and over. 'They're already dead. They're already dead.' Her parents separate, and Coral looks lost over which to follow.

My throat goes dry. I shiver just standing still in this flimsy uniform. So I do the only thing I can do well in the Stadium.

I overtake Coral, and I fight.

Coral's mother is first. She's no good with the staff. I knock it from her hands in seconds. She keeps looking behind me to her daughter. I can't tell whether it's for help or in—

Pain splits across the side of my head. My knees scrape against the sand as I fall forwards. I rush to get up. My left eye throbs where I was punched. I look around, and Coral takes my place in front of her mother, turning her back on me. So much for trying to help.

'Isn't she beautiful?'

That voice which triggers my automatic retch reflex creeps over the sands. Mr Winters stands paces away, watching the two women in his family stare each other down.

'I think she's going to kill us.' He speaks leisurely, as if the whole thing is some mix up and we'll all have a good laugh later. Eventually, his cold eyes settle on my face. There's the scent of decaying soil in the air. Is it possible for someone to smell like death?

'I've always liked you, Sola.'

Ha! He practically chokes on my name. I keep one eye on him, one on Coral and her mother.

'Perhaps you could take her on? If you kill her, they might cancel the Demonstration.'

A horrible crack rings out. Coral has broken her mother's neck. I gag.

'Please, Sola. I always rooted for your father. I was going to promote him.' He speaks faster now, backing away despite Coral not moving from the spot where she sits cradling her mother's shoulders.

It's up to me to finish this fight. I breathe deeply, ignore the throbbing pain from the side of my face, and leap forwards to attack.

Mr Winters is a surprisingly good fighter. His narrow eyes take in everything while his arms dart to deflect my blows. His scythe allows him to block from a distance, and he glides backwards, not letting me an inch closer. Yet this kind of parry is hard to sustain—a perfect example of Gideon's words: *if you can't run this field forty times before you go out to fight, you'll lose.*

Mr Winters' moves become less definite; his arm slower, less precise. My sword collides against his curved blade and his face twists as he tries to push me off. I throw my weight forwards. He stumbles back, panic and desperation breaking his usually calm gaze. He keeps looking behind me although I know no one is there.

I press on, waiting for that weakness in his defence. Eventually, his thin head shakes, and his cold stare finds its way into my eyes.

'I always helped you, Sola. I could have told Shepherd Fines about the sword that boy gave you in your tryout,' he says, and his words resonate within me. 'That night I saw you sneaking around at Zulu, I could have reported you.'

My hand wavers in the air. He's right. I stare at the white grains of sands below as if they could give me answers. Could he have cared, all this time? Shepherd Fines already knew about the sword, but my creeping around—

The crowd gasps. There's a red hot burning in my belly. Far too late, I figure out the ruse.

Stupid, stupid!

Blood seeps through my school uniform, spreading like a river over my shirt then down my leg. It's dark. Darker than it should be. I see the large slash to my stomach in the screen and then up close. It doesn't look real. It doesn't even hurt. Just burns. Mr Winters draws his scythe back, the blade now painted crimson.

All I hear is silence. Mr Winters swings for my neck. I block him instinctively. My body works for me, deflecting and attacking, not letting his blade come close again. I'm persisting, but resisting is much harder. The slow burning churns into a searing torment deep in my gut. I just think of injections. It's like the sickening pain as someone roots around with a needle inside of you, trying to find your vein. All you can do is sit there, waiting . . . waiting.

Energy is seeping from my body. I stagger forwards, the scene before me blurring.

Mr Winters' scythe clatters to the floor, the sound like claws tapping a table. I didn't even realise I'd knocked his weapon away. My limbs are so heavy. Sleep calls to me. Why is the sand so unsteady? I draw my sword back. Mr Winters doubles in my vision and all four eyes widen in terror.

'Sola, your father. He's watching. You don't want him to see you do this, do you?' Even now, his voice seems full of authority. I'm not sure if he's alluding to the fact that *he* could be my father. My feet stumble to keep me upright.

'My dad would understand,' I say. Using both hands, I swing my sword down and separate both of Mr Winters' heads from both his bodies. The last I see of him is a flash of memory: him standing in my kitchen the day I was chosen for the Debt.

Far away, people cheer. Every sense except my smell has dimmed. Metal, iron and rot. It's revolting. I wrap an arm around my belly. It's hot, but I'm so, so cold. I squeeze, try to stop the blood. I need to keep some for me. Medics are coming this way . . . so is something else.

A person. Rushing towards me. A sword high above her head. Coral.

A medic grabs to stop her and she cuts him down.

I back away on treacherous feet. Then I run. RUN!

Under the gateway where the prisoners were. Down through dark tunnels. Hands meeting stone and metal—I bounce off the walls and force myself onwards. I skid past workers who yell that I can't be here, but I keep on going, hoping they will slow Coral down. I'm leaving a trail of red in my wake. It reminds me of an old fairy tale. I fall. My knees cracking against a hard, cold floor. I force myself up, running down steps, forcing doors open, setting off alarms. Trying not to remember that Coral has a gun.

Only when I'm deep into the bowels of the Stadium do I slow down. No footsteps behind me. No screams for my death. I stumble towards a door. Something is jamming it. My palm finds the scanner but it beeps red. With the last of my strength I curl my fingers around the side, wrench it open and force it shut behind me. Coral can't get to me here.

I slither down the back of the door with a low screech as my blood lets me slide. I land in a heap on the floor. I'm pretty sure I'm dying.

For some reason, that's funny. I think I'm giggling. Tears wet my face. My body shudders violently. My eyes adjust to the dark. I squint and blink to make sure I'm not seeing things.

Just inches away from my leg, someone's outstretched hand is curled into a ball like a baby's is when it's born. They're dead.

I need to get up. They're everywhere, covering every inch of the ground in this low-roofed basement. No—wait. They aren't dead. Their chests heave. They're alive and for some reason, that's worse. Blacked-out windows built into the walls blur in my vision.

Maybe I'm hallucinating. Death must be catching up with me.

Or the tryouts. They might be here for the tryouts.

Yet something's not right. My brain is slow, useless. I force myself to think through the fog. On each of their brown uniforms there's a piece of paper pinned to their chests. I crawl to the nearest person. A man. He's old. Maybe seventy.

The ink on the paper wobbles before my eyes.

December Sales—Juliet—East Bound

Flight booked: 2nd Jan 2100

I don't know what that means! Despair catches up with me in overwhelming waves. How can I help? I can't help. I'm dying.

My eyes struggle to stay open despite the cold adrenaline pulsing through me. I grapple at the door now. Need to get out of here. Need to breathe. Need to tell someone—

'Hey, Kim! Quick! One's awake!'

A voice from somewhere—behind the windows? It's muffled. I open my mouth, but there's no sound. My bloody fingers scrape at the door. Someone's walking towards me. Must be another entrance somewhere. Using all my strength, I haul myself upon the door one more time. It doesn't budge. I slide down.

'She's wounded. Wait a minute . . .'

The voice dims. I blink as the blackout edges in.

I list the things I know for certain.

-I'm dead.

forty-four

VOICES. Smothered. Then shouting. One of them is familiar. I want to say their name but I can't move. The dark turns to grey. I breathe in and awake a deep burning down my throat.

Needles. No more needles, *please.*

Red light blazes behind my eyes. I'm being dragged—no, carried.

'What did she see?'

Angry, worried voices.

I blink. Shepherd Fines' face hovers above me. He's joined by medics with sanitary masks. They stare with big, goggling eyes.

'She's waking . . .'

Another long needle comes towards me. I think of Mr Winters, clench my eyes tight. Then there's nothing but the black cold.

CR

A DRY, FIRM HAND strokes my forehead. With each touch, I wake a little more. A hard pillow supports my head, while a smooth cotton sheet winds around my legs and over my arms. Something beeps. The stench of antiseptic and bittersweet medicine surges up my nose.

253

Before I've even opened my eyes, I check my body. Bare skin meets my hand. I'm totally starkers, but at least my stomach's not oozing blood. I touch the usual array of bumps along my skin that signal my collection of scars, but I stop when I reach a thick gash just right of my belly button; there's the fuzz of hundreds of tiny stitches. The pain has disappeared along with every other sense in my body. I don't want to think what's in the IV drip that lives in the crook of my elbow.

'Sweetheart, you're awake,' a smooth, soft voice says. For some reason, it puts me on edge. I open my eyes gradually. Shepherd Fines sits next to me, stroking my forehead.

'What happened?' I croak. My mouth's as dry as a fur rug.

'How . . . how much do you remember?' Shepherd Fines asks, his voice notching higher. When I look at him, I mean, *really* look at him, it's the first time I've ever seen him worried. A small part of my drowsy mind tells me to shut up. Whispers that I shouldn't say the truth. But my mouth seems to talk without my permission.

'Bodies,' I say. 'Sleeping people with signs on their front. They were being sold . . .' I trail off.

'I was afraid you were going to say that.' He sighs, looking at me as if I were in a coffin, not a bed.

'Don't worry. The Liaisons wanted to kill you. Announce that you died of the wound, but I wouldn't let them. I'd never let them.' He clicks his tongue. 'I can't stop them telling the other Shepherds, though.' Another long, whistling sigh.

'What's going to happen to those people?' I ask, although deep inside my throbbing mind I think I already know.

Shepherd Fines peers around although we're in a private room. He takes hold of my hand through the thin sheet. I'm way too conscious of the fact I'm naked.

'The Debt, Sola. It's huge.' He gives a little chuckle. 'We owe nearly every country out there billions. You

Demonstrators earn a tiny bit in ticket sales, but that mostly goes into keeping the specific cities happy. It doesn't touch the real deficit.'

My head hurts. What's this got to do with—

'Every month, we choose people to help us pay the Debt. The young and reasonably healthy of those who are chosen go into the tryouts. That was your journey. Others, however, are sacrificed to help us get this country back to what it once was. Great Britain.' He says the words with reference, pride.

'No, they're not. They come and work here at the camp,' I say, although I already know that's not true. I'm like a kid trying to cover their ears when they're told their pet has died.

'I'm surprised you haven't already worked out that's not the case. Many Demonstrators question that lie rather quickly. That's why they don't survive their final fight.'

I recoil at his answer. But my desperation to understand gets the better of me.

'How?' I whisper. 'How do the others help the country?'

'Through sales, of course. Each person is worth thousands of pounds. Some countries will pay five, maybe six figures for the right medical experiment subject. Others want servants.' He looks at me through the corner of his eyes. His eyebrows slant.

'Of course, my dear, people would object if they knew. My father used to say everyone wants to be a hero. They don't understand the practicalities of our situation.' He speaks as though this is happening to some lowly beings disconnected from us.

I shake my head. All I see is William's young face, the word 'Greece' next to his name on Shepherd Fines' digipad.

'How can you be okay with this?' I ask, my voice small and breathy. 'Selling people?'

'Now now, my darling. You're tired and recovering and have a serious amount of drugs in your system. It might take a while to get used to, but please don't make a fuss. I'm hoping to persuade the others that you don't remember the holding room.'

'But why us? Don't the other countries care?' I'm not sure how much sense I'm making. Shepherd Fines looks down. Something registers in his features. It resembles regret.

'The citizens of these places don't know, of course. The leaders . . . well, how they see it is that we got ourselves into this mess, and they're helping us by purchasing our people and reducing our Debt. They wouldn't want to risk a revolt by using their own subjects.

'I know you all think you're reporting to us Shepherds, but we're reporting to people, too. We just owe *so* much money.'

I suck my breath back in huge, aching gulps. My skin burns hot. I suddenly want to scream, to rage against Shepherd Fines and scratch and him and hit him and—

'Why have you done this to me?' I shout, but it sounds like a sob.

'What?'

'If I'm not paying back the Debt—' I gasp, needing more air. 'If I'm not helping anyone, why have you made me kill people? Why have I killed so many people?' I ask the last question to myself.

Looking perplexed, Shepherd Fines takes a moment to answer.

'Now, now. It's obvious. Why do you think they are called Demonstrations? It's to *demonstrate* our power. Do you not realise what an uprising we would have if cities knew we were selling people at random? Whenever someone works it out, they go into the Stadium. And every other person watching knows how easily they can be eradicated.

'You're doing so much *good*, Sola. You keep the crowd entertained, their minds elsewhere while reminding them they can't change a thing.'

At my expression, he hastily adds, 'Look, I don't like what we're doing, but an uprising would only increase our Debt. Then we'd have to pursue more extreme measures to keep everyone contained.

'You and I, we're all doing this for the greater good. Once we're out of Debt, we will stop selling people. Eventually, as the cities are gradually built up, the Demonstrations will stop, and this nation will emerge as one of the best.'

I look away. Tears are pooling in my eyes, and I don't want him to see. I hate him. But I won't die now for knowing too much.

I pull my sheet up to my chin just like Tabby did days ago.

'Coral?' I ask.

Shepherd Fines grimaces one of those 'what-can-you-do' faces.

'She requested to stay at the camp as a Demonstrator. Of course with her ticket-selling ability, we had to grant her wish. The family of the medic she killed will be compensated, naturally. And you have round the clock protection while you're in here. Not that my best Demonstrator can't look after herself.' He winks. 'Anyway, I'm glad you're feeling better,' he says, although I never mentioned how I felt. 'I should go and blow all this under the carpet.'

Clicking his tongue, he stands and leans over my bed. He quickly lands a kiss on my cheek before stroking my forehead once more and heading to the door. Before he reaches it, I call him back. I have one last question.

'Sir, those brothers . . . are they sold?'

He nods slowly.

'Yes, my dear. One had anomalies in his test results. In a situation such as that, we had to sacrifice both of them, so the other wouldn't cause a fuss. I hope you understand.'

With a final smile, he turns his back to me. The light flickers off when he leaves.

For a horrid second, I wonder if he's lying about protecting me the way he lied about protecting Mr Winters. But the fear dissolves as soon as it comes. Although I never meant to, I know I make Shepherd Fines feel good about himself. He won't do anything to hurt his 'best Demonstrator.'

Gulping down air, I clutch my sheet before throwing it over my head and curling up in a ball. It settles back on me like a cool caress.

forty-five

TWO DAYS AFTER THE NEW YEAR, I'm dismissed, and I can't get out of the Medic's Cabin quick enough. Straight away, I run over to the field where Dylan trains the Demonstrators I fought on Christmas day. He didn't visit me, and although I know why, it doesn't stop me missing him.

At the sight of his floppy hair and kind face, my worries subside slightly. I give a little wave.

He stops still and even from here I see his face change. He sets the Demonstrators all-too-familiar fitness drills and sprints over, stopping an arm's length away. His blue eyes run over my body. It makes me smile. Instead of admiring me, he's checking for injuries.

'How's your stomach?' he asks, serious now. I grin, pulling my shirt up to show him my smile of a scar. His eyebrows raise and he exhales slowly.

'I don't want to say it, but—'

'I should have seen it coming. I know.'

He chuckles and steps forwards. Although I want so much to greet him properly, to repeat our perfect kiss from days ago and hold him close, breathing in every part of him, I throw a glance to Shepherd Fines' watchtower.

Dylan follows my line of sight, steps back, and straightens his back. This is the reason he hasn't visited.

259

We're all too aware that Shepherd Fines cannot know about us. Not with my final fight so imminent.

'Something has happened,' I say, my voice low and grave.

'Did he hurt you?'

'No, it's not that. It's . . . I found something. In the Stadium. I've known for a while something was up but couldn't figure it out.'

I breathe in deeply and glance around. The trainees are too far away to hear us, but I still whisper. I tell Dylan everything from seeing William on Shepherd Fines' digipad to why no one who is chosen ever arrives at the camp to 'work'. I tell him how Shepherd Fines is the only reason I'm still alive. How the Demonstrations are just a distraction. I end on my fear for Alixis' baby; that he or she will end up as another number for the January sales.

Throughout my rant, Dylan nods solemnly. Eventually he runs his hands through his hair, massages his temples, and then looks directly at me, eyes blazing decisively.

'What they're doing is awful, Sola.' He sighs. 'But you can't fix it.'

My expression must say it all. He continues, faster now.

'Aye, I know you want to save the world, but you have to look after yourself. Keep Shepherd Fines on your side until your tour ends. Don't mention the sales, and the other Shepherds will believe you didn't see anything. Get back to Juliet and eventually you'll be forgotten.'

I chew on my nails, shaking my head. 'Fine. That's me sorted out. What about William? What about Alixis' baby?'

As much as I hate myself for it, the bottom of my eyes begins to sting. There must still be some medication in my system making me emotional. I duck my head and speak to my boots.

'I hate this,' I say sheepishly, aware I sound like a child. 'I'm so angry *all* the time. I hate Shepherd Fines, he terrifies me, but I've tried so hard thinking he's a good person that I can't give up now. I really hate Coral, but she killed her *mother* last week. Worst of all, I hate myself for everything I've done. I can't breathe with all this *hate*! I just want—I just want to be *me* again.'

I half expect him to answer how I would—to say I need to grow up and that you can't always get what you want. Instead, he tucks his finger underneath my chin and lifts my head so that I'm looking into those endless blue eyes.

'Aye. You want to see the stars.'

What I said to him on that trampoline sounds magical when he repeats it. I smile, relishing in the warmth of his finger still hooked under my chin.

He casts a glance over his shoulder at his trainees. 'Will you meet me tonight? By the Wetpod. We can't talk here.'

'Our scan chips will show we're together on Debtbook if we go in there. I'm worried about—' I pause. I don't exactly want Dylan to know I'm scared of what Shepherd Fines might do to him if he found out about us.

Dylan takes his hand away and his gaze skims my face. My heart lurches.

'Don't worry, I'll figure something out. Just be there at midnight.'

I nod. 'You don't get to tell me what to do though, remember?' I say it like a joke, alluding to our fight that led to the most amazing moment of my life so far. Dylan gives a firm shake of his head.

'I don't get to *tell* you. I do get to *ask*.'

We stand there for a moment, grinning our sad smiles.

Just then Tabby steps out from behind Dylan's legs. I jump, which in turn makes her startle.

'Sorry,' she mutters, head down. 'T'others are asking for yer.'

Dylan gives me one last, amazing nod before taking hold of Tabby's shoulders and marching her back to the group.

Tabby's words remind me of what she said to me in the Medic's Cabin. *Where are the others?*

I wish I didn't now know the answer.

forty-six

I COULD KILL DYLAN RIGHT NOW; it's freezing out here. I try to see through the gloom and pull my blue jumper tighter around me. It's still unwashed, because the servers will confiscate it if I leave it out for cleaning. No movement. January frost surrounds me, tainting the whole camp, stealing my breath away and turning it into icy mist.

Leaves rustle behind me. I spin.

Dylan leans out from behind the back wall of the Wetpod, his hair silhouetted against grey surroundings. My heart flips at his wide grin. He beckons me over. Aware of every whispering sound around me, I run lightly on the grass to him.

Once I've tucked myself against the back wall, Dylan checks around the side of the building. I have to stifle a giggle at that, thinking that we might as well be wearing balaclavas and carrying swag bags over shoulders. As soon as he turns to me, though, I can't hold myself back. We've already wasted too much time. I leap close to him and wrap my arms around his neck. By some magical, unspoken agreement, he takes a firm hold of my waist. My smile is echoed on his face. This time, I won't wait for him to kiss me. I stand on tiptoes and brush my lips against his.

He kisses, too, pressing himself closer and moving his hands up my back. I breathe him in, smelling and tasting him all at once. When I run my hand through the bottom of

263

his hair, gently stroking my short nails across his neck, he shivers in what I hope is delight.

Dylan pulls away for a second, yet the cool touch of his nose against mine is like we're still kissing. His eyes run over my face before he nudges me gently with the tip of his nose and finds my lips once more.

Eventually, I pull away. He sways forwards and holds me tighter. I chuckle.

'Is this why you asked me to meet you here?' I whisper.

He murmurs a 'mmm', but it sounds more like a purr, as if he's imagining us doing this all night.

'No. That wouldn't be very gentlemanly would it?' His breath turns into cold haze around us. The hot touch of our arms wrapped around each other contrasts against the ice-cold chill, making me crave him even more.

Reluctantly, I step backwards so that his hands slide from my waist. He tickles my sides as I draw away.

Dylan closes his eyes and takes a deep breath, as if composing himself. My skin and lips are alive from where he touched me.

'Come on then,' he finally says. He takes my hand in his and leads me around to the outer corner of the Wetpod, where a thick drainpipe runs down the building and into the ground.

With no further warning, he grabs hold of the tiny ridges that support the pipe, and hauls himself up.

'What are you doing?' I ask, my voice no longer a whisper. He grunts as he pulls his strong body onto a higher ridge.

'Avoiding the scanners.' He cranes his head to look down at me. 'And I'm not *telling* you to come with me, but it's going to be mighty lonely looking at those stars on my own.' I see a hint of a laugh before he turns back and continues climbing the pipe like a koala.

I stare up at the never-ending Wetpod. It stretches into the sky, leaning as if it were about to topple. One wrong foot, one weak moment, and it's a long, final drop to the ground. Yet the thought of slinking back to camp and returning to my pod shaft without following Dylan is an empty one. Deep down, my mind is already made up.

I climb.

My fingers slip on the ridges as I strain to keep hold. Dylan is already way ahead of me, and there's no way I'm letting myself fall farther behind. I steady my breathing and imagine I'm in the Stadium. *Persistence and resistance.* And don't look down, in this case.

I think back to when I was a little kid and used to ride the lift up to the highest floor in my block of flats so I could be closer to the sky. This is like that. Apart from that I have no walls to keep me safe here, I'm breaking the rules in the Book of Red Ink and, once I reach the top, I'm going to be alone with a man I really, *really* like.

I get a pang of anxiety, which is not good considering I'm about thirty feet into the air. What's Dylan expecting? He's three years older than me. What if he has no idea he was and is my only kiss? What if he's expecting . . . *more?*

My fingers slip. Crap. I slide down a few feet before desperately grabbing onto the last ridge. I cling on so hard I'm practically straddling the pipe as I try to catch my breath.

'You okay down there?' Dylan calls down. The sound is too loud. It does nothing to calm my raging heartbeat.

I don't know. Am I okay? When I'm with Dylan, all I want are his hands on me, his lips on mine, his voice in my ear, and to hear that amazing laugh. He makes me forget the hate and despair which consume me every other second of the day. But . . . I don't know.

With a mixture of fear and excitement so intense that my body seems to thud with my heartbeat, I follow Dylan up and over the top of the Wetpod.

The top 'level' is exactly how I'd imagined it: open, with an oval pool built into the roof. It's as if I could stretch up on tiptoes and touch the sky. Small blue lights shine from the bottom of the pool, illuminating the still water. If I lean over the rooftop's edge, I can see the fields stretch out before me. They meet the gate and the landing pad. I can even see the fence that marks camp's perimeter in the near distance. The willow trees sway through the silver darkness. I think of my fight with Dylan and grin.

'How did you know the way up here?' I ask.

'I've climbed up before,' he says.

My heart flips painfully, my mind taunting me with visions of him and another girl standing where we are now. I look away.

'On my own,' he adds. I hope he couldn't read my expression. In my peripheral vision, I see him trying to catch my eye. I look up as he walks towards me. His hand curls around mine, leaning in close so that my jumper touches his polo shirt.

'Do you want to get in?' he asks.

'I don't have my costume.'

'Never stopped you before.' He's smiling, I can tell from his voice. I can't help but beam, too.

'All right,' I say, looking up. 'Just look away until I'm under the water.'

He squeezes my hand, chews on his lip, and turns, but keeps his eyes on me until the last second. It occurs to me that Dylan's seen me in my underwear before, when we swam together just one level underneath this one, but tonight is . . . different.

I pull off my jumper and trousers and sink into the glorious warm water. I can't watch Dylan get undressed, so I lean my back against the wall nearest to him, looking over the water and away from the door. There's some rustling, followed by a huge splash as he jumps over my head and dive bombs into the pool.

How does he do that—make everything so fun yet intense at the same time? I kick off from the side and swim over to where he's surfacing.

He nods his head for me to follow and backstrokes to the side of the pool. His clothes are close to the edge, and he hunts through the pile. After a moment, he pulls out his digipad and taps a few times.

'I know this isn't *exactly* what you wanted, but . . .' Leaning back, he holds the digipad up to the sky. I gasp. His screen has transformed into a midnight blue, with all of the stars illuminated in the image of the sky. They hang on the screen and behind it, I see them blinking through the layer of fog in the real world. When he moves the digipad, the image moves, too.

I take the screen and walk slowly through the shallow end, giggling at the constellations as they form before my eyes.

'How did you—?'

'I hacked into some of the forbidden digipad files. This is a really old one.'

His hands touch my waist under the water as he stands behind me. We explore the sky together, trying to see the stars from the digipad in the polluted sky above. It doesn't matter that we don't find them.

When I've allowed the images of Hercules the hero and Draco the dragon to burn crooked lines in my mind, I set his digipad on the edge of the pool. Now there's nothing left to distract us, I twist slowly to face Dylan. His hands lightly glide over my waist as I turn. I meet his eyes. A second later, he's kissing me. I explore his back with my hands; his bare skin is like a hot lamp.

I wrap my arms around his neck, kissing him deeper.

Forget floating in the water—*this* is what it feels like to fly. I never imagined love could be this damn good. He walks with me until my back touches the cool wall. My heart flips continuously.

Once I get the urge to wrap my legs around his hips, I pull away, breathing heavily. I rest my head on his wet shoulder.

As I look around the twinkling camp, I sigh.

'What am I going to do?'

It has to be clear from my defeated tone that I'm talking about the bodies I found. Dylan strokes my hair.

'I don't like to say it,' he says softly, 'but there's nothing you can do.'

'You know, I even think the other cities are safe,' I say, voicing something I've been considering for a while. 'The Shepherds don't want us to travel, because their secrets would be harder to keep if the cities communicated. So they've created this hatred between us all. We're so terrified of each other we've created our own borders we can't cross.'

Dylan murmurs something that sounds like an agreement.

'Our scan chips aren't a way of keeping us safe. It's so the Shepherds would know if we dared to try to travel between cities. All of this, just for some stupid Debt that the Demonstrations don't even pay back.'

I shake my head against his chest, thinking of the poor people who've been sold to who-knows-where. 'What do you think? ' I ask Dylan, realising I've never actually heard him voice any opinion on the Shepherds or the way we live.

'I try not to think about any of this stuff,' he says.

'Why?'

'Because there's nothing we can do.'

I look up at him.

'Think about it,' he continues. 'All of us are suffering because of this Debt, even the Shepherds. It can't be easy, trying to keep a country together. What if we gave up, and the whole nation became slaves, or servants or test subjects to bigger, richer places? At least this way, some of us are happy. And maybe people born after us have a chance for a future.'

'But surely we could find another way? Maybe if someone else took over? I mean, Shepherd Fines mentioned an uprising . . . '

'Aye, and he was right. An uprising, revolution or whatever would mean more deaths and would cost more than our nation has in the bank. Then all of those people sold would have been for nothing. Who would lead us then? Another bunch of people faced with a bigger problem.'

I rest my head back on Dylan's chest. He holds me tighter and kisses the top of my head.

'I know what you mean,' I murmur. 'It makes sense to wait this out, but I'd still rather fight, if I had the choice.'

Dylan's stomach moves against my own as he laughs.

'Aye. No one fights like you do.'

I'm about to respond when something shifts in the air. I tense. One look up to Dylan tells me he feels it, too.

Someone's watching us.

I look to the door.

Tabby stands in the threshold, clouded in the gloom. She hangs her head when I look over, her hands twisting together. I'm about to breathe a sigh of relief when another shape appears behind her.

Shepherd Fines.

He just takes one look at us. He nods, almost to himself, and turns back down the stairs. Dylan still holds me tight, and we're both left looking over at the child I saved from the tryouts. The light reflects on her wet cheeks.

'I'm sorry.' It's half a whisper, half a sob. 'She told me she'd find t'others what were chosen if I told on you.'

Neither of us answer, and Tabby scuttles away after Shepherd Fines. It doesn't take a genius to work out who 'she' is.

Dylan swears, his voice breaking the silence. The water splashes gently as he turns away. Another curse, this time louder. The pool's hard edge scratches my thighs as I haul myself out. The winter air bites every goose bump.

'Are you going after him? Tell him you still love him. Tell him I forced you if you have to.' Dylan hisses.

'No. I'm going to be honest.' I struggle into my clothes.

'Honesty is going to get you killed! Is that what you want?'

I pause at the doorway. 'No, Dylan, it's not. But there's no way for us both to get out of this. Just be careful, okay?'

With that, I shuffle my feet into my shoes and leave the light of the pool behind.

forty-seven

MY KNOCK on Shepherd Fines' office door barely makes a sound. For a moment I don't think he's going to let me in, but the door slides open. I squint through the bright light and step in blindly.

Shepherd Fines sits behind his desk, head down. My favourite copper wire lamp lies smashed on its side, broken fragments of rose-tinted glass spread across the floor like they're reaching for the exit. A tiny sliver of blood slides out of Shepherd Fines' clenched fist. My instinct is to help him, but I hold back, knowing anything I do will be wrong.

A lifetime later, Shepherd Fines looks up. Pain flashes in his eyes, only to be replaced with fury. When it's clear he isn't going to speak, I take a deep breath.

'I'm sorry, Sir. I didn't want you to find out like . . .' I trail off. My excuse sounds weak even to me.

His eyes narrow. I continue.

'I know you believe you like me, and I like you, most of the time. I think you're funny and energetic and great to be around. But you remedy everything with control. I mean, you tried to drug me! What you and the other Shepherds do, I know it's not your fault, but it's wrong.'

'The Shepherds do not need advice from you.'

I flinch at his tone. It's like all the hours spent together have disappeared. All that time laughing over his anecdotes, drinking late into the night together, and even our 'relationship status' on Debtbook—none of it matters. He sits before me as only what he is: a Shepherd. My ruler. One of the seven people who control everyone in this country.

'I wasn't—'

'I didn't let you in for a discussion. The twist in your final Demonstration has been decided. You will fight another Demonstrator. Coral Winters.'

I laugh because he's joking. He's joking. He has to be joking.

'She will be armed, you will not. She will have a gun, you will not. She will live.'

He doesn't need to finish the sentence.

'You—you can't . . . I have followers!' My voice is stronger than I feel.

He clicks his tongue. 'Followers don't approve when the final Demonstration seems unfair. You have refused a gun throughout your tour. You hardly ever fight with the weapon you're given. The hatred between you and Miss Winters is common knowledge. I'm afraid the crowd will see this as your chance to prove what you've been preaching this whole time.'

Another knock at the door. It slides open, and Coral herself steps in like an evil spirit summoned because we dared to speak her name.

'Was I right?' Coral asks sweetly. For some reason, I envision her curling her tongue around Shepherd Fines' ear. I think I dreamt it once.

'Yes. Thank you, Miss Winters,' Shepherd Fines says, although his voice is poisonous.

'You're injured! Shall I get a medic?' she asks, stepping towards Shepherd Fines.

'I'm perfectly well. Is that all, Miss Winters?'

Coral looks from me, back to him, and hesitates. Perhaps she hoped she would take my place once I was usurped as his favourite. Or perhaps—I recognise the flicker of fear in her expression—she's afraid. Afraid of leaving us alone in case he changes his mind.

'This means that Sola and I will fight, doesn't it?' Her usually controlled voice goes up at the end.

He nods.

'Fantastic. I'll do you proud, Sir. No one should make you look like a fool.'

I can't tell whether Coral is trying to manipulate him or speaking from the heart. Her face is serious as she bows her head slightly. Her hair tumbles over her shoulder and with a quick, hard glance to me, she leaves the office as soon as the door reopens.

The silence traps Shepherd Fines and me together once again.

'Sir, do you wish for me to die?' I whisper. No games. I'm not playing him. I only want to know. He looks away quickly, his face stressed as if swallowing a particularly large painkiller. But as soon as I register the expression, he's staring at me coldly again.

'Stop it, Sola. Stop treating me like an idiot.' Each word is pronounced perfectly, his flat voice full of control. 'Pretending to like me. Pretending we were friends. I protected you once. Now, you are no longer my concern.'

Shepherd Fines activates the door behind me from his desk. It slides open, my cue to leave. I turn to go, but can't help myself. I pause.

'You once said you didn't want to be like Dr Frankenstein. For the record, I don't think you are. You're a good person made to do bad things. You're the monster. Just like me.'

'Great stuff,' he says in a hollow tone. 'Goodbye, Miss Herrington.'

#

I TRAIN. Dylan refuses to believe that I'm going to die. At first, it's irritating, this never ending denial, but his fantasies begin to sweep me away, too. Maybe this doesn't have to be the end. Maybe I haven't killed seventy-three people just to lose a fight I never stood a chance of winning. Maybe I can find a way to survive.

So every day I'm not Demonstrating, I train. I'm in the middle of a parry with Dylan when the date of my final Demonstration goes on Debtbook.

20th January 2100.

Seventeen days.

My followers sky rocket. I hear the tickets are sold out within minutes. The Shepherds double the price of downloading the live footage. There's even an application that allows you to vote for whoever you think will win.

When Alixis checks the current results, she winces. That's all I need to know about that.

I even consider blackmailing Shepherd Fines. I know *so* much. I could tell the other Shepherds that it was Fines who told me about the monthly sales and get him into trouble. Or, I can say I will kill myself before the big fight so that he loses all the money for the tickets. But both of those threats are suicide, and I think Fines knows me well enough to know I'm not the kind of girl to give up on my own life.

No, it's time to face up to the situation I've made for myself.

Instead of counting down the days until my fight, I tick off the Demonstrations. City Foxtrot—where I practise fighting with my left hand. In Echo, I don't let myself kick. Right before my fight in Delta, I run laps until I hit the wall, and enter the Stadium exhausted—that was risky, considering the two contestants ended up being ex-Herd officers. I attempt—and fail—to keep my eyes closed the whole way through my Demonstration in city Charlie, and I nearly meet my maker in Bravo after refusing to eat the day before.

In Alpha, the biggest, most affluent city I've ever visited, I request for the contestant to be armed with a gun. The Liaisons comply, but it turns out they only put a blank in. I guess they can't let me die before my final fight. It's a good job too, because the blank fires right at me. My body becomes a canvass of cuts and bruises.

I don't see Shepherd Fines in those two weeks. His office light is sometimes on, but the few times I've knocked on his door, I've been ignored. My dad's profile is constantly open on my digipad, and each time I see that's he's safe, guilt pangs through me at thinking that Shepherd Fines would harm him. My life is a pendulum, relentlessly swinging in between assurance and paranoia. Fear and determination.

Four days before our fight, I spot Gideon training Coral. Gideon, who probably saved my life when he became my trainer months ago by pushing me harder than Dylan would have. Gideon, who still hates me for my connection to Shepherd Fines. Who is training another girl to kill me.

My tongue stings with how hard I bite it to stop me from crying out in frustration. They've obviously been watching my fights. Coral trains with her right arm tied behind her back. Her left arm darts out like a viper, hitting home again and again.

'She's taking every advantage away from me!' I scream when I reach the oak tree where Dylan and Alixis are waiting. It's unusually warm for January, and the air tastes stagnant, like a damp towel at the bottom of the laundry basket. I brush Dylan's hand away from my shoulder as I pace in front of the tree.

'Every time I think I'm getting ahead, she's there, doing it better than me. She's got a sword and a gun. What more does she want?'

'She wants you dead,' Alixis says casually.

In the silence that follows, she looks up from her digipad. At least she has the courtesy to look sheepish.

'Sorry, but it's true. Think fast.' She launches her digipad towards me and I catch it easily. The screen displays Coral's profile. Her picture is an insanely beautiful headshot of her after a Demonstration. She's updated her status as:

Coral Winters has an annoying itch which she is looking forwards to getting rid of. Only four more days!!

I can't help myself. I throw Alixis' digipad back to her, admittedly a little harder than I should ever throw anything at a pregnant woman, and pull my own digipad from my pocket. My hand is shaking as I type out a status. Pathetic? Yes. Childish? Yes. I can't care less.

Sola Herrington thinks an itch can often turn into something serious. Four more days.

Alixis must see the update on her own digipad because she cocks her head to the side.

'Are you suggesting Coral has an STI?' she asks.

'What? No. I'm saying she shouldn't underestimate me.'

'Oh, right.'

I ball my hands so tight my fingernails leave half-moon shapes on my palm. I'm sure I'll find this funny one day. But not right now. It doesn't help that Alixis is still examining my comment, her face scrunched up like she is solving a puzzle.

'I need someone to fight this instant otherwise I'm going to go insane,' I say through gritted teeth.

Dylan steps up to the challenge.

¦

'QUICKER!' Dylan barks. He comes at me again with the gun. I swerve to the side while grabbing his wrist and push it away from my body in a heartbeat. As soon as I have control, I twist his wrist and retrieve the gun.

'You're too slow! Again, quicker this time.'

¦

A NOW-FORGIVEN TABBY sits on my feet as I force my head up to meet my knees.

'Two 'undred an thirty-eight. Come on, Sola!'

She wants me to defeat Coral more than anyone, I think. I've tried telling her none of this is her fault, but she doesn't believe me. I had no idea that she had been sharing a pod with my enemy since she arrived. No idea that Coral promised Tabby she could go home if she did what Coral asked. Once Coral got what she wanted, she cast Tabby and the false promises aside.

I think of the child's expression when she realised she wouldn't be going home to spur me on. My stomach muscles scream out for release.

'Two 'undred an thirty-nine. Just sixty-somethin' more to go!'

¦

'WHY. Do I. Have. To. Punch a bag twice my weight?' I breathe between hooks. 'Coral's. Only. Taller. Than me.'

Dylan walks around the punch bag so he's facing me. 'You answered your own question. In two days, when you hit Coral like you're hitting this bag, she'll feel like a piece of paper. Now more attacking, less talking.'

When I shoot Dylan a murderous look, he grins. I lose what little strength remains in my arms. Just as quickly, Dylan touches the small of my back.

'Stay alive, for me,' he whispers into my ear.

With that, I rein blows down on the bag as if I was fighting for my life right then and there.

CR

MY ARMS SHAKE. I hang from the tree branch like a stick insect. I can't pull myself up. Not again. Sweat drips over my mouth and down my neck. I need to be sick, but I don't have the energy.

'One more pull-up, and I'll get Dylan to take off his top,' Alixis pipes up. I laugh, and hit the ground with a painful thud.

CR

THE NIGHT BEFORE MY FIGHT, I complete Dylan's tailored-to-me obstacle course in under a minute, but strangely enough, my body aches less than it has in two weeks.

As I catch my breath, Dylan announces that my training is officially over. There's a second of silence, before Tabby storms out of the indoor gym in a huff. Alixis shakes her head, pushes off the bench with great effort, and touches my arm on her way past.

'I'll see you back in the pod,' she says softly. Her gaze drifts to Dylan and back to me. I could kiss her in that moment. She always seems to know exactly what to do. It's not fair that she won't get to be a mum; she would be so good at it.

I turn to Dylan as Alixis' footsteps echo through the gym. His strong eyebrows come together, avoiding my gaze as I wrap my arms around his neck and pull him closer to me.

We both know that the time has come. We've got to say goodbye.

Even in the best possible scenario—I win against all odds—we can't be together. I might see him occasionally in Juliet's Stadium, or maybe at another Demonstrator event like Coral's party, but it's not as though we can make casual trips in the spinner to see each other. Even if Dylan gives up Demonstrating, he can only go back to city Victor; the Shepherds will never let us travel between cities.

How can I leave him? This person who makes me laugh and smile and giggle like the nervous school girl I am, who kissed me at a party and made me fall in love with him a little bit more every day since that moment. This person who yesterday told me he's loved me since he saw me bouncing within a torrent of leaves on a trampoline—arms reaching for the sky, sucking in air as if I could find answers in the wind.

He holds me tighter and buries his head into my hair.

'Not yet,' he says, his voice tight. He runs his hand over the back of my neck and kisses my lips so gently that my breath catches. I nod, although in my mind I know we're out of time. I can't leave without hearing him say 'I love you' once more. I can't die without telling him he's one of the best things that's ever happened in my life, even if it did lead to this.

'Okay,' I whisper, making a mental note to force him to say goodbye before we part. 'Let's go and check on Tabby.'

We find her on the brick wall that separates the camp buildings from the servers' homes. She has her arms crossed and looks away angrily when we approach. Seeing her makes me think of William, and I can't decide who has it worse. William, who was too injured to be any use in further Demonstrations and who they sent away to become a slave in Greece. Or Tabby, who will have to kill dozens of people just to get a chance to go home.

'What are you looking at?' I ask gently as I sit next to Tabby. She huffs dramatically and turns farther away. Dylan and I wait in silence, and sure enough, she evidently tires of the silent treatment and looks over. Her lips make an irritated pout.

'It int fair. Why d'yer have to die?'

'She might not,' Dylan says firmly. I give him a subtle shake of my head. This isn't the time.

279

'No one wants me to live more than I do, Tabby.'

She sighs again, less angry this time. 'If *you* die, then *she's* gonna come back here.'

I hate that fact myself.

'Alixis will look out for you. She likes you, you know.' It's true. With Tabby around, Alixis seems to have found something to hang on to again. Her lively personality is creeping back, bit by bit.

'Oh yeah, I know that,' she says as if it's obvious. I can't help but grin. 'But you don't like me. Or you'd come back to live at t' camp if yer won.'

Although I don't glance to him, I know Dylan's looking at me, gauging my reaction. This isn't something we've discussed, but from the moment the idea entered my mind, I've known my answer.

'I can't do that, Tabby. I have a dad to go home too. He'll be lonely without me.'

She stays quiet for a while, as if digesting the fact that I could have a dad too.

'S'pose he would. Oh all right then. You can go. Just tell Lixy she can't forget about me when that babby comes out her belly.'

'Will do.'

'And'— she eyes Dylan suspiciously as she steps down from the low wall. 'Be careful of him,' she whispers. 'He's right funny, always lookin' at yer when yer can't see.'

I stiffen my smile and nod seriously. 'I'll keep my eye on him.'

She seems satisfied, and after all of that merely gives me a little wave and a 'see ya' before skipping off to her pod.

Dylan pulls on a tuft of his hair.

'She makes it sound like I'm some weirdo. It's not like there's anything better to look at.' As soon as he speaks, he cringes. 'I meant because you're beautiful, not just the best out of a bad—'

I laugh. Once I start, I can't stop. This second is why I love Dylan. His voice is so mesmerising, and he's so charming when he tries hard. But as soon as he lets his guard slip, he puts his foot in it totally and completely. I let the giggles take me over, my voice mingling in with his chuckles. Even when tears roll down my cheeks, and I know they aren't from laughing, I keep going. I shuffle closer to Dylan and hold him as tight as I can. We cackle together until there's nothing funny anymore.

forty-nine

ON THE MORNING OF MY FINAL DEMONSTRATION, I wake up cuddling Alixis. I don't even remember snuggling into her bed last night after Dylan and I said a quick, 'see you tomorrow.' One of her arms curls around her slowly rising bump, and the other holds my hand. She smells homely, like wheat cereal after you add the milk. Loving Alixis as much as I do makes me wonder what I used to be thinking with Coral. I believed I was lucky if she spoke to me nicely. I hankered after all my old memories with her, convincing myself she was a nice person 'deep down'. As unromantic as the truth is, I see now that some people are just cruel. Fine, it might be because of some underlying circumstance, but haven't we all been through something? My mum was murdered, for goodness' sake. It didn't make me treat everyone else like garbage.

I finally found people who love me for who I am, not what I can do for them or how I can make them feel better about themselves. Tabby, Alixis, Dylan, and even Shepherd Fines, once upon a time. Even though I'm leaving them all today, one way or another, I'm so happy I met them, thankful I realised the world was a bigger place than city Juliet.

I shuffle away from Alixis and edge out of the bed. This isn't the time to get sentimental.

I've arranged to meet Dylan after my makeup and wardrobe is sorted this morning. But before all of that, there's something else I have to do. I scan out as a voice pips up behind me.

'Sola?'

Alixis leans up in bed, looking at me through bleary eyes. I go to speak but she cuts me off.

'I would have called him Felix.'

I start. Alixis hasn't even acknowledged her baby in months.

'If, for even a moment, you falter tonight, just remember that. She might not deserve to die but if one of you does, it isn't you.' She pauses, looks down at her six-month tummy. 'I would have called him Felix,' she repeats.

I nod. I understand what's she's trying to do, but she needn't worry. I won't hesitate to make the kill.

'Alixis, I—I'm glad I...' I trail off. I'm no good at goodbyes. I thought Dylan has been putting ours off, but maybe I have too. There's nothing to say.

'Look, get out of here and let a pregnant woman rest, would you?' She smiles and gives me her trademark wink. I try to remember every detail of her face but end up staring, unable to move or say anything. Alixis heaves a great sigh, jokingly rolling her watery eyes before flopping back down in the bed.

It's easier when I'm not looking at her.

'You're my best friend, Alixis.'

'Oh Sola,' she whines. Then, 'You're my best friend too. But if you wanted me to pray for you, you could have just asked.'

I laugh. Maybe that's why we get on so much, because everything has to be a joke with us. When I turn away I know I'll never see her again.

Still in my pyjamas, I head through the silver-grey dawn and take the stairs to Shepherd Fines' office two by two. When I reach the door, I place the book I've carried with me right outside it. I hope returning his copy of *Frankenstein* will say all the things I wish I could.

I'm sorry. You can be a good man. It's too late for me, but maybe you can help someone else. You're not Dr Frankenstein.

It's a long shot. I admit that.

I stare at the camp as if it's a snap shot as I make my way to the Wetpod: the office which I still think of as a watchtower; the playground which really isn't a playground at all; the shafts reaching up high with their pods sprouting from every side.

The few Demonstrators already awake stare and whisper as I walk past, but I don't care. They probably see someone going to their death sentence. Well, the fight isn't over yet. One woman wishes me good luck, explaining she once had the misfortune to accidentally step on Coral's foot. The look she gives me says it all.

The steam room is full of a sandalwood scent today. It's earthy and real, and I languish in my swimsuit for a while. The warmth is a stunning contrast to the late January air outside.

I turn the shower faucet from steaming hot to freezing cold, concentrating on every sensation. Suddenly, I need to experience every smell, sight, emotion, sound, and touch out there. I wonder if I've wasted my life even though I've done more in my seventeen years than most people in Juliet ever experience.

With damp hair, I whisper goodbye to the Wetpod wall. I eat my breakfast in the refectory alone, soaking in the smell of porridge and processed eggs. I roll every bite of my toast on my tongue, sucking the butter out and revelling in the salty taste.

It's only when I'm outside and see a flash of red leaving the Medic's Cabin that my heart seems to stop and my breathing quickens.

Unfortunately, Coral sees me. She stops walking, causing the three Herd officers who surround her to pause. Coral cocks her head to the side and just stares at me. This is the day she must have been waiting for. Everything she's done since her final Demonstration; trying to kill me in the Stadium, roping Tabby into spying on me; leading Shepherd

Fines to walk in on me when I was with Dylan. It's all led up to today. Our fight to the death. I don't know whether it's because she wants to avenge her father, or just to prove to the country that she's a better Demonstrator than I am. Maybe she just really wants me dead. Either way, the sentiment is mutual. After everything's she's done, I'm ready to say goodbye to my childhood friend.

Coral smirks suddenly—a long, slow, thin-lipped smile which has Mr Winters written all over it. Standing there, watching my enemy walk away with an already-victorious swagger, a fog clears in my head. It's been building up since the night of the Demonstrators' party, when I found out about Mum. When I thought Mr Winters might be my father.

He's not.

Dad is my dad, and I know it. The same way I know my mum may have had her faults, but she was still kind and loving. She still sang to me while I was in the bath. All those memories are real.

ℭℜ

I SCOWL AS I STEP OUT from behind the curtain and face the makeup girl. I'm wearing my school uniform, but the trousers are so tight they're practically leggings. The shirt is shimmering silver and the tie has been made loose and un-adjustable. So instead of having the knot at my collar, it hangs around my chest, which is also on show thanks to this too-small shirt.

At least they've left my running boots alone. I shove my feet into them angrily.

'We should have made the shirt cropped,' makeup girl says. 'Your stomach is too good not to show it off.'

'Shirt's fine the way it is, thanks,' I practically snarl, thinking of the grinning scar that runs down my side— courtesy of Mr Winters.

When I sit, she hums and gets to work behind me. I start to recognise the tune between tugs and pulls at my scalp.

It was Mum's favourite melody. I think it came from an old film soundtrack or something. She sang it on the morning of her death. Dad hummed it the morning I was chosen.

I join in, forgetting about how stupidly I'm dressed or how much I don't want to die today. Instead, I let the song's bittersweet nostalgia carry me away. When makeup girl stops, I smile.

'What's your name?' I ask softly. There's a pause.

'Why do you want to know?' She sounds cautious.

I shrug. 'I don't know. It's just that all this time, I've never asked you what your name is, that's all.'

Her comb runs slowly through my hair. 'If I tell you, will you let me make you pretty?'

I scoff. 'Yeah, why not?'

'Yes! Ok, it's Rochelle. You're going to look amazing!'

☞

AFTER I'VE BEEN painted, plucked, and preened, Rochelle secures my hair pin with some clips and steps back to admire her handy work.

'Wow. I'm good.' She beams.

I thank her and leave without looking in a mirror. If I could, I would stop by every room in the Medic's Cabin and memorise everyone's name, but I need to meet Dylan before my time is up. I scan out of the main doors and step right into a huddle of Herd officers. The same three who had just been with Coral, in fact. I apologise and try to swerve around them, but they cluster around me once again.

'Miss,' one of them shouts. 'Miss!'

'What?'

'We're escorting you to the spinner landing pad.' He speaks loudly, as if I don't understand English. Through their bodies, I glimpse Dylan waiting by the edge of the field.

'Look, I just need five minutes.'

A wide hand weighs on my shoulder. A warning.

'We have orders to escort you to the landing pad,' he repeats.

'I'm not ready,' I spit out.

'Well, *we* are.' He raises his eyebrows, daring me.

I briefly consider taking them on. There are only three of them; I've fought worse. Yet, they're armed and I'm not. And if I get injured before my fight then I'm pretty much dead.

Dylan's looking over now, alerted by the fracas.

'Please,' I beg as we begin to walk down the path across the field. 'I just need to see somebody!'

The officers ignore me as if I weren't anything more than a passing fly. Dylan walks briskly to catch up to us. I'm stepping backwards, pushed along by the officers as I try and see over their shoulders.

'Dylan!' I call.

We reach the gate. As the beep of the scanner goes off, I launch myself against the Herd officers.

I can't leave without saying goodbye. I don't even notice I'm shouting it until I hear my cries. For the first time all day, I hit that terrified wall. My heart pounds. I can't breathe. I need to get to Dylan. If I can say goodbye, everything will be all right.

Hands grab at me. Hold me back. One officer loops his arm around my waist, and I'm lurched backwards. I reach out for Dylan's running figure.

'Don't fight them!' His beautiful voice carries across the field. I dig my heels into the ground as they drag me away.

I go to shout I love you. The words won't come. All I can do is hyperventilate and reach out. My body is shaking, using all its energy to break free. It's no use. The second I'm through the gate, it slides shut and locks Dylan on the other side.

He curls his hands around the bars as I'm hauled into the spinner.

He stands there, crushed. Those lips I've kissed so many times part as he stares at me through the bars. His head shakes, eyes darting around to find a way to reach me.

The terrible machine shudders awake, and my chest aches as I'm lurched into the air. Words are so formed on my tongue that I can practically taste them. Yet, I'm silent as I watch his image fall away from me. The spinner pulls me higher into the air, and soon it's too late.

I'm flying away from him. His face becomes a blur. Then, just like that, he disappears from view.

I hadn't expected it to end like that.

fifty

I HARDLY RECOGNISE my home as the spinner looms over the blackened earth that surrounds city Juliet. My fight isn't for an hour, but the darkening streets are already infested with swarms of people cramming into the Stadium. From up here, they look like dark clouds morphing and moving through the roads.

Only a Herd officer and the pilot accompany me. Coral left in a separate spinner, and I'm not sure if Shepherd Fines is even watching. We swing through the city, and I spot new skyscrapers. The unsightly scaffolding I noticed a month ago has disappeared, as if the whole city had entered an ugly cocoon for a while but has emerged as a bright, beautiful new creature. Shiny, glass walls make up the Juliet Hall instead of the grey brick we've had since I was born.

I gasp. On the side of a block of offices, another amplified image of my face covers a billboard. On the building opposite, Coral's Debtbook profile picture shines on a similar-sized digital poster. We fly by too quickly for me to fully read the words underneath our faces, but I recognise 'showdown' as we go by.

How strange it must be for Dad or any of my school 'friends' to see my face looking over them every single day.

We swoop lower, only to see the streets lined with multi-coloured lanterns instead of streetlights. They join together like children holding hands and run around the city. The atmosphere smells familiar but different, kind of like a familiar perfume on the wrong person.

As we touch down, I realise too late that I will never fly again. This city will be my home until the day I die, whether that's today or in the years to come. It's as though I've lost something then. I sulked over being torn away from Dylan for the whole flight, and now I'll never get to savour that experience again. I'm trapped beneath this milky roof of pollution—forever.

More Herd officers meet me from the spinner. We take the lift down, and on every floor, it stops to reveal a flock of scrabbling people shoving their digipads into the shaft, trying to get a picture.

'Sola!' 'Miss Herrington!' 'Coral!' they shout. Some don't even seem to know who they're cheering for. The Herd officers close around me, not allowing anyone to gain entrance to the lift or to touch me with their grasping hands. What do they want from me? I have nothing left to give except my life.

As we near the ground floor, a Herd officer turns to me and grips my arm.

'Be careful now. An officer leaked what time you'd be arriving. We've already had someone try to assassinate Miss Winters.' I shrug as he blathers on. 'It's ironic considering she'll probably be killing her assassin in her next Demonstration now that he's caught.' The officer looks to me, eyes wide. 'Oh . . . if she wins, which I'm she sure won't.'

Guess I can tick tact off my list of Herd officer qualities. Thankfully, the lift beeps open.

Any fear I had dissolves as I step out of the lift and walk through the crowd of Juliet's inhabitants. The Herd officers make a tunnel around me, moving as I do, pushing back anyone who oversteps the mark. As I move forwards to sign a digipad, there's a sharp sting at the back of my neck. I briefly catch a young woman sobbing with joy over a lock of my hair before she's carried away by the surging crowd.

Rubbing my neck, I curse under my breath.

Right, no more signing digipads. No more eye contact. I walk until we reach the familiar back door of the Stadium. When it slides shut behind me, all the noise, light, and life from outside is squeezed out of the passage. The dank corridors echo only my footfalls as I walk through the foul-smelling guts of the Stadium.

In here, I'm not nice. I'm not kind or caring. I'm not even Sola Herrington.

I'm a Demonstrator. A Demonstrator who will do everything it takes to survive.

fifty-one

THE CLAWING ANGER grows with each passing minute. I imagine Coral laughing back at the camp tomorrow, telling anyone who'll listen about how she finally got rid of me. I remember how she tricked Tabby, the life to which she's subjected Alixis' son, the moment she lied and told me my only surviving parent had died. Finally, I think of Dad—all alone and waiting for my return.

Iron and soil. I can already smell combat in the air. The hatred inside me forms that gleeful creature, desperate for one last kill.

I'm led to a room with a closed gate instead of the open archway that I would usually stand underneath. It takes a moment to recognise why. I'm being presented as the contestant, not the Demonstrator. That makes sense, as people have paid to see Coral kill me, but it still feeds the rage inside and makes me want to eliminate everyone in that crowd.

I grind my teeth, becoming more and more like an animal waiting for its release. The crack of my knuckles reminds me of Shepherd Fines clicking his tongue. I keep my head down. Glare at the gate.

Of course, Ebiere bates the audience with her carefully chosen words designed to whet their appetites.

'Three months ago, two young women began risking their lives to pay back their Debts! Thanks to their sacrifices, Juliet is quickly becoming the richest city in the country!' Cheers rattle to life with this comment.

'Yet underneath the talented fights and smiles for Debtbook, a storm was brewing between your very own Demonstrators. You have the downloaded footage of Sola Herrington killing none other than Coral Winters' *own* father!'

Have they forgotten I didn't have a choice?

'You've kept up with the Debtbook statuses! You've seen Coral attempt to attack Sola once before! Now, for the first time in Shepherd history, you will be privileged to see not one, but two Demonstrators combat to the death. . . . The other cities are tuned in on their digipads, but only you will get to see this live!

'The school-girl Demonstrator has consistently refused a gun in the Stadium. She casts away her sword as if she loathes to kill. For the final twist in this warped battle of jealous rivalry, Sola Herrington must prove she is worthy of paying back her Debt indefinitely. To do this, she will embrace the rules she has given herself. She will fight unarmed!

'Daughter of the disgraced Liaison Albert Winters will fight with both sword and the trademark one-bullet gun. I leave you with this question: when the fighters are this well-trained and the stakes are so deliciously high, who will walk out of the Stadium alive? Who will you welcome back into your city as a hero?

'Brought to you by the Shepherds, I present Sola Herrington Versus Coral Winters in a final Demonstration!'

I stand, breathing in time to the climactic music. I roll my shoulders back, rotate my neck. In a way, there's irony in the fact I'm going to step out under the same gate as I did on the day of my tryout. I'm standing on the same trodden-down soil, near the now-empty weapons bench. Back then, I was about to make my first ever kill. Now, I'll make my last.

The gate rises.

And it clicks.

I'm seeing the sand from my tryout.

But William's gone. The arena is empty.

I'm staring out at Juliet's Stadium just the way it is. The mob screams with perverse pleasure. This is it.

One step. Two. The floodlights sting, but I stare through the light. My body tenses, strength rippling through each muscle.

My steps cause stomping and cheers so loud it's as if someone's yelling right into my ear. I have to admit, seeing my stern face on the screen, Rochelle was right. I look amazing. She's painted metallic silver all over my eyelid. The paint arches under my brow and flicks up to my temples like a glistening pair of insect wings. It matches the shimmer of my shirt exactly. What I wasn't expecting was a thick purple line running underneath my eyes and lining the very edge of my eyelid. It must pay tribute to the bruises I suffered on my first Demonstration. I look like an ethereal bandit, or a criminal ghost.

The rest of my face has been left natural, with only the loosely curled strands of hair falling from the knot on my head to frame it. My mother's four-leaf clover shines brightly through my locks.

I hold my head up high, smile an acknowledgment to the raging audience, and turn to the archway.

As if accepting my invitation, Coral steps out.

She's beautiful, but ugly all at once.

I hardly have time to register her loose, thick hair cascading around her shoulders or the bright splashes of red, yellow, and copper makeup which make her look as though her eyes are bleeding fire. She smiles that horrid, sickly sweet smile to the screen, blows a kiss to the audience, and then, like a tarantula which has been lying in wait for its prey, she leaps forwards.

The hate in her eyes is matched only by my own.

Blinding heat suddenly rages behind me. All around us, flames billow up from the ground. We both freeze, rotating circles as we try to figure out what's happening.

Another twist. I swallow. The inner rim of the arena blazes. Tiny metal pipes jut from the ground and spit out tornadoes of fire. We're trapped in a circle of deadly heat.

While I'm still staring, Coral rushes at me, her blade raised. In the time it takes to blink, I've read her body posture. She's feigning. I duck under her arm as she makes the false move, aiming a swift jab into her ribs. The touch feeds the monster inside.

I *want* to kill her.

The buzz of the crowd numbs my senses; all goes quiet except the crackles from the fire.

In a flurry of red and white, Coral twirls, swinging the sword around in a fast arc. Her perfume—sweet, flowery, and everything she isn't—makes me gag. I dodge the sword, once, twice, three—

Not fast enough. The tip of her sword slits my skin right underneath my collar bone like an enormous paper cut. I grit my teeth and cry out. Coral's smile blossoms as the blood expands on my shirt.

She's fast. But so am I.

All our training comes down to this—her slicing and swinging, me dodging, ducking, and swerving for my life. Each of us trying to keep two steps ahead of the other.

Persistence and resistance.

Hours pass, or maybe it's minutes. All I understand is the sweat sticking to me and our grunts as we dance in an effort to both kill and live.

Finally, though, Coral begins to slow.

A rush of triumph bleeds through me, and I could kiss Dylan all over for pushing me so hard on the tree pull-ups. I step closer, ready to disarm her gun and turn the sword on her.

I spot a glint in her eye. Then I track the easy way she swings her sword—too easily for someone who's tiring . . .

I try to backtrack, but she's too fast. She catches me again, this time dangerously close to my scar from her father. I scramble backwards as another ugly patch of blood seeps through my shirt. A sudden force of heat warns me I'm too near the edge of the sands and I roll sideways, clenching my teeth as I grasp at my cut.

It's bad, deeper than a flesh wound, but I'm not dying yet. The sand sticks to my injuries, marking them like the shadow of a beard.

She's cutting away at me. Piece by piece, as if she were preparing a slice of meat for dinner. She could end this all right now with one shot of her gun, but I figure she won't use the bullet unless she's backed into a corner. This is the public show she's dreamed of—a chance to prove she's better than me at everything: Killing, fighting, seducing, *living*.

She stalks towards me, taking her time, allowing me to languish in my pain.

An involuntary groan comes from my shaking body. I spit black-red blood onto the sands. The jab to my stomach is worse than I thought.

Coral takes another lazy step, and I rush forwards, rolling ahead and barrelling into her legs before she can register I'm moving. I pull her ankles towards me, ducking her frantic sword throws as she tumbles to the ground.

She lands like a cat, but before she can push herself up, I yank out my hair pin and jam it through her right hand as though I were ringing a gong. Her scream gives me a feverish thrill. She flops to the floor, breathing in a mouthful of sand. When she lunges upwards, I'm thrown off her back. Her white Demonstrator's uniform is stained with my blood.

She swears at me, spitting sand from her lips as she transfers the sword to her left hand. I coax her forwards, revelling in her anger.

She fights well with her left hand, but not well enough. I deflect her blows, and leave my defences open for a moment. She falls for the ruse, eyes lighting up at the opportunity to slash me once more. Unfortunately, I have to sacrifice a hit for my plan to work. I can't swerve the attack without giving up my chance to hit back. Her sword comes down and I leap towards her. There's a vicious ripping sensation in my cheek. I ignore it, spinning into her side while grabbing her arm. I kick her hand with more force than I ever used on the punching bag. Dylan was right. Her fingers give in easily, and the sword flies from her grip.

We're so close, I can hear her high-pitched wheeze. Without warning, agony darts through my face. My nose cracks under the side of her head as she head-butts me.

I'm choking on blood. It covers my face, inside and out. I wrestle from Coral's grip and gulp down breath. Maybe now I'll match Dylan with his twice-broken nose.

A flicker of movement tells me I shouldn't have given myself a moment to recover.

Coral is going for the sword.

So do I.

She moves so fast I swear I'm watching her dance. She skids on the sand, launches herself on tiptoes, spins around, and grabs something from her belt.

The gun.

Don't think, don't look, don't scream. Just act.

Lean.

Grab the gun away as she brings it from her belt. Just like I did with Dylan—only faster.

Coral's eyes widen as I wrench her wrist around. I'm still running, so we crash to the sands together. This time my hand clutches something solid. She punches and scrapes, but I loop an arm around her scrawny neck and pull the back of her head up against my chest.

I don't even know what I'm doing until I look up to the screen.

I sit, legs apart, flanking Coral. She's frozen with fear, her chest thumping as hard as my own. The black makeup covering my eyes has smudged into the sticky red blood pulsing from my nose. My cheek is barely recognisable; a dark gash runs from the side of my nose to my jaw. And in my hand, barrel hard against Coral's temple, is the gun.

All I can feel is calm. It's as though time itself pauses just for me. I see every jaw-slacked face in the crowd staring down at us from above the layer of fire. I see the hatred in my own eyes. The fear that lives in me and everyone in this Stadium. All this time I've been embracing it, letting that monster inside fight for me to survive. Just like everyone in Juliet embraces their fear of other cities.

Dylan was right, I can't change the world.

But I can make my own choices. I can find a balance between who I was and who I am now. I can still be a fighter, a Demonstrator, and not lose *me.*

With a heavy, slow hand, I pull the gun away.

'I can't shoot you,' I say, but my voice is a wheeze. Coral rolls sideways, quick as a slap. I cast the gun behind me and hear short, high-pitched laughs coming from Coral.

'You're still obsessed with me. Why, Sola?' Her eyes dart to the sword, an equal distance from both of us.

I drag my bleeding body to my feet.

'Don't you understand that the more you try and be nice to me, the more I hate you?' As she talks, she edges towards the sword. She thinks I haven't noticed. I close the gap between us with stumbling steps.

'My whole life, you've been there. Like a whiny pet. You take things which are mine, then act like an angel. What do I have to do to get you to despise me like I despise you?'

She rushes towards the sword. I barrel into her, and she ricochets from me onto the sands. I don't turn to watch her scramble up. I'm forcing my body towards the sword. My hand clamps around the cool handle, and I haul it up.

Coral's speech was wasted. I never said I couldn't *kill* her. I only said I couldn't *shoot* her.

I turn.

Coral stands opposite. One arm dangles by her side, the other points towards me. In her hand is the gun. All my hope evaporates from my chest.

'You really need to work on predicting your opponent's move. Why would I go for a sword when there's a gun right here?' she asks. Her face looks almost disappointed.

I drop the sword. I'm a fool.

I'm still expecting something more. Some grandiose event or word to mark the end of my life. But there's just a sound like a champagne cork popping and a sting in my chest.

I look down. My shirt's so saturated that the black blood pumps right out of it. I don't know whether everyone is really this still or if time has stopped.

As I'm staring at my wound, the sting wakes up. It spreads pain through my chest, like a giant claw tearing my body to shreds.

I can't breathe. My breaths are half screeches, half notes of a song. My knees hit the floor. My body curls itself around the wound, like those old paper fishes that twist in your palm to signify your mood.

The flames lining the arena edge singe my back. I must be lying down, because Coral's legs walk up to me sideways-on. Behind her, the night sky beckons me towards it, the smoke from the fire making swirling patterns in the air.

I try to get up, scrambling around on the sand just like I did that day on Coral's trampoline. It's no use. I'm dying in so many different ways, and Coral hardly has a scratch on her.

'Sorry, I missed. I've never used a gun before.' She talks to me as if we're discussing a burnt dinner or something. 'No matter.' She crouches down.

Hot tears mingle with blood on my face.

'I don't want to die,' I whisper. My body hiccups with each painful sob. I know she just shot me, but as my vision clouds around the edges I reach my hand out for Coral to hold. I can't go alone.

My hand is left cold.

'Please, Sola. This is embarrassing. None of this is fun if you don't hate me!' Coral snaps.

I close my eyes against the image of her face.

'How about this. Listen to me.' She sounds desperate now, more concerned than she has this whole fight. 'What about if I tell you I celebrated when your mum died?'

My muscles clench, the agony making me cry out.

'That's doing it, isn't it? Not only did I celebrate, Sola, but I think of it every year and smile to myself. It's the 20th of May, isn't it?'

My back slams into the floor. I think I'm convulsing.

She giggles. Her laugh is like a thousand needles injected into my ears. The pain travels through my body, translating into manic shouts in my mind. The fire behind us blazes and ebbs as if it's responding to my scattered thoughts.

'I guess this year, I'll have two dates to celebrate,' she whispers.

Something's pulling at me, dragging me down. Coral's words slither like a snake towards me. I make sense of them, arranging them so I can understand.

Then, it's clear. Once more, that white calm washes over me. It could be that I'm dead, so I smile and hum the notes of my mum's favourite melody. They drift from my mouth, encapsulating me. Giving me strength. Lifting me up.

I'm not dead. Yet.

I'm Sola Herrington.

A Person.

A Demonstrator.

Unafraid.

Coral doesn't even have time to pout as I push my ruined body to its feet and grab her shoulders. She's still laughing. I sing.

And I twist.

I push her towards the fire.

Her arms flay up like hair underwater. The surprise in her wide eyes turns to realisation, and then to fear as she tries to grab onto something to stop her fall. I step away, pulling my hands far from reach. There's a second of disbelief on her face when she falls. She didn't think I could ever do it. That I would ever let go.

Her red hair goes first, burning like a crimson halo.

My knees hit the ground once more. I can't watch the flames consume Coral. My old best friend, my possible sister, my attempted killer.

Yet I feel it—the moment she dies. The link holding us together for so long breaks, as if I've had a rope binding me to her all this time. I lean backwards with the full weight of myself.

The edges of my vision blur and cave in on me. The screen shows my dying face while music blares. I read the dancing words.

Sola Herrington has paid back her Debt.

 fifty-two

I'M FREE, flying high above a field full of four-leaf clovers. Stars burn bright in the sky, and I'm so close I could touch one. In a rush, the sun swings down. It heats my face, and I was right—it *is* like having a bath, but more magnificent. The ocean thunders below, crashing like it does in films. Just like in the spinner, the breeze lifts my hair from my shoulders.

I wince in my paradise. Something cuts into my chest, collar bone and stomach, making them ache. That isn't fair. Nothing should hurt here.

The sun dips below the water, its light fading away until there's nothing above me—no pollution, no stands, no crowd. Just open air with stars and impurities and never-ending opportunity. When the rain comes, I open my mouth to catch it, and water flows through me.

Then there's pain. It's not welcome in this place. Suffering weighs me down, dragging me from the sky and into the ocean. I thought I would like it here, but waves crash down on me again and again. Knocking me against jagged rocks, letting the hate in through my old wounds, reviving the animal inside I thought I'd killed. I can't breathe. I can't swim. I gasp.

And gasp.

And gasp.

Until air rushes into my body. The field, stars, sea, sky, wind, sun, and rain shine so bright that they become one white hot light.

A bitter antiseptic smell fills my senses. Pins pierce my skin. Eyes loom above.

Eyes I recognise.

Shepherd Fines.

'She's awake!'

Am I? I blink. And blinking hurts . . . because everything hurts. The sea has disappeared and left me in a room. A bright, colourless room that I've seen before. Not the Medic's Cabin, but the hospital in Juliet. Someone squeezes my hand.

'Sola, Sola, if you can hear me say Shepherd Fines.'

'Shepherd—'

'Great stuff! Great stuff!'

Machines surround me, chiming in a melody of beeps. Medics stand back, congratulating themselves and Shepherd Fines. What have they got to be so happy about?

Then, I see him. A face I would recognise even through a torrent of pain and fire. A face I never thought I would see again.

He has red, glassy eyes. When he looks at me, his chest pulses as he gasps in relief. He stands well back. I know he wants to come over. I can sense it in the way he leans towards me despite his unmoving feet. If the link between Coral and me was a thick, thorny rope, then what connects me to Dylan is a silk thread.

Coral. The Demonstration. The gunshot.

I jolt upwards, running my hands down my body.

'Calm down, Sola. You're okay, you're okay. I told them to do whatever they could to save you. The shot just missed your heart, although you won't be using your arm for a while.' Shepherd Fines speaks. 'Also, you'll be left with a few pretty scars.'

I suck air through my teeth as he ushers the medics away. They trail out, chattering excitedly amongst themselves.

Once the door's shut, terror claims me. I don't understand why Shepherd Fines is here. Aren't I free?

'I won't go back. I won't do it again. I've finished, I don't care if there's another twist. I'm not fighting!' At first, I don't even realise the blurry words are coming from me.

'No, no. No one's making you do anything again. You've finished your tour. You won the fight!' Shepherd Fines says.

'Why are you here? Where's my dad?'

My questions upset him. He looks away.

'My dear, your father is waiting outside. He's been at your bedside for days.'

Days? How long have I been lying here?

'I'm here because . . . because I was wrong. Actually, it's not exactly *wrong* to organise an unfair fight for your last game.' He chuckles and looks at Dylan as if seeking reassurance. He doesn't find any. 'However, I think my own personal regard for you affected my judgement. When I thought you were going to die, I kept remembering the times you made me chuckle. And although there was a time I might have desired *more*, I've recently come to the decision that we are probably better as friends.' He squeezes my palm, looking down at me with a pitying smile. I get the impression he thinks that he's letting me down gently.

'Between us boys—' He grins to Dylan. '—that Ebiere is really rather something. I got chatting to her after the Demonstration yesterday. *Really* chatting. She's got quite the wit!

'Anyway, Sola, my dear. I wish to make this mess up to you. I'm a powerful man. I want to give you a gift. I can't change the laws, so don't you be getting any ideas!' He waggles a finger at me. 'However, I am willing to make one exception. Anything you want. I will even—' He looks to Dylan and sighs. 'I will even allow Mr Casey here to move to city Juliet, if you so wish.'

My heart leaps. There's a foreign sensation in my face—
I'm smiling.

But, just as fast, my body sinks down.

When I tell Shepherd Fines what I want, he looks
surprised, but nods all the same.

'Very well.' He clicks his teeth again. 'I guess I better
leave you two alone for a moment then.'

I don't have the heart to tell him he's still holding my
hand.

Eventually, he stands. He leans down as if to kiss my
forehead, but settles on running his hand over it instead. I
give Shepherd Fines a smile as he leaves. When he reaches
the door, he looks back.

'You really don't think I'm like him? You know, Dr
Frankenstein?'

The truth is that I don't know, but instead I say, 'Not if
you don't want to be.'

He grins.

'Hmm, I didn't think so. I'm more of a Don Corleone,
wouldn't you say?' He laughs at his reference to *The
Godfather* and walks out of the room, nodding to himself as
if to reaffirm his decision.

I stare as long as I can at the back of the closed door
once it has slid shut. Now that I'm alone with Dylan, fear
and anxiety creep over me. I've won an impossible battle,
yet I'm nervous about being alone with the man I love.

He steps forwards. I swing my legs out of bed, pain
shooting through to my fingers and toes as I perch on the
edge. I'm glad to see I'm dressed in pyjamas and not naked.

'Sola, do you remember me?' he asks tentatively. It's
enough to make me burst into giggles.

'I definitely remember that voice,' I croak out, my
nervousness evaporating. I reach for his hand with my good
arm and pull him close.

His touch is gentle, apprehensive. As if he's scared of breaking me. I seek his mouth with mine, and he gives in with a loaded sigh. He kisses me deeply, wrapping his arms around my shoulders. Although it hurts, I don't let on.

'I'm sorry,' I whisper when we part. My lips brush his mouth as I talk. 'I'm sorry I didn't choose you.'

He shakes his head, soothing my worries with a gentle, *shh.*

'It's one of the reasons why I love you,' he says, tracing my cheek with his thumb. 'You're being kind, Sola.'

I don't know if he realises that his words mirror our first conversation. For some reason, they bring tears to my eyes. But I don't regret my choice. Knowing Alixis will be allowed to return home with her son goes somewhere to make me feel okay again. In a way, it repairs some of the damage Coral has done to my family and me over the years, like putting flowers over a grave.

Fed up with hospital beds, I try to stand. Dylan helps me gain my balance.

'Dylan,' I whisper. 'How bad does it look?' I'm not so stupid that I haven't noticed there are no mirrors in this room. The bumps of healing skin on my body are as thick as folds in a sheet.

Dylan doesn't reply. Instead, he places his hands on my waist. Keeping eye contact, he pulls my top up slowly, so that it shows my midriff. I take hold of the top, and Dylan kisses every stitch, staple, and scar until he reaches my nose. It isn't sore, but I can tell from touching it that it's changed shape. When he runs his lips over my cut cheek, I wince. It's hard to bring myself to feel the thick line which runs over half of my face. At some point, I'll look at the damage. The first time, I'm sure I'll cry, but I'll get over it. I'm alive; who cares what my face is like?

Finally, it's time to let go.

'Dylan,' I say, 'you never told me why you stayed on as a Demonstrator.'

Dylan smiles. 'You're right, so I didn't.'

'I think I know,' I whisper.

'Oh yeah?'

I think about how Dylan has never mentioned his parents, yet somehow I don't think they're dead.

'Your family didn't want you back, did they?'

He tucks a piece of hair behind my ear easily.

'No, they didn't. The Shepherds encouraged my ma to have another child. By the time I finished my tour, I had a baby brother.' He shrugs, still smiling—not happily, but like he has made his peace with this long ago. 'Would you want a ten year old killer around your newborn baby?' he asks.

'That's not really fair.'

Another shrug. 'Probably not, but it's life. I got to meet you, didn't I?'

He's grinning now, that mischievous sparkle is back in those blue eyes.

'Aye,' I say, faking his accent, 'that you did.' I'm definitely getting better at that. I take his hands in mine, and duck my head. 'So . . . are you attending any parties in Juliet in the near future?'

Silence. I dare to look up. Dylan chews on his bottom lip. He's keeping something from me.

'Actually, Sola, I promised myself that if you woke up, I would find a way to be with you. If you want that—that is.'

'Yes! I mean, yeah, I want that. But how?'

Dylan chuckles at my response.

'Can't you predict what I'm going to do?' he asks. I glower at the reference to my failure as a Demonstrator. 'Okay, okay,' he puts his hands up, still grinning.

'I don't know if it will work, but I'm going to try and make a deal with Fines. I've finished my tour so I can threaten to go home. *Or*, I could offer to continue to

307

demonstrate if I'm allowed to live here. With you. Well, maybe not with you—I mean, I'll get my own place.'

I shut him up with a kiss—a glorious, arms-wrapped-around-his-neck, never-going-to-let-you-go kiss. It might take time, it might not work, but there's a chance that we still get to be together. After everything I've been through, that chance is enough. Without warning, Dylan pulls away and glances nervously to the door.

'Oh, I forgot. Your dad is outside. I met him.'

I manage to laugh. 'Did he like you?'

'Aye, of course. But he won't for much longer if he sees us like this.'

With that, we both know our time is over. Outside this room, my life is waiting for me.

'Okay,' I say.

'All right,' Dylan whispers, almost to himself. 'Hopefully I'll see you soon. Until then, don't forget about me.'

'You're not allowed to tell me what to do,' I joke, although I hold onto him. We kiss as our fingers dance together. I savour the moment, which is gone all too soon. He breaks away, and in four controlled footsteps, he's at the door.

For some reason, I imagine that silk thread following him out, connecting us forever. Dylan steps through the door. It slides shut.

A moment to myself is all I need.

I let my mind dwell on Coral. In this stark, white room, without a Debt hanging over me, she seems so simple. All the nasty words that ever came out of her mouth, were they even true? I never questioned it before, but what proof do I have that Mum had an affair with Mr Winters? Perhaps Coral invented the whole thing; perhaps she believed it herself.

I guess I'll never know if she really did celebrate Mum's death, or if it was a lie to make me hate her. Unfortunately, not knowing means I'll still have regret for what I did to Coral. Yet it's no more regret than I have for all the other people I've killed. They will stay with me forever, just like my scars.

I've been alone for long enough. Through the shuttered windows I see a silhouette standing in the hallway outside my room. Dad.

Mum's four-leaf clover hair pin gleams on the bedside table. I hesitate, but pick it up and slide it into my hair.

My legs wobble, and I steady myself for a moment. I run through the list of things I know for sure:

- *My name is Sola Herrington.*

-*I'm in love with Dylan Casey.*

-*I've killed ninety-three people.*

-*I know the Shepherds' best kept secret.*

-*I'm not afraid anymore.*

For now, I want to tell Dad I'm proud of him. I'll enjoy every second of living until the inevitable happens and the Shepherds' rules re-enter my world. I'll fight, then, if I have to.

Because that's part of who I am.

I'm a Demonstrator.

After the Fear

BIO

Rosanne writes for children and young adults and hopes to bring readers to an unfamiliar yet alluring setting. Rosanne was inspired to write when she read the Harry Potter books, and at age fourteen, she wrote romance fanfiction on just about every pairing you could dream up from the HP series. She currently lives with her partner and two bunny rabbits and is working on a new adult fantasy novel.

acknowledgements

My first ever reader, Faye.

Darren, for your constant love and support.

My family: Nana, Mum, Dad, Joe, Pete, Alice, Tom, Faye, Claire (and everyone else!) for your help and for listening to me ramble about the book for hours on end.

Ted and Raj, for being the best writing friends a girl could have.

All of my tutors on the MA in Writing at Warwick.

Everyone at Immortal Ink Publishing, for making the book ten times better with your advice, amazing editing talents and beautiful book cover. Thank you for having faith in the book. You've made my dreams come true!

Made in the USA
San Bernardino, CA
19 August 2014